Vote for Murder

Jacqueline Beard

ISBN: 978-1-91-605067-9

This book is published by Dornica Press

First Printing 2015 PublishNation

Also, by this author:

The Lawrence Harpham Murder Mysteries:

The Fressingfield Witch

The Ripper Deception

The Scole Confession

The author can be contacted on her website
https://jacquelinebeardwriter.com/

While there, why not sign up for her FREE newsletter.

To Lee, for his encouragement
and
Jill, for her unwavering support

Contents

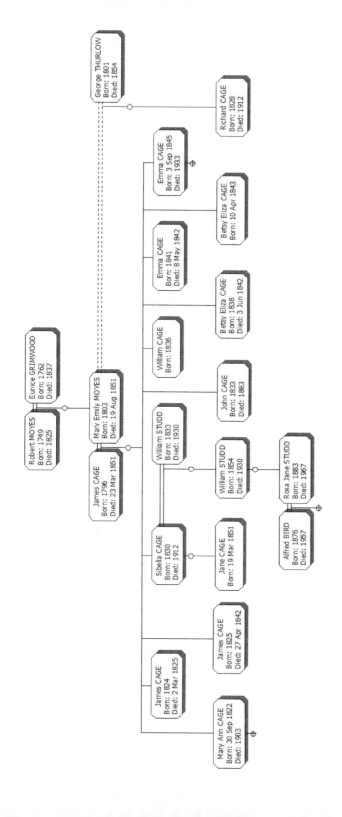

Prologue

Mary patted her belly and sighed. "How do I look?" she asked, flattening the pleats of her stiff cotton skirts.

"As lovely as the finest lady, Mary Emily," replied Anna, ignoring the obvious baby bump distorting the pleated fabric. "Here," she continued lifting a tattered red check cloth from her basket. "I've made you a present."

She peeled back another layer revealing a lovingly hand-crafted headdress made from bluebells and cowslips, each purple and pale-yellow flower head trembling as she passed it to her friend.

"Oh, Annie," gasped Mary reaching for her gift. "It's exquisite."

She placed the headdress over her dark curls.

"How does it look?" she asked. "Never mind, I want to see for myself." She grabbed Anna's hand, giving her no opportunity for reply. "Come with me."

Mary threw open the door of the gloomy cottage, and they ran up the muddy track into a field where a group of bedraggled sheep chewed grass next to a stone trough.

"There," said Mary, peering into the algae-infused water. A smiling, tousled-haired young woman returned her gaze.

"Annie," she exclaimed, "you have done me proud. James will think me the prettiest girl in the village."

"And rightly so," agreed Anna. "It is hard to believe you will be Mrs James Cage by the end of the day."

Mary took Anna's hands and pulled her onto the flat stone bench in front of the trough until they faced each other. "You have been patient, Annie," she said. "I know you have reservations, and you may be right, but James will love me in time, and with the little one coming, I must marry."

1

"And marry, you shall," said Anna. "I wish you nothing but joy." She kissed her friend on the cheek before turning towards the cottage.

Her smile slid into a frown as a recent memory returned to her consciousness; an unwanted recollection of James Cage trying to steal a kiss. She could almost smell the stale sweat and alcohol; a drunken kiss from an idle waster - poor choice Mary, a man not fit to speak your name in church.

Anna had resolved to keep the incident secret. The truth could not help Mary. Her child was due in three or four months, and her father was determined to eject her from the house unless she was married before the baby arrived. There was no choice. Anna could only hope for the best outcome for her friend.

Mary sat alone by the stone trough, swishing her fingers through the stale water. Short and slight with dark lustrous hair and fine features, high cheekbones enhanced her delicate face. Mary's full lips set naturally in a broad smile, but her eyes were sad as if something dark loomed in her future. Anna watched and wondered then embraced her friend.

"James will change when you are married, and the baby arrives," she reassured her. "He will become responsible and hard-working, and you will have lots of children and live in a happy home. You already start married life with rooms of your own which is more than most."

"We are lucky," beamed Mary. "Our home is not grand but having two rooms for our own use is a blessing. I am fortunate, Annie and I know James likes a drink, but I believe he cares for me."

"As do I," agreed Anna, "and you a wife and mother before you are twenty."

"But what else could I be?" asked Mary, "I am not educated like you. I spent my childhood days picking stones in the fields while you learned your letters."

"What of it?" asked Anna, straightening the headdress and tucking a loose curl behind Mary's ear. "I will marry a local man and live close to you. We will be neighbours, and our children will grow up together and how will it matter that I can read a book and you cannot? Besides, you sing like an angel, and I cannot carry a tune in a pail."

Mary laughed, "I know," she said, "and I do not mind so very much. I don't long to live elsewhere and will be quite content as long as you don't leave to seek your fortune without me."

2

"Never," said Anna scanning the fields as she heard voices in the distance. "No," she cried. "James is on his way. Run indoors. He cannot see you before the wedding."

Mary lifted her skirts and ran up the pathway laughing, then waved to Anna, and slammed the door.

"I'll see you later," called Anna picking her way up the stone path to the front of the cottage.

The cream-coloured building fronting the road stood side by side with three similar dwellings. Dirt and debris covered the lower walls grey. Anna noticed another hole surrounded by a spider's web of cracked panes and a shabby red curtain which had been squashed into the gaps in a vain attempt to retain the heat.

The sight of Mary's mother bustling along the street distracted Anna from her thoughts.

"Good day Mrs Moise," she said. "How are you?"

"I am well," said Eunice Moise. "Have you come to give Mary some last-minute advice?"

"No," laughed Anna, "I made her a headdress for the wedding."

"That was kind," she replied. "Will you join us when we walk to church later?"

"Oh, yes," replied Anna. "It will be an honour to walk with you and a joy to see Mary wed."

"It is necessary," said Mary's mother. "We may have peace in our home at last when Cage makes an honest woman of her." She smiled wryly. "Mr Moise has not been pleased of late."

"Today is a happy day," smiled Anna chatting for a few more minutes before taking her leave. She walked up the street towards the Ten Bells beerhouse swinging her basket as she went.

"Hello, Annie." A shadow loomed large in her path. She looked up to see the bulky form of James Cage staggering from the beer house with two of his friends, a quart of ale in each hand. He grinned. "Some well-earned lubrication," he added nodding at the beer.

"Be sensible with it," said Annie. "Mary is happy. Do not spoil her day."

"I will not," he said, "unless you decide to marry me instead. Then I will send Samuel to the church in my place."

"Not I," smirked Samuel, "You bring up your own bastard." He patted James on the back, and they laughed.

3

Anna shook her head, "I know you don't mean a word of it," she said, "but you should not joke about such things. Now get yourself clean and ready for church. Off with you now."

The three men sauntered up the road swigging from ale jars. Anna followed keeping a safe distance behind until she reached her father's tidy detached cottage.

Anna was proud of her ivy-clad home painted in Suffolk pink. A smart, red-tiled porch graced the front of the cottage which nestled in a little patch of garden. It was a happy family home in which she felt secure and loved. She opened the door and retired to her room until it was time to change into her Sunday best dress ready for the wedding.

The bells pealed as a train of villagers meandered down the stone road towards the church. It was a bright, sunny June day, and the softest breeze ruffled Mary's headdress, making the flowers quiver. Mary dressed in cream pleated skirts, and a white laced bodice yellowing with age walked at the head of the procession. She carried a posy of freshly picked wildflowers, and the gentle scent of lavender was just discernible whenever the wind changed direction. Anna followed behind, holding the soft, warm hand of Mary's young niece. The little girl clutched a small basket filled with crimson rose petals.

The wedding party approached the square flint tower of the church, standing sturdy in the distance. They continued up the path and into the vestibule, leaving Mary and her father at the gate. A few minutes passed, the peals stopped, and the resonant tones of an organ filtered through the doors.

Robert Moise straightened his cravat. "Make me proud, Mary," he said, taking her arm before leading her into the flower-filled church.

They walked up the aisle in time with the music until they reached the altar where James leaned casually against a carved, wooden bench end. He grinned at Samuel, who covered his mouth and whispered. James laughed aloud and slapped Samuel on the shoulder.

The vicar gestured for quiet as he peered at the congregation over horn-rimmed glasses. "Be seated," he commanded.

James pointed a dirty nail at the vicar. "You be seated," he slurred.

Anna gasped. A woman cried "shame," while others tutted and shook their heads.

James swayed from side to side, grinning at the congregation while Mary stared blankly at the altar, her face expressionless. A slow burn of colour spread over her cheeks, but otherwise, she did not react.

James hiccupped and theatrically slapped a hand to his mouth, before reaching towards Samuel for support.

Anna watched James Cage as he humiliated her friend, dreading what he might do next. Dressed in a faded worsted jacket, and the same breeches and boots he'd worn while working in the fields earlier that day, James cut an unkempt figure. His face was pallid, covered in a smear of grey and in no cleaner state than his nails. Anna wondered how she'd failed to notice the condition of his clothes earlier.

"I said sit down," boomed the vicar. James slumped upon a wooden seat; legs splayed in front.

The vicar embarked upon his sermon as Robert Moise rose from his seat. Silent as a cat, he picked his way across the floorboards until he reached James, then he crouched down and whispered, in a voice too low for Anna to hear.

James frowned and pursed his lips then sat up straight-backed, watching the rector through narrowed eyes.

The rest of the service passed without incident. Anna held her breath as the vicar asked if anyone knew of any impediment to the marriage. To her immense relief, there was no objection. James and Mary took their vows and exchanged wedding bands then Mary's niece Sarah tossed rose petals to the floor as the organ ground back to life. They walked up the aisle side by side, a newly married couple.

The wedding party strolled the short distance to the Ten Bells public house where Frederick Abbot grabbed his fiddle and scraped a tune. The younger people danced and frolicked, but Mary remained sitting quietly beside Anna.

Anna smiled. "How are you feeling Mary?" she asked, holding her hand.

"I am well," replied Mary softly.

"You are quiet."

"I cannot dance in my condition," replied Mary watching James in the distance.

"He is young and foolish," said Anna as James consumed another quart of ale.

"I can live with that," said Mary, "but he is twenty-six and already drinks like a hardened lag. Is it too late for him to settle? Do I hope in vain?"

"He will change when the baby comes," said Anna, "Have faith."

"He must," replied Mary. "Or I will make him."

Mary's eyes flashed gimlet grey. Anna shuddered, acknowledging a steely resolve in her friend not previously apparent. For a moment, she felt she did not know Mary at all.

Chapter One

A call to action

"If we must obey the law, shouldn't we have a say in who makes it?"

The clear pitched voice cut across the buzz emanating from the crowd of women milling around a podium in Christchurch Park. The crowd, composed of middle-aged, smartly dressed women, moved reluctantly aside as two younger girls squeezed their way through the gathering. They pushed to the front, attracting unwelcome attention in their enthusiasm for the cause. When they reached the foot of the podium, the dark-haired girl stopped in front of the stand. She stood with her hands on her hips, leaning towards her shorter, fair-haired companion.

"Marvellous, isn't she?" she whispered, nodding towards a strident sounding woman standing high on the podium above. The woman was an expressive speaker, accompanying every word with an earnest gesture which made her argument passionate and sincere.

"She is inspiring, Louisa," replied Sophia, "but who is she?"

"Constance Andrews, leader of our Women's Freedom League. If she can't get us closer to the vote, I don't know who can."

Louisa watched the throng of women listen to their figurehead with rapt attention. Her full voice carried across Christchurch Park and over the chatter of the assembled women. After a few moments, the audience quietened, mesmerised by the eloquence of her argument. Constance Andrews talked with authority and confidence.

"I bring news from London," she declared, "from Millicent Fawcett. She plans a peaceful demonstration against the census. From north to south our suffragette sisters mean to boycott the census next Sunday. They will make themselves unavailable if their vote does not count. Whether they live in London or Scotland, women will leave their homes on census night and hide from the enumerator. They will not appear on Prime Minister Asquith's statistics." Her face darkened at the mention of the politician. "The government cannot be trusted," she continued. "Even now, their promises, their mealy-mouthed words, count for nothing."

"Hear hear," trilled a fine-featured woman dressed in a soft plum hat and matching jacket. Her clothes were cut from the finest cloth but pinned with purple and green 'Vote for Women' buttons, leaving no doubt of her commitment to the cause.

"That's Grace Roe," whispered Louisa. "She is beautiful but much more radical than Constance. She runs the Women's Social and Political Union office in Princes Street and is great friends with Emmeline Pankhurst."

Grace Roe spoke. "May I?" she asked gesturing to Constance Andrews who nodded her approval.

"I believe in this course of action," said Grace. "But is it enough? We have only empty promises from the government for all our negotiations though we kept our word and ceased militant action months ago. There have been no hunger strikes and no smashed windows, but what advantage has it brought us?"

"Come now, Grace," Constance replied. "Radical action does not have to mean violence or self-harm. I keep to my militant principles. I have not paid for Spartan's dog licence though they threaten me with prison."

"A dog licence indeed," said Grace shaking her head. "It is hardly going to bring the government to its knees. We should do more."

"We will do more," agreed Constance. "But for now, this is a valuable demonstration of our will. The census is a historical document. Our action on Sunday night will skew the statistics forever. They will never be correct."

She addressed the crowd of women. "What say you, ladies?" she cried. "Will you support us?"

A dozen women raised their hands chanting, "we will," in unison, but many more stared at the ground, unwilling to commit to the cause.

"Lydia Marshall, will you not join us?" asked Constance.

"I would if I could," replied Lydia. "But I cannot. My husband would not brook law-breaking of any kind. He tolerates my attendance at these meetings. He even expresses some level of understanding. But if he thought I intended to go against the government, he would stop me."

Several other women nodded empathetically.

The two women on the podium fell quiet. The expression on Grace Roe's face left no doubt as to her feelings about husbands' claiming their authority. Constance Andrews was more sympathetic.

"I understand your concerns," she said, "which is why it is important that those of us able to avoid the census do. I have secured premises at the Old Museum in Museum Street on Sunday night. I will provide food, shelter, and warmth. We will be quite safe and away from the public eye. Again, I ask, who will join me?"

This time more hands shot into the air. The realisation that shelter provided discretion and secrecy lifted their spirits.

"Oh, I will, I will," cried Louisa enthusiastically.

"Thank you," said Constance singling Louisa out. "I welcome your enthusiasm."

Louisa blushed with pleasure at the attention.

"I too," said Sophia raising her hand uncertainly and looking anxiously towards Louisa.

By now, more than forty hands were in the air, representing almost half of the women in attendance.

"We will meet at The Old Museum at six o'clock on Sunday night," said Constance. "Please come. If we can raise enough attention throughout the country, our inconvenience will be worthwhile and helpful to the cause. I thank you for your attendance today and look forward to seeing you Sunday week."

A spontaneous round of applause erupted from the gathering. Constance waved and smiled until the crowd melted away. Once the park was almost empty, a smartly dressed man helped her from the podium.

"Thank you, Mr Bastian," she said. He released her gloved hand and smiled before returning to his waiting wife. Henry Bastian was one of half a dozen men standing in support of the suffrage cause. Some married men attended in a show of solidarity to their wives, but other liberal single men joined because it fitted with their political beliefs. They were vocal in their support, clapping eagerly through the speeches. Constance approached the small group of men, shook hands, and gave thanks to each of them for his time.

"I cannot wait until Sunday," said Louisa clasping her hands together. "I want to do my bit to help. It is a great opportunity."

"But how will we get away?" asked Sophia. "My father will never give permission."

"Has he no sympathy with suffrage?" asked Louisa.

"None at all," said Sophia shaking her head. "There is not the smallest chance he will allow it. Besides which, Father is in a frightful rage with one of the servants and talking of dismissal. He is hardly in the right frame of mind to ask, even if there was a chance of his agreement. Surely your father does not allow you out at night unchaperoned, Louisa?"

"My father lets me go anywhere as long as I am sensible and do not indulge in violence. It is a lost cause for Papa. My cousin is married to Millicent Fawcett's sister and committed to the suffragist principles. Indeed, Millicent has visited us several times over the past few years. Mama has given her word that she will not get involved, so my father turns a blind eye to anything Charlotte, and I wish to do."

"You are lucky," sighed Sophia. "My father has never allowed much freedom. I would be in a great deal of trouble if he knew I was here, and he has been even worse since we left Chippenham. I won't be able to join you, Louisa. I should not have raised my hand."

"Well, you must say you are staying with me that evening," Louisa replied. "We can invent a reason. With luck, we may not need to. My brother Albert is coming home in the next few days, and he often brings friends. You must come to dinner. I will make a proper invitation."

"That might work," said Sophia, her face brightening. "A written invitation will make a great deal of difference. Father is all about appearances and will undoubtedly give his approval to a formal dinner. Mummy will not mind anyway."

The girls left the podium and walked along the pathway and past the tall stone memorial to the Ipswich martyrs. The cross-topped monument stretched skywards casting a lanky shadow over the path ahead. The recently completed carved round pillars caught the light of the morning sun, and the engraved inscription stood fresh and clear.

"Do your sisters support us?" asked Louisa.

10

"Oh no," laughed Sophia. "Ethel is too busy raising her children and has no time for such things. And as for my sister, Catherine, you may be surprised to hear that she took holy orders two years' ago and lives in a convent in York."

"I had no idea," exclaimed Louisa, "but I forget how little time we have known each other. We are such good friends that it feels as if we have known one another longer. I did not realise your family were religious."

"We are not," said Sophia, "Mother is somewhat, but Father not at all. Religion has always attracted Catherine, and there are other reasons why she has chosen to live in relative obscurity. She has a simple life which does not involve speculating about women's politics."

"Understandably," said Louisa. "So, shall I send you an invitation tomorrow and you can speak to your father?"

"Yes, please," said Sophia. "My cousin Daniel is visiting tomorrow, but his arrival will not affect our plans for next week. He will have been with us for several days by then."

"Is he staying long?" asked Louisa.

"For the foreseeable future," said Sophia, "Which will hopefully please father - male companionship may improve his mood. Daniel is an engineer. He begins a new career in Ipswich soon and will board with us until he finds a permanent home. I am looking forward to having different conversations. I miss my sisters, and John Edward is too young to be interesting company."

"Do you know Daniel well?" asked Louisa.

"Not at all," replied Sophia. "He was fourteen when we last met, and I only ten. He dwelled in London until recently and will have much to tell us about the capital. He will brighten up our dreary old house."

They left the park and walked up Ivry Street stopping outside Sophia's imposing gothic style house standing angularly at the end of a wide stone drive. Ivy clad, with mullioned windows and a turreted roof, the property was more prominent and far grander than Louisa's red brick house next door, but for all the opulence it carried an air of gloom.

They reached the drive as Sophia's father emerged from the arched front door and strode towards a gleaming Ford automobile parked on the driveway.

"Sophia," he barked, nodding towards Louisa before climbing into a Model T parked at the foot of the drive. Sunlight glinted from the brightly polished chassis, and the brass lamps gleamed like goldfish eyes. The vehicle purred into life, and he pulled out of the driveway, turning left into Ivry Street.

"I should go in," said Sophia as the engine noise faded.

"Not before I thank you for coming to the rally with me," said Louisa. "I hope you enjoyed it. I will organise your dinner invitation tomorrow. You simply cannot miss the census night evasion."

Sophia smiled. "I will be there," she said, waving to Louisa before entering the house.

A pair of familiar faces greeted Louisa on her return. "Ada, Bessie," she squealed, seeing her two cousins standing on the front lawn of The Poplars. "You missed the rally in Christchurch Park."

"Yes, it was rather unfortunate," said Ada, "but we have been involved in the planning and will attend the evasion at the Old Museum next week. I guarantee you will not see the names of Ada and Bessie Ridley on the 1911 census return. Come inside. We have much to tell you."

Chapter Two

If women don't count, neither shall they be counted....

Sunday lunch at The Poplars was a merry affair with Louisa's father, Henry Russell his engaging, convivial self, providing much welcome and entertaining conversation to his dinner guest. Sophia, usually quieter than Louisa, was encouraged to chat about her family and enjoyed herself so much that the afternoon slipped by.

Albert Russell was home, having returned from his lodgings in Camden Town and was charming and attentive to his sister's new friend. Charlotte Russell was equally welcoming.

At half-past four Maggie, the housemaid provided a platter of sandwiches, a selection of cakes and pots of steaming hot tea for the family. The girls sat together in the drawing-room watching Louisa's spaniels play on the flat rear lawn.

"This has been a wonderful day," whispered Sophia as she passed the cake stand to Louisa. Your family are welcoming, and your house is so lively. There are more of us than you, but we are quite gloomy in comparison.

"I am fortunate," said Louisa smiling.

"What are you girls plotting?" asked Henry Russell. "Are you involved in this suffragist business your cousin Ada mentioned?"

"We plan to go to the Old Museum with Ada and Bessie later," Louisa replied, "with your permission, of course."

Henry Russell placed his teacup down and spread jam on a scone with his customary precision. "I give my consent to you Louisa, as always, with the usual proviso that you do not place yourself in any danger or commit any act of violence. As I am assured this is a peaceful protest you may go, but I cannot speak for Mr Drummond so please be sure that Sophia has obtained his permission."

Sophia stared at the floor as the colour rose in her cheeks.

"Indeed," said Louisa reaching for a cake. She returned to her seat and sat down with a bump, tipping her plate which dropped to the carpet.

"Oh, I'm so sorry," she said, jumping to her feet while purposely stepping on the edge of the cake and grinding it deep into the carpet pile.

"Oh Louisa," exclaimed her mother, "That was careless. Look at my poor carpet."

She pressed a brass bell, and moments later, a housemaid appeared.

"I'm sorry, Maggie, but can you clear this mess up, please?" she asked.

"Yes, ma'am," said Maggie returning with a dustpan, brush, and damp cloth.

Louisa took the opportunity to excuse herself from the drawing-room. Taking Sophia by the hand, they climbed the stairs to her bedroom on the first floor.

"Oh Louisa, you shouldn't have made that terrible mess on my account," admonished Sophia. "Your family have been so kind. Today was wonderful."

"It was a necessary distraction, Sophia darling," said Louisa. "My father is indulgent, where I am concerned, but he would have felt obliged to ask you if your father had given permission. He is suitably distracted now and will think no more about it. Let's change into warm clothes. It will take half an hour to walk, and we don't want to catch colds."

They donned coats, gloves and hats and left the house pausing only to say goodbye to Louisa's mother, Marianne, who waved them off from the hallway.

"Take care, Louisa," she said, "how I wish I could join you."

Louisa kissed her mother's cheek. "Thank you, Mama," she said softly.

Sophia murmured her thanks, and they walked up the crunchy gravel drive into Ivry Street.

Louisa took Sophia's arm. "No talking until we are a long way from your house," she commanded.

They scuttled past Sophia's driveway, but were no more than twenty yards from her house when a deep voice boomed, "hello Sophia, where are you going at this time of day?"

A tall, dark-haired young man emerged from behind a dense bush at the top of the driveway where he had been enjoying an evening cigarette.

Sophia gasped. "It's cousin Daniel," she whispered, turning to Louisa before facing her cousin.

"Where is Father?" she asked softly.

"Why are you whispering?" asked Daniel.

"Walk with us a little way," Louisa suggested, attempting to move the conversation away from the house.

They walked to the top of the road before Daniel stopped. "Enough now," he said. "You're obviously reluctant to talk outside your father's house, Sophia. What are you afraid of? And as for you," he continued, turning to Louisa, "who are you, and why have you deliberately drawn us away from Sophia's home?"

Sophia stared at Daniel, eyes brimming with tears as she trembled like a frightened child. "Please don't tell father," she implored.

"Don't tell Charles what, exactly?" asked Daniel. "There is nothing I could tell him if I wanted to. I've no idea what you are doing or why you feel this apparent need for secrecy."

Louisa sighed. "We are visiting friends in Museum Street," she said, opting for a half-truth.

"Charles may be strict," said Daniel, "but even he would permit Sophia to visit her friends. It must be more. Tell me the truth."

Sophia swallowed, staring at her gloved hands in abject misery. "We are going to the Woman's Freedom League meeting at the Old Museum," she confessed. "We are avoiding the census enumerator."

"For goodness sake, Sophia," Daniel exploded. "Your father would be appalled. I don't wonder you are hiding this foolishness from him. What are you thinking?"

"She wants to be able to vote," snapped Louisa. "And she is willing to do something about it."

Daniel glared. "What utter nonsense," he said. "Your father looks after your political interests, and if you are lucky enough to marry, your husband will take over those responsibilities. What could you possibly know of parliament and politics? That is not your domain."

"Why do you think you know better than me just because you were born a man," exclaimed Louisa, then stopped herself pontificating further on hearing Sophia's sobs. She was crying with deep, undignified breaths.

"Now you've upset Sophia with your nonsense," thundered Daniel.

"My nonsense," Louisa exclaimed. "She was perfectly happy until five minutes ago when we met you. You're to blame."

Daniel opened his mouth to reply, then changed his mind before putting a protective arm around Sophia.

"Are you resolved to see this through?" he asked.

"I must," sniffed Sophia between sobs. "It matters, Daniel. It is the first time in my life that I feel any purpose in my privileged existence."

"Your father will never give his permission," Daniel replied. "He will react badly if he ever hears of this." He exchanged a long look with Sophia. She held his gaze, and a mutual understanding passed between them. For a moment, Louisa felt like an outsider watching a carefully crafted family tableau.

Daniel inhaled. A plume of smoke from his cigarette dissolved into the air. He tossed the cigarette butt onto the path and ground it to dust with a well-polished shoe. "I was not here. I did not see you," he said as he walked away.

The girls watched as Daniel strode up the road, waiting in silence until he disappeared into the leafy driveway of The Rowans.

"Will he tell?" asked Louisa.

Sophia shook her head. "I do not believe he will," she replied. "But I can't return home in any event. If he tells Father, I will willingly delay the confrontation for a few hours, and if he does not tell, then all is well. Let's continue as planned."

Louisa hooked her arm through Sophia's and watched her friend's pale face as she stared back down the street. Sophia slowed, her eyes darting between Louisa and the road beyond.

"Don't worry. We will be discreet," said Louisa, pulling her forward. "The anti-suffragists have heard of the planned evasion and may seek to stop us. As far as anyone is concerned, we are taking an evening walk around the park."

Sophia exhaled. "Then I shall enjoy our walk," she said.

Picking up the pace they continued through Ivry Street, passing the crossing to Constitution Hill. They walked alongside Christchurch Park until they reached the junction of Anglesea Road and Fonnereau Road. Dusk was falling when they heard whispered voices and several women emerged from the shadows.

"Louisa." A voice hissed through the air.

"Ada, Bessie, you have come," whispered Louisa. "This is my friend Sophia. She is joining us tonight. We will be a merry party."

"Welcome," said Bessie shaking Sophia's hand. "We are pleased to meet you."

"Not a merry party yet," warned Ada. "We have serious work to do tonight, and there are trouble-makers afoot."

"Yes," said Bessie. "A large crowd has gathered at the other end of Fonnereau Road. "Men and women with banners, bells and whistles; no weaponry that we can see but they know of the proposed meeting and seek to disrupt it."

"Did they try to harm you?" asked Louisa, clutching her cousin's arm.

"No," Bessie reassured her. "It is too difficult to tell a suffragist from any other respectable woman, and that rather hobbles them. They don't know whether we go about our normal, lawful business or are involved in something more sinister."

"We should hurry, though," said Ada. "We don't want to take any chances with such a crowd afoot. If they reach us and see us enter the Old Museum, they will know our business and have reason to cause us harm."

They hurried into the High Street where the gas lamplighters were starting their evening's work. The few lamps already ignited partly illuminated the way to Museum Street which they reached just before six o'clock.

"Stop," called Louisa, watching a group of men milling around the entrance to the Old Museum. "Don't go any further." She grabbed Sophia's hand and pulled her back.

"Don't worry," said Sophia. "They are friends. I recognise two of them from the meeting at the park."

Ada and Bessie strode forward, greeting the men in friendly voices. "Good evening to you, Mr Tippett." Ada shook the hand of a smartly dressed gentleman in a bowler hat and double-breasted jacket. "Is Isobel inside?"

"She is," replied Mr Tippett gesturing to the doorway.

"It's good to see you here," said Bessie. "We met some of the anti-suffragists en route."

Tippett raised an eyebrow. "We thought there might be trouble," he said. "We intend to stay outside the building through the night and offer what protection we can. Whatever happens, we will make sure you are safe inside."

"Thank you," said Bessie. "We appreciate your support. "Come, Louisa," she said, beckoning the two younger girls.

Louisa smiled at the men as she walked towards the doorway of the stucco-fronted building with its fluted Doric pilasters standing sentry either side. The building had been retired as a museum long before Louisa was born, and she did not know what it had subsequently become. With a frisson of excitement, she anticipated an opportunity to explore the old building as well as participate in the night's events.

The doorway opened into a hall from which a staircase with an ornate balustrade rose into a galleried landing. Constance Andrews stood at the foot of the stairs with a jug in each hand which she placed on a smartly dressed trestle table containing glasses and a box of Huntley and Palmer's Royal Sovereign biscuits.

"My favourite," whispered Sophia.

"Good evening, ladies," said Constance in clipped tones. "Please help yourself to refreshments and go through." She gestured to a door on the right. "There are several ladies here already and more expected from Felixstowe and Lowestoft shortly. I'll provide supper at eight o'clock, and you will have a good breakfast before you leave tomorrow."

"Thank you," said Ada leading the way.

Louisa was disappointed that the room, once full of interesting exhibits, had been converted into dull offices. Constance and her helpers had rearranged the furniture to accommodate the night's events with dark wooden desks cleared to the side of the large room and a selection of wood and leather chairs placed at intervals around the perimeter. A fire burned brightly beneath a marble mantelpiece, and half a dozen women warmed themselves in front of the flickering flames, chattering excitedly.

"I'll introduce you," said Ada, ushering the girls towards the group of women. "Isobel, Lilla, please meet my cousin, Louisa and her friend Sophia. They are joining us tonight."

Louisa shook hands with the well-dressed women to her front pleased to see Sophia's natural shyness evaporate as she joined the conversation.

More women entered until there were thirty or so present and the room filled with chatter until Constance joined them.

"Ladies," she began, "Everyone we expected has arrived, and the doors are closed until tomorrow. We are protected and safe. Let the revelry begin".

The evening passed in a happy medley of rousing speeches, songs, and party games. Constance provided an excellent supper of sandwiches, salads and devilled chicken legs with the centrepiece, a raised game pie. She apologised for the lack of hot food, but her concerns were dismissed by the other women who complimented her on a tremendous effort, considering the lack of facilities.

The clock was ticking towards midnight when Louisa finished the last of the strawberries in jelly. Her attempt to disguise a yawn beneath her hand failed, and she turned to Sophia.

"I am so full and contented I will fall asleep if I don't move around soon," she said.

"Don't be alarmed if you do," laughed Sophia. "Others have." She pointed to Mrs Vincent, a woman of sixty years or so, slumped in a leather armchair. Her ample bosom moved up and down in time with her audible snores. Louisa giggled.

"I know, but I would like to explore this fine old building. Do you mind?"

"Not at all," said Sophia. "Will it bother you if I don't come?"

Louisa smiled, "Of course not," she said. "I am pleased to see you enjoying the company of our new friends. May I take this candle?"

Sophia nodded, finishing a small piece of cake before moving closer to Ada and Bessie. They huddled together around the brightly lit chimney breast, warmed by the well-stoked fire. Louisa carried the candle holder, guarding the flame with her hand.

She crossed the room and entered the hallway climbing stairs that creaked and groaned beneath her boots. The stairs opened onto a galleried landing occupied by sturdy dark wood cupboards. Glass framed, polished cabinets still contained remnants of fur and feathers, and Louisa presumed that they once housed the museum's exhibits when it was still a museum. She passed the cabinets and opened a narrow, latched door leading to a corridor.

Louisa wrinkled her nose as a smell of damp assailed her nostrils but continued, tiptoeing through the corridor until a noise stopped her dead in her tracks. Tap, tap, tap – the sound was rhythmical like the tick-tock of a clock. Louisa shone the candle against the wall with a trembling hand. There was no timepiece; not even a piece of artwork - just white painted walls and four closed doors. For a second, the only audible sound was her heart beating in time with the tapping. Too terrified to retreat down the corridor and back downstairs to safety, she waited as the seconds ticked by. Then a draught swished the curtain at the far end of the passage, and Louisa saw the branches of a tree tapping against the window.

With the source of the noise revealed, she exhaled and clutched a hand to her chest. "I should return and join the others," she whispered aloud.

She waited until her hands stopped shaking, then tried the first two doors at the top of the corridor. Both lead to identical offices, each with ornate desks positioned centrally on the far wall, a leather chair behind and two visitors' chairs to the front of each desk. The mirror-image rooms were devoid of character. Louisa was disappointed, and her disappointment increased as the third door failed to open at all. It was tightly locked.

The fourth and final door from the corridor squealed open, and Louisa entered, holding the candle high. She almost dropped it again at the sight of a skull staring sightlessly towards her from a crate at the end of the room. Logic triumphed before fear got the better of her as she reasoned the skull was a previous exhibit, and she must be inside a storage room. On further examination, she found other boxes, one containing a frame filled with butterflies and another with a moth-eaten, stuffed polecat. She touched one of the tiny pointed teeth, and the jaw wobbled.

"Perhaps not," she murmured, moving to another box.

This container was full of tin cups, spoons, and other assorted pieces of household crockery. Sighing, Louisa turned to the final box housed on top of an iron safe lodged in the corner of the far wall.

Hanging over the edge of the box were several pairs of handcuffs and an enormous bunch of rusted keys. Underneath, were pay books, files of minutes in shabby folders and a register of prison officers dating from the 1840s. Louisa rummaged around the bottom of the box and pulled out a packet of letters and a dog-eared, black leather diary with mould spores spotted across the spine. Louisa heaved the box to the floor, set her candle on the safe and pulled up a chair from the stacked pile in the corner. Blowing dust from the cover, she opened the front page of the diary. The flickering candle illuminated the fading letters. They read:

"The last days of Mary Emily Cage; a truthful record by Anna Tomkins."

Chapter Three

The Cracks Widen

The shabby, battered diary commanded Louisa's full attention as she puzzled over the title. Who was Mary Cage? Why had her last days been recorded?

She opened the diary and began to read.

"I scarcely know how to start this account, so great is the shock of the news my dear Alfred brought home tonight. I am heartbroken to hear that one of his prisoners is my dear childhood companion, Mary Moise. She is Mary Cage now, of course, having married in haste many years ago. I should know. I was at her wedding, smiling and hoping she would have a good life even though all the portents implied not. She has been in the cells for a whole week, and I did not know until today.

This week I returned from an extended visit to Ireland where my cousin, Margaret, endured the last gruelling days of her pregnancy at her farmhouse in Galway Town. Margaret had always suffered from delicate health and was bed-bound in the final weeks of her confinement. My presence was a boon to her husband, Patrick, who struggled to cope with a sick wife and two young children. He arrived at the station to collect me wearing an expression of undisguised relief across his face, thanking me regularly and often. His unfailing appreciation of my efforts, while Margaret remained incapacitated, made me grateful and embarrassed in equal measures. Despite her frailty, Margaret birthed a fine son called Francis named after her father as he is the second son. Francis thrived, and by six weeks old, had grown fat legs and a powerful pair of lungs. I was no longer needed and returned home, where Alfred greeted me with a beaming smile, delighted to see me after an eight-week absence. Mary, our eldest, minded the younger two children but Alfred said it was lonely while I was away, and they are happy I am home and have told me not to venture away any time soon.

But what sort of homecoming is this? My dear friend is confined in the cells and waiting to die. How can I bear it?

I'd heard of the accusations against her. It was widely known that Mary had been charged with poisoning her husband, but I knew just as well that she could not have done it. Not my Mary. I expected they would find her innocent in last Saturday's trial, but the judge donned the black cap and said she was guilty. They are wrong. They must be.

I will go to see Mary Emily tomorrow as early as I can. Alfred will make the necessary arrangements before my visit, and I will do whatever it takes to bring her comfort. I must atone for neglecting her these past twenty years.

I am at a loss what to do with myself in the meantime. Since Alfred broke the news this evening, I have paced the floor and can find no peace. It is well past midnight, and I sit penning this journal by candlelight as it helps to write about Mary if I cannot talk to her.

I have broken from this account to examine the bookcase in our back bedroom where I keep my old diaries. They are all there; every page I ever wrote. I stole into the room and removed them while the children slept, my youngest Alfred junior snoring quietly as I tip-toed past.

I was luckier than most. My Father kept the village store, so he learned to read, and he sent me to school so I could learn my letters too. I learned to count unlike most village girls and signed my name in the parish register on my wedding day. We both did. All four of our children read. We made sure of it.

I am still a long way from sleep and have resolved to copy any entries from my childhood diary, which contain Mary's name into this journal. Then I will remember properly ahead of our meeting tomorrow."

June 30, 1822 – James and Mary wed yesterday morning. It was a fine day, and all the villagers attended. We celebrated at the Ten Bells Inn after the wedding. James Cage was drunk and disrespectful when he arrived at the church, but Mr Moise admonished him, and the rest of the ceremony passed without further incident. James recovered his usual good humour by the evening, but Mary sat quietly complaining of tiredness. After gentle persuasion, James took her home in an old cart dressed in bows and ribbons. He carried her ever so tenderly onto the seat and drove the cart home to their new rooms to start married life. I will give them some time together before visiting later in the week.

July 3, 1822 – I saw Mary today and found her in good spirits. James has been very attentive since they married, and she thinks he is over the worst of his bad behaviour and minded to be a good husband and father. She invited me into her small parlour furnished with a table, two wooden chairs, and a carved rocking chair her godmother gave her on the day of her wedding. Her bedroom is sparse and empty, save for the bed and a small dresser but she says she is content and will make a happy home.

July 15, 1822 – I watched Mary walk past our cottage today. She has grown fuller with child in the short time since I last saw her. Mary waved to me through the window but did not stop, and I noticed a bandage tied around her arm. I hope she has not had an accident. She will surely call on me if she needs my help.

September 30, 1822 – Mary's first child has come - a new baby daughter called Mary Ann, who was delivered by Mrs Woolner and her daughter, Kezia today. The tiny creature, with a precious face and a shock of dark hair, entered the world quickly for a firstborn. I visited Mary as soon as I heard the news to find her tired but eager for me to meet her new daughter. An absent James could not be persuaded away from his toil in the fields but was told of the birth and sent word that he would meet the baby on his return that night.

October 27, 1822 – Poor Mary; she has scant milk to give and little Mary cries and cries. Mary Emily is exhausted. I have taken the baby to my rooms several times this last week so Mary can rest. James shouts at her and says she shouldn't expect him to work in the fields all day if he can't sleep through the night.

November 11, 1822 – Unexpected news arrived for me today from Ipswich. Last month I applied to teach at the schoolrooms in

Tuddenham Road and the headmistress has written to offer me the position. I will travel to Ipswich in two weeks to reside in nearby Christchurch Street. My working days are Monday to Friday and one in every three Saturdays, which means that I can come home most weekends. Ipswich is no distance at all. Mother and Father are delighted to see me in such a fortunate position.

August 16, 1823 – I returned to Stonham Aspal on Sunday, visiting Mary for the first time in several months. She is still aggrieved at my decision to move away from the village, and we are not such good friends as we once were. I purchased a delicate navy ribbon at the haberdashers in Ipswich Butter Market and used it to trim my old bonnet as a present for Mary. I called on her and gave her my gift. She thanked me but left it on the side and did not try it on. Mary Ann is a lively baby and in good health, praise the Lord. Mary loves her but says she is in no rush to have another.

December 24, 1823 – A wonderful yuletide lies before us. Mother and Aunt Jane have spoken of nothing else for weeks and planned all the festivities by the start of the month. I arrived in Stonham Aspal Christmas Eve morning by carriage and spent the remainder of the day helping Mother trim the house for Christmas Day. We gathered moss, holly, berries, and pinecones from the woods behind our house, assembling a respectable wreath, which Father hung on the front door. Father's fortunes have significantly increased of late since we acquired more space to stock our wares. He used some of this extra money to purchase a weighty turkey for dinner tomorrow. We are all looking forward to Christmas Day.

December 26, 1823 – Christmas Day passed in a haze of enjoyment with as much food as we could wish for and the best company. We attended church on Christmas morning, as always, but Mary was not there, so I visited her today. She is with child again and not looking forward to carrying it for the next six months. There were no signs of Christmas festivities in her parlour, and Mary looked thin and tired. She says James has been out of work for the last four weeks but will not consider any alternative to labouring in the fields preferring to spend his time in the alehouse. She is glum and listless, depressed at James' suggestion that they move to Wetheringsett for farm work. It is two miles from here and means I will see even less of her.

July 7, 1824 – Back home again to visit Mother. Father was in Colchester these last weeks, and Mother tends the store alone. We enjoyed a happy few days together and expect Father to return tomorrow. We will be exceedingly pleased to see him. Today I visited Mary in Wetheringsett. Her new baby arrived early in May and was small and sickly. She called him James after his Father and says she hopes her husband will show more interest in this child than he does in Mary, but so far this has not been the case. I invited Mary to take tea with us, but she declined; a great pity as she is thin and looks exhausted. I asked her if she gets any sleep, and she tells me her mother minds the children from time to time, so she can rest when they are away. Mary says the men are to trim the old barn for a big dance after haysel. I asked her if I should return to the village so we could go together, and she has agreed if she can find someone to watch the babies. So, it is settled. Mary will be her old self again if she has some cheer in her life.

September 24, 1824 – I returned for the harvest dance and it was a jolly affair. Mary's mother minded her children, and we spent the afternoon together, laughing and joking as we did when we were young. Mary wore the bonnet I gave her last year and her best blue dress with the flowered bodice. We danced and sung throughout the evening. All night, Mary was her former happy self, but James grabbed my arm and tried to dance with me. I was polite and danced with him, but he was drunk and touched me inappropriately. I did not tell Mary, and she did not see as she was singing with the village girls at the time. James was not alone in his enjoyment of alcohol. I was surprised to see Mary drinking too. She does not usually but seemed quite merry with it by the end of the evening.

April 5, 1825 – Sad news followed my return to the village with the death of Robert Moise. At his age, and living so close to poverty, death is never wholly unexpected, but Mary grieves, and her distress is terrible to behold. Mr Moise projected a natural authority despite his years, and James appeased him. There will be nobody to restrain his excesses now. Eunice Moise is head to toe in black. She has drawn the curtains in her little cottage and cannot face the world, and Mary has little help with the children.

Baby James has grown little these last few months. He rarely cries but lies in the dresser drawer, seldom raising his tiny head. I lifted his frail body as soon as I entered Mary's parlour, and he snuggled into my shoulder, shallow breathing in my ear. For such a scrap, he is a dear boy, and the love I felt overwhelmed me as I held him, smelling his baby hair, and concealing my teary eyes from Mary. Little Mary, in contrast, is as plump as a butterball and a happier little girl you never did see. With boundless energy and a child's natural curiosity, she tears around the house asking questions about everything she sees. I ruffled her hair as she ran to my side and thought how wonderful it would be to have children of my own one day if I ever meet a man I want to marry. Mary said she will have another mouth to feed by the end of the year. She is with child again and three months gone already. There is no excitement in her for this child. She does not relish motherhood.

May 2, 1825 – I returned home at the behest of my mother. She hastened my return to tell me awful news, so terrible she would not send it in a letter. Baby James has died. My innocent little scrap faded to nothing and was cold and stiff in his dresser drawer one morning. Mother fears Mary is too isolated in Wetheringsett. It is only a short distance from our village, but with small children and no means of travel, it might as well be London. I hailed a waggon that afternoon to visit Mary and console with her, and I cried throughout the journey as I remembered little James' soft skin and his sweet baby smell when I last held him; chiding a God who would take such a dear boy for his own.

When Mary opened the door to me, I held her close and told her how sorry I was for her loss. She was still numb with grief for she barely acknowledged my words, save to say she will name the new baby James if it is a boy. I tried to help her, offering to watch little Mary or perform some household chore, but our conversation was stilted and full of awkward silences. I felt unable to intrude upon her grief any further, so bid her goodbye.

As I left, her sleeve slid down as she reached for the door latch, revealing blotches and bruises stark against the pale skin of her arm. She dragged her sleeve over her forearm, claiming the marks were from a fall against the dresser. I wanted to believe her and did not pry.

When I returned to Stonham, I walked to St Lambert's and prayed for Little James at the altar. The Reverend approached me, and we said the Lord's prayer together. He told me God would look after his little soul, and it gave me comfort, so I am minded to tell Mary next

27

time I see her. Perhaps she will benefit from the succour of the church.

December 22, 1825 – I returned home for Christmas to catch up with the comings and goings in Stonham Aspal. Frederick Abbott is to wed the prettiest girl in the village so we will have another celebration soon. Old Mrs Tydeman and the widow Wright have both died this quarter, but neither death was unexpected. They were both poorly with Mrs Tydeman bed-bound these last two years. The blacksmith has employed another apprentice, and there is a new assistant at the butcher's shop. I love meeting new people and will walk by later and introduce myself.

Mary's new baby is born, and it was a boy, much healthier and heartier than poor sickly James. As expected, they named him after his elder brother. I will visit Mary tomorrow and bring her all the village news.

December 23, 1825 – I witnessed such horror today I scarcely believe my eyes. James Cage is the son of Satan with a dark hole where his heart should be. But I rush to get my words out and must form my sentences in an intelligible manner before I write them down, even though I cannot imagine wishing to recount them again.

I visited Mary earlier and found her tired and despondent, as is her usual demeanour these days. Mary Ann played contentedly in the corner, but baby James bawled, red-faced and angry. Mary raised her eyes and scowled as she opened the door, wasting no time on small talk and warning me that James was lying in the bedroom and must have quiet. I picked up the baby, rocking him in the hope that he might sleep, but he continued to bawl. Mary put him to her breast, but he did not settle, and the crying became a scream. I took him from Mary, inserting a fingertip into his angry mouth when the door to the bedroom slammed open and James Cage strode into the room. Without uttering a word, he struck Mary about the face with one mighty blow. She reeled backwards, falling onto the table. Crockery lay shattered on the floor surrounded by a puddle of water from the jug. Mary lay where she had fallen with the broken items about her. She did not move and laid quite still, conscious, but stationery.

"You cannot ill-treat her like that," I cried, but Cage raised his hand to me and told me I would get the same if I did not leave his house. Mary lifted her head and said 'go' in a firm voice, and I took the children and carried them back to Stonham Aspal, where I left

them in my mother's care. I sought Mother's advice, and she cautioned me to be careful not to get in between a husband and wife, but the thought of Mary lying immobile on the floor for fear of making James angrier was unbearable. My conscience would not let me leave matters alone, so I hastened to the police house and informed Constable Dawson. He told me he was familiar with the ructions between James Cage and his wife but could do nothing unless he committed grievous injury upon her. I told him that in my opinion, the harm he had already perpetrated was sufficiently heinous for police involvement, but he said it was not. Must she be permanently damaged before they will act? Now I know how bad things are for Mary, and I do not think she will thank me for bringing them to the attention of the authorities. Mother still has the little ones. I can only imagine what tomorrow will bring.

December 24, 1825 – Mary walked to our house from Wetheringsett today. She trudged through sleet with holes in her boots, wrapped in a thin, fraying shawl. I invited her into my mother's parlour, but she declined and stayed shivering at the front door without stepping across the threshold. I asked whether James was violent towards her before yesterday's attack. She pursed her lips and stared sightlessly down the hallway without responding. I made another attempt. She shook her head, then in a flat, monotone voice, told me not to visit again.

I do not know what made me act so impulsively, but I pulled her through the door and pushed her into the chair by the fire. I knelt on the floor, holding her frozen hand. "Do not ask that of me, Mary," I said. "I am your friend and will not stand by and watch. Ask anything of me, but do not tell me I am unwelcome in your home." Her steel-grey eyes momentarily filled with tears, and then she recovered. She said she would not ask me to stay away forever, but I should not return to her house in the immediate future. She picked up the baby and, taking little Mary's hand, marched from the parlour without further discourse. I ran straight to John Firman's and asked if his cart was available for hire. It was, and he agreed to collect Mary and take her to Wetheringsett so she would not have to walk across fields in the bad weather again. I paid him the fare, and he left to find Mary. I expect that is the last I will see of her until she is prepared to allow me to visit again.

April 13, 1826 – Today I spoke with Mary for the first time this year after several abortive visits to Wetheringsett in January and February. On both occasions, I knocked at her door, but there was no answer. Whether the house was empty or not was impossible to tell, but I left Mary no opportunity to avoid me today when I spotted her entering the chemist in Debenham. My aunt, Jane Fairweather, lived there and I was in town on a long-overdue visit. We were taking tea in the parlour when I saw Mary through the window facing the High Street. Pausing only to ask my aunt if she minded me leaving her briefly, I ran up the street after Mary. I reached her towards the end of the High Street and tapped her on the shoulder. She turned and smiled, her old self for a moment. Then her face clouded, and she turned away. "Talk to me Mary," I pleaded, and she relented, suggesting we walk together to the churchyard. We settled on a wooden bench amongst the gravestones of our ancestors, for we both had kin in Debenham, and she began to talk.

She said that James had mistreated her since the first days of their marriage. He was more restrained when her Father was alive but since his death, had no fear of the consequences of his actions. James was tolerable when sober but a cruel drunk, and as he was drunk most of the time, she was often the subject of his bad temper. I asked why she did not leave him, but she pushed my hand away. "Where do you think I would go?" Mary asked scornfully. I suggested her mother might take her, but she shook her head and said her mother can only feed herself because she receives poor relief. I said I was sorry to hear this. We sat in silence as she twirled a ringlet of hair around her finger, deep in thought. Then she took a deep breath and talked frankly of James' meagre income and his inclination to spend the little he earned on ale.

As much as I tried to conceal my pity, a tear stole down my face as she talked of her troubles, but she remained aloof and distant, in complete command of her emotions. I recognised nothing of the warm, joyful girl who was my childhood friend and wondered at the change in a human soul when hope dies. We sat together for a while longer, but the conversation tailed away. I thought of my aunt waiting for my return and bid Mary goodbye promising to visit early summer. She leaned towards me, dry lips pecking my cheek, and said she looked forward to my visit. Then we left the churchyard and went our separate ways. Furrows line this page where my tears fell into the ink earlier while writing the day's events. I would offer money, but Mary is too proud to accept it. I want to help her, but I don't know how.

Louisa broke from the diary at the sound of footsteps echoing down the corridor.

"Louisa, where are you?"

"I'm here, Sophia," she called watching as a shadow loomed large in the doorway, followed by Sophia bearing a lamp.

"You've been away for ages," said Sophia. "We were worried. It is past two o'clock in the morning, and the women are asleep. Are you not tired?"

"Not in the least," said Louisa. "I found a diary about a wretched woman and her cruel husband. It is a true story, and I am only partway through. I want to know how it ends. From the inscription at the front, I fear it does not end well".

Sophia laughed. "Surely you do not favour this story over the tales of suffragette escapades we have enjoyed all evening?" she asked. "It is most unlike you, Louisa. You are the ringleader in our adventures."

"And will continue to be," smiled Louisa, "but I am in the grip of this diary. Let me have another half hour with it, and I will return to you. I cannot read for much longer anyway. My hands are blocks of ice".

"Bring the book downstairs," suggested Sophia. "It is warm and cosy, and Constance is about to make another urn of coffee."

"What a wonderful idea," smiled Louisa, "although I am not sure whether I ought to take the book downstairs. It is not mine and belongs to the Old Museum."

"It will pass unnoticed for the rest of the night," said Sophia. "Replace it after breakfast tomorrow, and no one will be any the wiser."

"I shall," said Louisa, taking her candle in one hand and carrying the diary with her index finger marking her place in the other. Shrugging off the cold, she headed back down the corridor and into the welcome warmth of the reception room.

Those women who had previously laid claim to the leather chairs were dozing while those in the hard, wooden chairs were resigned to a sleepless night. An ever-diligent Constance Andrews kept the fire burning, and flames leapt and crackled while providing a comfortable ambient temperature.

"Have my chair," said Sophia, directing Louisa to her seat next to the fire. "Your poor hands are freezing."

"Thank you," said Louisa. "Will you think me rude if I keep reading?"

"Only if you do not recount the story to me in full tomorrow," smiled Sophia, and Louisa continued reading.

July 9, 1826 – The inevitable has happened, and Mary lies gravely ill in my mother's spare bedroom after a beating that left her black and blue. Her poor lips are swollen and her chest and neck a purple mess of bruising. Mary arrived at mother's door two days ago in the dark of night with her two bewildered children. They walked by moonlight with no candle or lantern to light the way, only seeking help because Mary lost so much blood, she feared she would die, leaving her children alone with Cage.

Mother sent word to Ipswich, and I arrived today to see her battered and broken in my home. I asked her to promise never to return to Cage, but she has no other means to live and will not give her word. Fortunately, both children are hearty creatures and have settled well. After much persuasion, Mary agreed to remain with us until the end of the month.

July 15, 1826 – Mary is much recovered and relieved to be living in Stonham Aspal once again. Her health has improved, and she felt well enough to visit friends at Lasts' farm this morning. Mary was so much her old self when she returned that it gladdened my heart. She says she will go again tomorrow and all the other days until she leaves us.

July 17, 1826 – I feel uneasy today. Mary talks not just of her girlfriends, but of a young man she met at the farm. He is employed by Mr Last to repair a brick wall around the stable yard. She tells me they have talked together frequently, and it is clear that she admires him a great deal. Regardless of her justification in staying away from James Cage, she must remember that she is a married woman. I have advised her to avoid this friendship.

July 25, 1826 – Mary continues to see her bricklayer, George Thurlow. She says they only talk together, but I know her well enough to be sure she is excessively fond of him. I made some discreet enquiries about the village to see what kind of character Mary has acquainted herself with. George was born in Stonham Aspal and, although I do not know him well, others do. They say he is charming and a bit of a rogue. He is a favourite with the village girls but has shown no interest in them, or so I am told. I believe this friendship is unwise and have been quite forthright in telling Mary about my concerns. I have not mentioned George to my mother as she would not countenance this behaviour under her roof.

July 31, 1826 – Mary tells me that she must return to Wetheringsett. I wish she would not go, but she says she cannot remain here and has no money to go anywhere else. James Cage turned up a few days ago and offered to have her back and mend his ways. He admits an excess of beer makes him violent and has told Mary he will not drink so much if she returns. She understands her friendship with George cannot continue and could lead to a great deal of trouble if she stays in our village. I said my goodbyes with a heavy heart. I neither trust James Cage nor believe a single word he utters. But Mary seems to love him still despite his heavy-handed ways, and I am resigned to her returning to Wetheringsett.

November 8, 1826 – This is surely the saddest day of my life. My gentle, loving mother died suddenly in her bed Sunday evening. She retired early feeling out of sorts, and my poor Father found her marble cold when he returned from the store. I will never feel her gentle touch or hear her words of comfort again. I cannot bear it. I am accustomed to the solitude of being an only child, but the burden of trying to console my dear Father alone while my grief is so raw is more than I can endure.

Fortune favoured me with a kind and loving family, and I have grown up with such affection that the loss of it makes me almost wish I never had it at all. Our homely kitchen is dark and cold, the fire unlit, the table bare. I sit beside Mother's chair in the parlour at night, the arms worn away where she sat and sewed. Grandmother's old shawl lies across the back and carries the scent of my mother. The indentation where she sat remains, but she will never occupy this chair again. Last night I woke after a fitful sleep to muffled noises downstairs. I tip-toed into the hallway to see Father sitting at the kitchen table with his head in hands, sobbing like a small boy. It broke my heart to see him, and I could not comfort him for it would have made him feel worse to think I had witnessed his grief.

My mother will be interred at St Lambert's tomorrow and will lie in the cold frost-bitten ground. I will never see her again and can only pray that God will keep her safe and guide her to heaven.

November 9, 1826 – I am numb, and my heart is broken. I write because I cannot sleep. Perhaps I will never sleep again. We bade our final goodbyes to Mother early this morning. It was even colder today, and our breath hung heavy in the air. Many more people than we expected joined us at church. Mother's kin arrived from Debenham and Fathers from Kenton. And in the cold November air, we laid her to rest.

I am all cried out now. There are no more tears left to fall even though I am sadder than I have ever been. My Aunt Jane remained with us. She will keep house for the next week until her return to Debenham. Mother was the last of her sisters, so her grief is considerable. She tried to persuade my Father to eat a little for he has hardly touched a morsel in days. He tried some bread and butter but pushed it away after a few bites. I have never seen him so upset. He has not opened the store since my mother was taken from us.

December 24, 1826 – Christmas Eve is a hollow day this year, a mess of warm memories of Christmases past and the cold horror of our present reality. I travelled home to spread what Christmas cheer I could, but Father has lurched from one extreme to the other and keeps to his shop until late at night. He cannot face Christmas without Mother. Indeed, he seems reluctant to set foot in the house if he can avoid doing so.

I tried to make a Christmas wreath this morning and ventured into the woods carrying Mother's wicker basket. I gathered ivy, moss, and pinecones from the dewy forest floor, but it was the loneliest walk I have ever taken. I knew that Mother would have wanted me to trim the house for my father, so I persevered with tears coursing down my face. I spent an hour sitting on the edge of the well fashioning a wreath of sorts from the collection of foliage, then tied a bright red ribbon around it. The wreath is not as good as the one Mother, and I made together. My sadness is woven into its very structure, but I think she would have been proud that I tried. I prepared a small chicken for tomorrow's dinner, as there will only be two of us. I usually look forward to Christmas, but this year I dread it.

December 26, 1826 – Christmas Day was an ordeal better forgotten. We tried to be cheerful as Mother would have wished, but it was an impossible task. From the moment I saw Father sitting in his chair in the parlour staring misty-eyed into the fire, I knew I did not have the strength to carry on. A lump grew tight in my throat, and I could not swallow it down. I could not move, could not pretend. My Father looked into my eyes and the grief seared through my body emerging in an agonised moan as the tears coursed down my face like drops of molten metal. I cried in great shuddering sobs until I could cry no more and my father cried with me.

When there were no tears left, we sat together, watching the rain streak down the windows. Father reminisced about life with Mother before I was born, telling tales of their courtship and her family and many things, I never knew. By the end of the day, we had grieved so much that we were exhausted; but it was cathartic. For the first time, I thought we could be happy again one day.

December 27, 1827 - I visited Mary as I had not seen her since Mother's funeral. She came alone to the church that day, leaving her children I know not where. I can hardly imagine they were with their father, but she spoke kindly of my mother at the funeral, which gave me some small comfort. Her living quarters are unchanged. They are cold and spartan with her roof in a poor state of repair and leaking badly. I asked her how things were between herself and James. She changed the direction of the conversation and talked about other matters without answering my question, so I think they cannot be right.

She said she missed my mother dreadfully. Mother made her feel safe, and our home had been her place of sanctuary. She held my hand, saying how sorry she was for my loss and that she also felt mother's absence keenly. I was grateful for her appreciation of my mother, yet irritated that she mentioned the loss of her safe house. I know she recognises my loss and grief, and perhaps it is unfair, but I am not minded to be charitable while my pain is so raw. I stayed at Mary's only half of an hour. She was not in a talking mood, and the silence became uncomfortable. Mary Ann, usually so lively, was subdued and listless. Little James was quiet too. Mary seemed pre-occupied, so I took my leave.

May 5, 1827 - I have left Ipswich four times this year to spend time with Father. Each time I return, hoping his spirits will improve before the next visit, even if only a little. But sorrow overwhelms him, and he does nothing but work and sleep. He is thinner than he should be, despite employing Mrs Johnson to cook and clean while he minds the store. Even her renowned baking cannot tempt him to eat.

I decided to visit Mary today, and Mr Firman took me to Wetheringsett in his cart. Mary was not at home, so it is a good thing I did not walk miles across the fields for a futile visit. After I returned from Wetheringsett, I stopped at the church to pay my respects to Mother and met Alice and Susan Hunt at the lychgate. They talked of village matters and told me that James Cage was making free with his fists again. Perhaps that is why Mary was so quiet during my last visit. I cannot be sure this is not idle gossip, so I will try to put it from my mind. Mother has a gravestone at last. It is a sombre granite stone with a simple inscription. "Florence Saunders, 1781 – 1826 - Well loved by all who knew her"

Chapter Four

A new acquaintance

August 20, 1827 – I have not returned to Stonham Aspal this month, and Father's letters have brought the village news. Although I have been busy, truth to tell, I have become acquainted with a pleasant young man who occasionally walks with me from my lodgings to the school. He works at the prison here in Ipswich but lodges nearby, which is how we met. Alfred is kind and full of interesting stories about his work. I am reluctant to leave town this early in our acquaintance. Am I selfish to stay away from my father? What would Mother think of my neglect?

August 27, 1827 – I received a further letter from my father bringing alarming news. James Cage and three others were caught stealing plate and silverware from The Old Hall. Naturally, he was apprehended as it is not the first time he has been charged with larceny, although he was treated leniently on the previous occasion. This time, it is a different matter. He has stolen from influential people, and I cannot think that he will escape without a custodial sentence. How will poor Mary live? James already squanders most of what he earns, but if they gaol him, she will be dependent upon poor relief, possibly even the workhouse. We must hope they show mercy, but he has come to the attention of the authorities too many times to expend much hope.

November 1, 1827 – I returned to Stonham Aspal last night with Alfred. We travelled together in the wagon but decided it was too soon for him to meet my father. My mother has not lain in the earth a whole year yet, and we think it insensitive for him to make Father's acquaintance this soon even though we are walking out together. Perhaps next year would be better. My father was pleased to see me. We talked at length, and he admitted he was lonely without Mother even with the comings and goings of his customers. As soon as I reached the village, I learned that James Cage had been committed to trial and sentenced to nine months hard labour inside Ipswich Gaol. It is ironic indeed, for Alfred works in the gaol house and will no doubt encounter Cage in the course of his duties. I am saddened for Mary and do not know how she will cope without his income; however small it is. I will visit her tomorrow and offer her what little comfort I may.

November 2, 1827 – Mary was at home when I visited earlier and in good spirits. Though James is absent, and she has no income, her mother agreed, after much persuasion, to let her live at her house in Stonham Aspal for a few months. It will be a tight squeeze for her and the children in the cramped little cottage, and I do not know how they will manage, but it is an improvement for Mary to be back in the village where people know her and can help. James is two years old now and Mary Ann five, so they are less demanding. Mary Emily seems happier and is excited about the prospect of returning to Stonham. A cart is due to collect her and her scant possessions on Sunday, and she will be installed at Mrs Moises' house by the end of this weekend.

She was in such good spirits that I felt able to tell her about Alfred and how much I like him and what a gentleman he is. She asked if we might marry, and I told her I could not say, for he had not asked me, and I did not know whether he ever would. But I do like him, so very much, and Mary is the one person I can tell.

December 21, 1827 – I arrived early for Christmas this year to be met with the most scandalous news. Mary resolved her problem of how to live without an income by taking up with George Thurlow who she met last year. On hearing this information, I hastened down the street to Mary's mother's cottage and asked to see Mary at once. The children were still living with Eunice, but Mary had moved into George Thurlow's lodgings by the Green, where she dwells with him in sin.

I found her there some half an hour later in a state of great contentment and fully cognisant of the damage to her reputation. "I love him," she told me," and he loves me." When I asked her what she would do when James left prison, she put her nose in the air and told me she did not care. She said George would look after her and see that no harm came to her when James returned. I asked her if she was sure of this and she said he had told her so. I met George when I returned later that evening. He is an affable chap and good company, but he is young with no ties. I cannot see why he would wish to take on a married woman and her children. I have not told my father that I visited Mary. The village gossips have blackened her name, and I am sure he would prefer me to keep away from the scandal.

April 4, 1828 – I took much pleasure in visiting Stonham accompanied by Alfred, who was meeting my father for the first time. Alfred lodged at the Ten Bells for the sake of propriety while I stayed with my dear father as usual. Mrs Johnson cooked a hearty supper today and father invited Alfred to dine. My Aunt Jane arrived from Debenham and joined us. Father talked at length with Alfred. It appears that Alfred's aunt is distant kin to us by marriage. This first meeting seems to have gone well. Father asked Alfred to join us for lunch tomorrow, so I am exceedingly happy that the people I care most about seem easy in each other's company.

April 5, 1828 – Today was good and bad in equal measures. Alfred, Aunt Jane, and I spent a pleasant morning in Debenham later returning to Stonham by cart where we joined father for lunch. He seemed much taken with Alfred and shut the store for an extra half-hour when they went to the Ten Bells together for a drink, while Aunt Jane and I helped Mrs Johnson clear the dinner dishes away. I cannot remember the last time Father went to the public house, and though I am not a great lover of beer drinking, I think it will do him good to be sociable and join the other men, for once.

On their return, Father re-opened the shop, and I asked Alfred if he would mind if I visited my friend, Mary. He wondered if he might join me, but I made my excuses in case George Thurlow was present. I don't want him to know details about Mary's life or judge her only on this recent misdemeanour, so I made an excuse and said Mary was shy. Alfred accepted my explanation and returned to the Ten Bells to read the local newspaper, as was his inclination.

It turned out to be a wise course of action as I quickly discovered the extent of Mary's shame. How it is not public knowledge about the village, I know not, but Mary's stomach is much pronounced, and she

39

is quite obviously with child. It is equally apparent that this is not the child of her husband, who has been incarcerated since October. Anxious to avoid an argument but unable to pretend I had not noticed, I asked outright whether she carried George Thurlow's child. She said she did, but it was of no consequence as they would continue to live together as husband and wife when James Cage returned from gaol. She cared nothing for public opinion and was content for the first time in many years. George treated her kindly, and she had known only cruelty from James. Her behaviour is morally wrong, but her logic is impeccable. How can I condemn her for her shameful conduct when living with her husband would surely be dangerous? I told her I understood but did not invite her to meet Alfred. There is too much potential for trouble.

July 1, 1828 – I was delighted to see my father when he visited my lodgings in Christchurch Street today. We spent an enjoyable time together with Alfred in Christchurch Park where we lunched on sandwiches and fruit. It was a beautiful, cloudless day and the sun shone so brightly that we were sunburnt by the end of it. Father walked me back to my lodgings at the end of the afternoon before boarding the coach to Stonham Aspal.

On the way to the coach, he said two things, both of which caused me great consternation. Firstly, he asked if Alfred intended to make an honest woman of me. I could not answer as Alfred has never spoken of it. I know he likes me a great deal and treats me with the utmost respect. Alfred holds my hand, kisses my cheek, and has dined more than once with my beloved father, but he has never discussed a future with me. Perhaps he does not love me and sees this more as a friendship. As I write this diary, I am in a state of considerable confusion.

The second disconcerting utterance from my father was the news that James Cage has returned to the village. I might have known this sooner had I risked speaking to Alfred about Cage, but I did not want Mary's shame reflected upon me, so I have said nothing of it. It turns out that James returned over a month ago to find his wife taken up with another man and big with child. He confronted George Thurlow, struck him hard and chased him off. George Thurlow has not been seen in the village since and is rumoured to be dwelling here in Ipswich.

Cage took Mary and the children back to Wetheringsett. I dread to think what treatment she will endure at his hands after this and I am even more surprised that he has taken her back at all and not abandoned her to the workhouse. I asked Father if there was any word of Mary's condition, and he said he had heard nothing but would make enquiries.

July 5, 1828 – I could not rest for worrying about Mary and ventured back to Stonham Aspal for one night only. Father was surprised to see me but pleased as it gives him company. Father had business in Wetheringsett, and we rode together by cart. I went to Mary's rooms while he visited Mr Allen, the blacksmith.

Mary was there, but James was not, thank the Lord, so we were able to speak undisturbed. But she is broken. She is but a shadow of how she was only a few short months ago. She sat upon one of her hard wooden chairs for her rocking chair is gone, and I know not where and dare not ask, staring at the dying embers of the fire through faraway eyes. Her hair is unkempt, her clothes dirty and, God forgive me for noticing it, but she smells. The whole dwelling, leaking and musty, gave an air of melancholy that bought me low. Depression had settled across the household, and even the children lay still on the floor, utterly subdued by the all-pervading atmosphere of gloom.

I must have gasped aloud for she asked me how I was without moving her gaze from the fireplace. I took her hands and, ignoring the smell of her, looked into her eyes, and asked what ailed her. She stared back at me with unfocussed eyes. "He is gone," she said. I asked her who was gone, and she answered George and then she cried, and I held her close until her sobbing ceased. Not since she was a young child has Mary cried in front of me. A mistress of composure, she has never given in to tears before, no matter how justified her circumstance. She must be distraught at the loss of her man.

I asked her where George had gone and whether he would come back again. She said she did not know where he had gone, but he would not come back, and she knew this because he sent one of his kin to tell her. He told her to remain with her husband and forget all about him. Their love could be no more. He was not cruel in the words that he sent, but he was firm and resolved never to return to the village again.

I watched as she stood from the chair and dropped two dirty white pills into a cup of liquid, gulping it down with such a lack of care that

41

the liquid fell onto her clothing. She told me that James intended to raise the child as his own. I professed astonishment at this news which appeared wholly out of character. She further surprised me by saying that James was not entirely wicked and that although he did not take time with the children, neither was he cruel or neglectful to them. He reserved that behaviour for her but that he had not been violent since her return. She is due to birth her new child imminently, so I pray this peace continues.

August 15, 1828 – Father writes to tell me that Mary's child has arrived. She birthed another little boy and has called him Richard. I mentioned Mary's baby to Alfred but have not told him the circumstances of the birth. As far as he is concerned, Richard is a child born of wedlock. I asked Alfred if he ever thought to have a child of his own one day. He smiled at me and said that he hoped fate would give him the opportunity. I do not know how to interpret this.

September 18, 1828 – I arrived back in the village late this evening, as father had written and asked me to come home. He wanted to discuss a matter of great importance but in person and not in a letter. We dined together, and he disclosed that he proposed to sell the store and use the proceeds to retire to Ipswich but would only do so with my blessing. I was taken aback by this news. Not only I have lived in Stonham Aspal my entire life, but Father has lived there the vast majority of his. He told me what I already knew. He is lonely without my mother, and the house carries too many memories of happier times. He has a few kin and a good friend in Ipswich, and with me living nearby, thinks he could be happy away from the village. I said, of course, he must do whatever is necessary for his fulfilment and that I would support him in this endeavour. Father anticipates that it will take many months to find a purchaser for the store and the cottage, so it will be sometime in the next year before he moves.

We sat by the fire and talked of happier days, remembering my childhood and our precious time with Mother and then he enquired after Alfred. I could not bear the thought of him asking about Alfred's intentions towards me again, so I feigned tiredness and went to bed. Out of earshot of Father, I curled up in my blankets and cried for my mother. My heart ached at the loss of her, and now the loss of my childhood home where her love and kindness still lingered.

September 19, 1828 – It was a warm, if slightly breezy autumn day, and I walked across the fields to Wetheringsett passing several other people along the way. The door to Mary's house was wide open when I arrived, and I knocked before entering, to find her sitting on the wooden chair, nursing her new son. She seemed tired and wan. Mary Ann stood beside her, stroking the baby's head, and patting his cheek. He has a head of dark hair just like George. There is no doubting the father as James is fair-haired, as are their other two children. I asked Mary if she felt any better, and she replied that her mood was somewhat improved, and she would recover fully before long. I did not believe her, but she has regained a little of her steely determination, so perhaps she will. I asked about George, but she said never to mention his name again. He is gone from her thoughts forever.

December 22, 1828 – I have returned to Stonham Aspal for Christmastide, as is my custom, to find Father no further forward with the sale of the store and quite despondent about the prospect. He longs to leave the village now and says he cannot face another year here among the memories. I asked him if he would miss being able to visit Mother in the churchyard nearby, and he replied that she was not there anymore. She was with him and would always be with him wherever he chose to settle. I was glad to hear that as he has suffered enough.

My Aunt Jane joins us for Christmas again this year. She arrived a few days ago and has trimmed the house for us, ready for Yule. She has placed a wreath upon the door, which is a considerable improvement on my poor effort last year. I was pleased to be spared this task, as it upset me sorely Christmas last. I intend to visit Mary tomorrow, although I cannot profess to be looking forward to seeing her. She has been in such low spirits of late.

December 23, 1828 – I did not visit Mary for such a momentous event occurred that she went right out of my mind. All my hopes and prayers have come to fruition, and I am truly happy for the first time since Mother left us. Father is overjoyed, but I digress and must write this down chronologically for my future pleasure.

Father and I breakfasted early this morning, and I walked to the butchers at his behest to purchase our supper. On my return, I was surprised to see a carriage at our front door. I entered our home to find Alfred and my father in earnest discussion in the parlour. Father saw me and waved me away, and I stood in the garden puzzled and upset to think that Alfred was here unexpectedly, and Father did not wish me to be privy to their conversation. I paced the garden in my confusion watching the chickens, only half hearing their throaty clucks, when the kitchen door opened, and Alfred strode towards me with a big smile on his handsome face.

He approached me and said, "my dearest Anna, how I love you so." Those were his exact words, recorded here for posterity. 'My dearest Anna...' I could listen to those words all day long. Then he knelt on the frozen earth and asked me if I would have him for a husband, and he reached into his pocket and pulled out a golden ring. I cannot say how surprised I was and how much I had longed to hear those words. At first, I could not answer for the tears streamed down my face, but once I composed myself, I said 'yes' so loudly and firmly that he could have been in no doubt about my devotion. We are now betrothed, and I am sublimely happy.

I told Alfred that I did not think he wanted to marry me, and he said that he had wanted to almost since the day we first met, but he did not feel his prospects were good enough. Mr Bowden, his superior, retired last week and they have given him extra duties at the prison, together with a higher salary. He has taken advice about purchasing a property and should be able to acquire a small house soon. My father has given his consent with much pleasure and will relocate close by so we can see him regularly. I cannot believe my good fortune. Alfred stayed for supper, and Father opened a bottle of his best port. We enjoyed a merry evening and raised a glass to Mother. It was like old times. Then, Alfred left for the Ten Bells where he will stay for the Christmas period and in two days, he will join us for our first Christmas lunch together. I am overjoyed.

December 25, 1828 – We rose early and made our way to the church where Alfred joined us for the Christmas morning sermon. After the service, Father approached the reverend and asked him if he would marry us, which he eagerly agreed to do. Alfred wants to marry next autumn, which will allow enough time to save money and purchase a property. This timescale will also give Father ample opportunity to sell the store and his cottage.

Aunt Jane and Alfred walked back to our house while Father and I tended to my mother's grave. I whispered my news while I cleaned the tombstone as I wanted her to know it from me. Father took my arm as we returned to the cottage and told me how happy he was and what a sensible young man he thought Alfred to be. After saying Grace,

Father, Aunt Jane, Alfred, and I ate a hearty Christmas dinner. It was a happier and more substantial repast than last Christmas.

December 29, 1828 – I returned to my lodgings in Christchurch Road and soon realised that I had forgotten to visit Mary in all the excitement of Christmas. I write this diary entry as an aide to memory and will arrange to see Mary at the first opportunity in the New Year. I must not forget my obligation to my old friend.

March 15, 1829 – Alfred and I arrived in Stonham Aspal on a beautiful spring day to cobalt blue skies and a welcoming procession of daffodils along the roadside. I love my village but especially in the spring. It is a magical season invoking boundless optimism for the year ahead. The weather was so alluring that virtually every able-bodied villager found a reason to be outside. Women bustled about the village carrying out errands while the fields were full of working men in shirt sleeves; jackets and smocks lying in heaps on the ground.

Alfred lodged at the Ten Bells as usual; glad to reacquaint himself with Mr Pepper, the proprietor, with whom he has built a steady and enduring friendship. Alfred tells me they talk into the small hours when he visits, but what they find to speak of for so long, I do not know. Alfred took his bag to the inn while I sought Father in his shop. He was in high spirits, having secured a buyer for the store who will purchase it imminently. Father also found a separate purchaser for the cottage who is willing to wait until October, enabling him to settle in Ipswich after we are married.

Mindful that I had not visited Mary for some considerable time, I stopped at Mr Firman's on the way back to the cottage and asked him to drive me to Wetheringsett on the morrow. He told me that Mary has moved to another smaller abode within Wetheringsett as James could not find work over winter and money was scarce.

March 16, 1829 – I travelled to Wetheringsett today with Mr Firman. Alfred was dismayed that I did not ask him to join me but was too polite to ask why. I am not entirely sure of the reason myself. I am not ashamed of Mary, so why do I feel unable to introduce her to my betrothed? Suffice it to say I visited Mary, but alone.

Neither Mr Firman nor I knew the location of Mary's new dwelling, so I asked a passing villager, and he pointed towards a little wooden structure leaning against the crumbling wall of a nearby cottage. My heart sank. Mary's former rooms were of the most basic kind, leaking and cold but this shack was barely standing, and I dreaded what I might find inside. I knocked on the pitted wooden door. Mary was home and answered the door to me. She stood at the doorway, dusty and unkempt with the same glazed eyes with which I had grown accustomed.

"What do you want?" she growled. I was taken aback at her hostility but said I had come to visit her and was sorry that I had not seen her at Christmas. Time had been pressing, and I could not manage a visit within the time allotted. She replied, saying that it was a shame that I had not thought to tell her about my engagement before she found out from the village gossips. She asked me if I was too grand for my old friends now that I was to be married. I said "no, not at all," and she said if that was the case, why did I not introduce her to Alfred? And I had nothing with which to counter her. Nothing at all, because I had battled with this thought myself and did not know or could not admit the reason why. Then she told me to go and slammed the door in my face. I stood, shocked for several moments, then knocked again but she did not reply. I believe I have lost her, my childhood friend. I have been careless of her feelings, and now she is gone.

October 14, 1829 – I marry in a few days and have returned to my village for the last time as Anna Saunders. Soon I will be Mrs Anna Tomkins. How wonderful those words sound? My father took leave of his store in early summer and since then has lived a work-free life as a man of means. His cottage is sold but will not be vacated until the end of this month when he follows us back to Ipswich forever. I attempted to visit Mary yesterday in the hope of repairing our friendship before I leave Stonham Aspal. She was not at home, but a neighbour asked what I wanted with her and told me she was about the village somewhere. The neighbour spoke disparagingly of Mary and said that the overseers had summoned her lately and quizzed her about her bastard son's father. They wanted a sworn statement so they could claim maintenance for the child. She said that James Cage had worked little these last months, and the household is in extreme poverty and want. I walked the streets of Wetheringsett for half an hour but could not see Mary, so left with an unfinished task and a heavy heart.

October 18, 1829 – I was married today and now carry the name, Mrs Alfred Tomkins. My heart is full of love for my husband, and I am excited to return to Ipswich tomorrow to make a new life at our home *in Woodbridge Road. I could not be happier save for one thing. I hoped against hope that Mary would attend my wedding, as I did hers, but she did not appear. Nor has she sent me good wishes or congratulations. I have lost her forever. I start tomorrow with a bright new future and a heart full of hope and do not wish to remember things that I cannot change. This, my first diary entry as a married woman will also be my last. I pray I shall have a happy life, and I wish Mary all the love and luck in the world.*

Chapter Five

Come the Dawn

"But that can't be the end of it," exclaimed Louisa. "There is a substantial part of the journal left to read."

"You're back with us," said Sophia, smiling indulgently at her friend. "And just in time too. Breakfast isn't far away, and I am exceedingly hungry."

"I am hungry too, "said Louisa, as the aroma of coffee filled the air, and her stomach growled in an unladylike manner. "I quite lost myself in this diary, Sophia," she confessed. "There is much more to read, but I don't have time to indulge in it now."

"No, you can't," agreed Sophia. "We have lost you to your reading for most of the night. You've missed some dreadful stories about the suffering of our comrades in London. Bessie's account was harrowing. Her friend, Marion, was arrested in Kensington last month and the conditions she endured were shocking. The violence and language used by the police is barely imaginable."

"I heard about it," said Louisa, "but not the whole account. I have been self-indulgent tonight and left you on your own with women you do not know well. Forgive me, Sophia."

"There is nothing to forgive. I have been perfectly at ease with my new friends. Life has brought me few challenges, Louisa. My family have means, and I have never known a day's hunger in my life. I may not always be happy, but I am all too aware of my privileged existence. You have opened my eyes to politics and the enfranchisement of women, and I have never felt more useful. I will always be grateful to you for introducing me to these brave women and their noble mission."

"You have truly altered Sophia. Where is my shy friend who would not say boo to a goose?" teased Louisa.

"She is still here," said Sophia, "but now she has a purpose."

"Coffee, ladies?" asked the bright, authoritative voice of Constance Andrews. She bustled into the room and passed the girls two delicate china teacups full of steaming hot liquid. The cups clattered against the saucers with the speed of her delivery.

"Thank you," they said in unison.

"She is marvellous," sighed Sophia again. "She has been awake all night long, given speeches, kept our spirits high and now she's making breakfast with little help from anyone else. Is there anything she can't do?"

"She amply illustrates the importance of the suffrage movement," agreed Louisa. "There are many strong and capable women like her who should be allowed to take the lead in national matters."

"What are you ladies talking about?" asked Ada Ridley as she joined the two girls at their seats by the dwindling fire.

"Louisa has finally taken her nose out of the book," said Sophia wickedly, "and has remembered why we are here today."

"A good thing too," said Ada. "There is much progress still to make. We're in the middle of a long journey, and there's a fair distance left to travel."

They looked up to see Constance Andrews standing at the entrance to the doorway, clapping her hands. "Breakfast is served," she said, gesturing to the hallway where loaves of bread and sumptuous pastries lay neatly on trays. A delicious aroma of bacon permeated the room and Louisa was left wondering how on earth Constance had found the means to cook food.

"I will only keep you for a few moments," announced Constance. "I don't want the food you have earned to go cold, but I would like to express my heartfelt gratitude for your attendance here tonight. I hope it has not been too uncomfortable. There is a small gift for each of you," she continued, gesturing towards a square metal tray upon which thirty or forty button badges in the purple and green colours of the suffragette movement, had been placed. "It is not much, I know, but I hope you will wear it with pride and remember our night of peaceful protest."

Another woman well past her prime creaked unsteadily to her feet. She was unfamiliar to Louisa who had begun to regret the opportunity she had squandered in failing to get acquainted with the other local suffragists during the night.

"We would like to thank you for your endeavours, Constance," the woman said in a deep, hearty voice. "This protest was successful due to your planning and efficiency. We are indebted to you, as always."

Louisa jumped to her feet, "Hear, hear," she cried. The elderly woman acknowledged her with a nod before asking the other women to express their appreciation. Applause echoed around the room, and a red-faced Constance clapped her hands again and asked for silence.

"Breakfast is getting cold. Go and enjoy the food."

After they had eaten, small groups of women began to leave until there were only half a dozen left in the building.

"I must return this journal," said Louisa. "But how can I finish the tale?"

"It is highly unlikely you will come back here," said Sophia. "If you return the book, you will never know how the diary ends."

Louisa bit her lip and considered the matter for a few moments. She studied the journal as she fought with her conscience, then thrust it into the pocket of her coat.

"Finish your coffee and let's go," she said.

The girls emerged from the Old Museum into a chill April morning. Raindrops tumbled from the gloomy grey sky, bouncing on the sodden earth while two men smoked pipes as they sheltered by the door under a large black umbrella. "Good morning, ladies," they said, doffing their hats.

"Good morning," said Louisa smiling, "and thank you for your protection."

"Our pleasure," said the taller of the two men.

Louisa and Sophia waited momentarily for the Ridley sisters, but the sky darkened, and they left before the drizzle turned into a downpour.

"We should go straight home," said Sophia. "My father thinks I'm at your house, and if I arrive home soaked to the skin, it will give the game away."

"Yes, we will go straight to The Poplars," said Louisa. "We can't avoid getting wet as we have no umbrella, but we can hasten back and dry ourselves by the fire before you go home."

The two girls hurried through town glad to take advantage of a sudden break in the rain. By the time they walked to the bottom of Christchurch Park, the drizzle had virtually stopped, and a feeble sun pushed through the clouds. But the sun was no indicator of a change of fortune. From the moment they turned the corner of Ivry Street, it was clear that something was awry.

"Who is that?" asked Louisa, pointing to the shiny black carriage of a hansom cab. A man tickled the ears of a chestnut-coloured horse, as it pawed nervously at the ground.

"I don't know," said Sophia. "But it has stopped outside The Rowans, and we are not expecting visitors."

"Perhaps they are visiting my house?" suggested Louisa, "or they have settled in the wrong location. They could be there for Mrs Elliot at The Laburnums."

"No, I think not," protested Sophia, standing still as she eyed the carriage warily. "I hope they haven't discovered my absence from your house. Perhaps they've found out that I wasn't there last night. I will be in terrible trouble. What if Father won't permit me to see you again?"

"Stop," said Louisa. "It is not the police if that is what you think. I can't see any insignia on the carriage, and the cabman is wearing a bowler hat, not a policeman's helmet. Stay calm; don't worry."

Louisa slipped her arm through Sophia's. They crossed the road to the opposite side walking hastily towards the cab in the hope that it would mask them from Sophia's family when they passed the drive. But Louisa could not resist glancing towards the house as they tip-toed past noticing Daniel and several of the servants waiting in the turning circle of the driveway. Sophia suddenly stopped as Minnie ran towards her.

"Miss Sophia," she called. "Come quickly."

"What is it?" asked Sophia. "What is wrong?"

"Come here, Minnie," commanded a hard voice in an unmistakable Suffolk accent. "Don't interfere. Mr Daniel will deal with this."

"Sorry miss," said Minnie, lowering her head, as she scurried towards the upright figure of Jane Piggott.

Daniel strode down the driveway towards Sophia, who flinched as he came closer.

Louisa instinctively walked in front of her friend. "Leave her alone," she said.

Daniel ignored her, turned to face Sophia and gently took her hand.

51

"What is wrong?" asked Sophia. "You are not angry with me. Has something happened?"

"Dear Sophia, try not to worry," said Daniel. "Your father was taken ill last night and has been in a great deal of pain and distress ever since. The doctor was called at first light and is treating your father as best he can. Your mother needs your support. You must come inside right away."

"Poor mother," exclaimed Sophia. "She must be distraught."

"She is more at ease now the doctor has arrived," said Daniel, "but she has had little sleep and will be pleased to see you. "

"Do they know where I was last night?" asked Sophia.

Daniel pursed his lips. "They have better things to think about," he said curtly. "Your secret is safe. I have no wish to make trouble for your parents at this difficult time though I must insist that you do your duty and return with me now. Please leave all this nonsense alone, at least until your father has recovered."

Louisa opened her mouth to protest but stopped as Daniel put his finger to his lips.

"I am sure you agree that Sophia should return and comfort her mother," he said abruptly.

"You should," conceded Louisa. "I will look in on you tomorrow, Sophia, and hope to hear of an improvement in your father's condition."

She watched as Daniel escorted Sophia up the driveway and into the house then rushed towards The Poplars, bursting through the door and into the path of her sister Charlotte.

"Take care, Louisa," exclaimed Charlotte. "You nearly knocked me over."

"Charles Drummond is sick," said Louisa. "The doctor has been called."

"Hold the front page," said Charlotte. "That is hardly news. What ails him?"

"I don't know, but it is serious and painful," said Louisa.

"It sounds unpleasant," replied her sister, "though I am sure he will soon recover. Try not to worry about it."

"You are right," said Louisa, "it will pass. You should have come with us last night though," she continued. "It was everything I hoped for with speeches and songs and horrifying tales of arrests and beatings. Constance was astounding. We were warm and well-fed through the night, although I feel tired to the bone now." She put her hand to her mouth and yawned.

"I don't feel as you do about such matters," said Charlotte. "Good luck to you and the others but count me out."

"I'm going to my room", said Louisa. "I can't go another minute without sleep. Let mother know I am back and will be down for dinner," she continued, trudging wearily up the stairs.

It was several days later when Louisa finally found the time to visit Sophia to ask after her father's health. She knocked on the front door of the Rowans, and waited anxiously for the door to open, hoping that Daniel would not be at home.

Louisa watched as the slouching; grey-frocked form of Jane Piggott loomed in front of the bevelled glass of the door. She seemed to take forever, almost as if she was deliberately making Louisa wait. After several minutes of frustration, the door opened, and Jane Piggott stood on the doorstep with her arms crossed and her hair pulled back into a tight bun secured with a white hat and pins. She peered disdainfully towards Louisa. "Good day miss," she said in a thick Suffolk drawl.

"Good day Mrs Piggott," said Louisa. "Can I see Sophia?"

The housekeeper frowned. "You had better come in," she replied and ushered Louisa into the oak-panelled library at the front of the house.

Louisa untied her bonnet and sat in the red leather armchair next to a globe in the corner, which she spun absent-mindedly. A few moments later, she stopped, examined her dusty forefinger and wiped it on the cushion. The study was oppressive. Heavy red drapes covered the windows, and the dark panelling did nothing to alleviate the gloomy air inside the room. Louisa was relieved to hear footsteps echoing down the tiled hallway. The door swung open to reveal the tall, suited form of Daniel Bannister.

"Good morning, Louisa," he said, entering the room.

Louisa rose from the chair. "Where is Sophia?" she asked.

"Sophia is in the morning room," he replied, "where she will stay."

"Doesn't she want to see me?" asked Louisa.

"She doesn't know you're here," replied Daniel. "Louisa, please don't think I'm unduly harsh, but Sophia's father, though slightly improved, is far from well. Sophia is needed here, and you must not tempt her to embark on any more of your schemes. You can't know how difficult it would be if her father came to know of her recent transgressions."

"Please tell her I am here," cried Louisa. "She will think I don't care. You wouldn't want her to think she is friendless at a time like this?"

"I don't," said Daniel, "and I will tell her you called upon her when you are safely away."

"But she is expecting my visit," said Louisa plaintively.

"She was expecting your visit yesterday," chided Daniel.

"I couldn't see her yesterday," said Louisa, "my Godmother visited without warning. I was duty-bound to attend to my own family."

"As Sophia is to hers," said Daniel. "You won't see her today or any other day this week, and you should reconcile yourself to this. I will ring for Mrs Piggott to show you out, and I wish you a good day."

Daniel nodded his head and left the room without looking back. Mrs Piggott appeared almost immediately from the nearby dining room, her thin-lipped faced set in a stony stare. She opened the door without further discourse and waved Louisa outside.

Louisa stood open-mouthed on the doorstep of The Rowans, then stomped up the driveway and through the entrance of The Poplars. She knocked impatiently at the door of her father's study.

Henry Russell's deep voice boomed through the door. "Come," he said.

Louisa entered to see the usual pile of papers strewn across his desk, each paper marked with diagrams and drawings of things she did not understand. Across the room, the door to his laboratory stood ajar, and she smelled the unmistakable odour of sulphur.

"That's revolting," she said.

"I doubt you are here to discuss the condition of the air in my quarters," said Henry, smiling benevolently. He closed the door to the laboratory. "Sit down Louisa," he said, gesturing to the window seat beside his desk. "What is troubling you?"

"I've been refused entry to The Rowans," she said, dramatically.

"Who stopped you? Were you left on the doorstep?" asked Henry.

"No, not exactly. The housekeeper showed me in, but Daniel wouldn't let me see Sophia."

"Why?" asked Henry Russell.

"Because her father is unwell and Daniel thinks her duties lie with the family," said Louisa.

"He is right. They do," said Henry. "With Charles' health in such sharp decline, she must surely be needed by her mother."

"But I only wanted to ask after her father and let her know she was in my thoughts."

"Louisa, you must abide by the rules of their household," said Henry reasonably. "You may not like it, but you must do as you are asked."

Louisa sighed and gazed mournfully at her father. "We were becoming such good friends," she said.

"Why don't you use this opportunity to visit your Aunt and Uncle in Kensington?" asked Henry Russell. They have invited you several times recently. Perhaps it would take your mind off your friend and give her time to minister to her father."

"Perhaps I will," sighed Louisa, staring at the floor. If she was enthusiastic about the prospect of a trip to Kensington, there were no visible signs.

"Then I'll write to them tonight," said her father firmly. "We will settle the arrangement."

Louisa thanked him politely then wandered back into the hallway where

Charlotte stood in front of the dresser removing browning leaves from a vase of flowers. "There's a letter for you," she said, gesturing towards the piece of furniture where a cream coloured envelope leaned against the inkstand. Louisa picked up the letter and looked at the London post-mark. Intrigued, she took it to the morning room, pulled up a chair and sat at the round breakfast table nodding towards the new cook and housekeeper, Janet McGowan who was sweeping crumbs from a side table.

"Would you like a cup of coffee, Miss Louisa?" Janet asked in clipped Scottish tones.

"Thank you," said Louisa and Janet returned moments later with a tray of coffee and a small plate of shortbread.

"I don't suppose you are acquainted with the housekeeper at The Rowans?" asked Louisa.

"Jane Piggott? Janet replied. Louisa nodded.

"A little," she said. "Harold knows her better."

"Does she know how Mr Drummond has fared since the doctor's visit?"

"He is feeling better," said Janet. "Maggie is friendly with their young housemaid, Minnie Cole and keeps us well informed of the news."

"Did they find out what it was?" asked Louisa.

"They think it is probably a stomach ailment," replied Janet. "He is still in his bed and not very well, but not nearly as bad as he was yesterday."

"I am glad to hear it," said Louisa. "And Miss Sophia, is she well?"

"As far as I know, Miss," said Janet. "I expect she will appreciate the peace for a few days until Mr Drummond is back on his feet."

"Thank you," said Louisa reaching for the drawer of the morning room dresser. Her hands closed over a letter opener, and she deftly slit the envelope. The letter was in a familiar hand.

"Dear Louisa, we were glad to see you at the Old Museum on Sunday night and wondered if you might be interested in a forthcoming Suffragette debate at Caxton Hall in two weeks. Bessie and I are staying at our club in London for the next month. We do hope that you can join us at the debate. There will be influential suffragette speakers, and it will give you a better understanding of our great and noble cause. Do feel free to bring your friend along if you want. Write to me at The Empress Club in Dover Street and let me know if you can come. Yours ever, Ada Ridley".

"How marvellous," said Louisa aloud.

"What's that darling," asked Charlotte, who had joined her sister in the morning room.

"Ada and Bessie have invited me to a suffragist meeting in London, and Father has just written to our Aunt and Uncle Cowell in Kensington, so I will be wonderfully well-placed to join them. How fortunate."

"Take care," warned Charlotte. "Father knows you will pursue your political aims and is resigned to it, but only if he is nearby to watch over you. I doubt he'd permit a visit to Westminster. Ada and Bessie forget how young you are sometimes. It might be a kind thought, but it is an unwise invitation."

"It's only an idea," said Louisa. "Don't tell Father, please. In any case, he hasn't received a reply from my Aunt and Uncle yet. It might not be a convenient time for me to visit."

Charlotte sighed. "Just stay out of trouble, Louisa," she said. "The whole idea fills me with foreboding."

The next days passed in a blur of boredom for Louisa as she waited for the post to find out whether she would go to London, or not. It rained heavily outside, and she did not dare try to see Sophia again for fear of Daniel preventing access.

Louisa wandered aimlessly around the house recalling the camaraderie of the census evasion night when she suddenly remembered that the diary was still in her possession.

She ran to her closet, felt around inside her coat pocket, and removed the journal with a sigh of relief. Sitting on her bed, she opened the book where she had left off. The next page was blank, so she opened the one after and read.

Chapter Six

From bad to worse

Saturday, August 9, 1851 – This is my first diary entry since my frenzied attempt last night to reproduce the earlier entries concerning my dear friend, Mary Emily Cage. Transcribing these excerpts focussed my mind on previous times in my life, causing me to re-examine my past conduct, of which I am not at all proud. I was selfish and thought only of my life, carelessly disregarding the needs of my best friend. As Mary's life descended into chaos, not always of her own making, my fortunes increased until I was happily married and had enough food and shelter for all my needs. How it must have hurt Mary that her life was in turmoil while mine was always comfortable. Why did I think it was acceptable to neglect her and fail to consider that she might compare our fortunes and suffer more by it?

I visited Mary in her cell today. Before I left home, Alfred took my hand and asked me to sit. He looked directly into my eyes and watched me with tender concern, stroking my hand as he spoke. "Anna," he said. I must tell you something that you will find upsetting, but you must know certain facts about Mary before meeting her again. You may not wish to reacquaint yourself when you find out the depths to which she has sunk." I smiled, grateful for his concern, and said that it did not matter what I heard, I would not desert Mary now, nor would I take her account any less seriously than the official records of her misdemeanour. Alfred said he was afraid of this but continued without preamble and said that Mary had been found guilty of murder by poison and would die within a week. There was nothing that could prevent her execution, and any renewal of our friendship would inevitably be of short and painful duration. I reminded Alfred that I had abandoned Mary once and must do all that I could to make up for my past disloyalty. He kissed me tenderly and told me he had arranged a visit and would take me there immediately but warned me that the conditions inside the prison were not what I was used to and that I should not be shocked at anything I saw.

Clutching Alfred's arm, I walked the twenty minutes to the gaol with my husband, my rock, by my side. We did not talk, but every so often he stopped and smiled at me, his hand firmly grasping mine. Poor Mary – how sad that she never knew the love and care of a good man. Eventually, we arrived at the gaol; a vast, brick building surrounded by a high wall. Tall chimneys stood stark atop the roof against the skyline. Our entryway, through a large wooden gate, was positioned where the straight sidewall met the curved wall to the front of the structure. Alfred escorted me through the gates and up the long pathway to the front of the building. He nodded to the guards at the door and was granted easy access, as a man in his position should be.

I did not know what to expect of the prison, for in all the years we were married, I never went near the place. From the outside, the grounds were pleasant. The door through which we entered was located at the side, and a large, mullioned arch-window stood centrally above occupying several floors. The sun shone brightly, and I thought perhaps my visit would not be as bad as Alfred feared, but that thought only lasted until I went inside. Alfred escorted me through the dark reception hall, and we passed the first of many solid, metal gates, each with a prison warder within easy sight. We weaved our way through corridors avoiding the men's cells as Alfred did not wish to subject me to the worst of the prison, then we descended dank, shallow stairs and walked through whitewashed passages beneath the ground floor. Each side of the corridor contained a succession of single cells. Alfred explained that these were the condemned cells, and prisoners usually shared the space. A single cell was a privilege granted to those inmates due for execution. Many of the cells were empty, and it sent a chill through my spine when I realised why. Alfred quickly propelled me past two cells occupied by men, and I did not have the opportunity to glimpse inside them despite the lack of private space. At the end of the corridor was a further door which Alfred opened before stopping and putting a hand on my shoulder. He smiled, then gestured to a cell on the left.

Fully exposed to the prying eyes of anyone who might pass by, floor to ceiling bars enclosed the small cell composed of whitewashed brick with a clay tiled floor. A barred window set high above the end wall illuminated a hard wooden bed pushed firmly against the back wall. A small figure clutching a book was sitting on the bed, her lips moving silently as if she was reading aloud, but the book was firmly closed.

"Mary," I whispered, for it was she and she looked up and smiled radiantly, then walked to the barred walls of the cell, reaching towards me. She said my name over and over and grasped my hand, and I sobbed so hard I could not speak for several minutes. Alfred called the guard, took the keys to the cell and allowed me access. The guard picked up his chair and set it down beside Mary's bed, and we spoke for the first time in twenty years. Before I had the chance to ask her anything, she said she had something she must tell me. Alfred had sent word in advance of my intended visit, allowing Mary the opportunity to consider our impending meeting. She had given it a lot of thought and planned what she would say. With her head bowed, Mary said how sorry she was for her past conduct. She regretted her dissolute life and, above all, her resentment of me. I said there was nothing to apologise for and that I should say sorry to her for my lack of consideration, but she disagreed and said that I should not.

Mary had not aged as one would expect of a person having lived a difficult life. She was still small and relatively slight; no more than five feet high, if that, with only a slight thickening of her body through age. Her face was unlined, and grey streaks peppered her once dark hair, but her eyes were kinder and less hard than I remembered. Mary wore the black garb of prison, and her hair was pinned back though not at all neatly, and rebellious tendrils escaped through the pins, softening the overall effect. She grasped a bible in her hand as if her life depended upon it.

Even as I uttered the words, I realised what an absurd question I was asking, but still felt moved to enquire how Mary fared. It seemed only polite to ask. She said she was managing well under the circumstances; that the prison chaplain was a frequent visitor during her incarceration and had provided her with much comfort. She was not afraid to face the next life and was fully reconciled to her fate. She *told me she had been a most grievous sinner and was ashamed of her actions. She hoped God would grant her mercy and that she would die forgiven. She asked to know everything about my life, which I revealed with a degree of reluctance as I have fared so much better than she.*

Mary confessed that she stayed away from my wedding in spite, resenting that I had never introduced Alfred. I immediately apologised for making her feel she was not good enough to meet him, but Mary said the fault was hers alone. When I told her about my four children, her eyes filled with tears at the milestones she had missed. But when she discovered that my eldest girl, Mary Elizabeth, was named in her honour, she beamed. Mary asked after my father, and I smiled, remembering how he had enjoyed ten happy years in Ipswich close to our home before passing away, and leaving the proceeds of the sale of his house to Alfred and me. We talked about Alfred's progression within the prison system, and I explained how he came to occupy his current senior position in Ipswich Gaol. While not wishing to cause any further resentment, I felt moved to honesty and revealed that our good fortune allowed us to purchase a larger house in Christchurch Street where my original lodgings were when I was a teacher. She did not seem to mind, though and said she was pleased that my life was comfortable and would not wish it otherwise just because hers was not.

I asked if there was anything that I could do for her to bring some comfort in these last few weeks and she said that there was. Mary had three sons and four daughters still living, who would dwell in the shadow of her misdemeanour forever, and she was sorry and ashamed for the notoriety her conduct would bring. Mary intended to ask for their forgiveness and for God's mercy. But to be truly repentant, she wanted to make an account of her transgressions as part of her redemption. Mary was adamant that this account could not be made public for the sake of her children and asked if I might listen to her story and write it down as she could neither read nor write. Even after so long a time, Mary felt that she could trust her words to me as she could trust them to no other. She said that it might be difficult for me to hear her story, especially the narratives involving me, but that an accurate account must contain both bad times and good. I did not have to think for long and said, of course, I would do this for her no matter how harrowing the details. So, it is settled. I will come tomorrow, sit with her, and record her story.

I left the damp confines of Mary's cell, and, at my request, Alfred took me to the prison chapel. I knelt at the front pew praying fervently for Mary's soul, while Alfred conducted some business in the nearby reception hall. Presently, I heard footsteps and the prison chaplain joined me in prayer. When we finished, I stood, and he engaged me in conversation, and I took the opportunity to ask him about Mary and tell him about our friendship. He said Mary was a guilty sinner but that she had confessed to her loose conduct and depraved way of life and wholeheartedly wished to atone for her misdemeanours in the eyes of the Lord. The chaplain had told her to confess to all her sins, including her husband's murder. But she would not do it, even though God would never forgive her. The chaplain said that if I were a true friend, I would help her to understand the importance of a full confession, and I said that I would do anything for Mary as I had failed her too many times before.

Then we left the gaol, and I write this at home now. The next entry in this journal will be Mary's story in Mary's own words.

I, Mary Emily Cage, was born to good but poor parents at the turn of the century in the village of Stonham Aspal, where I dwelled for most of my life. My childhood was hard; none of us were adequately schooled, and we all worked for our living from the age of seven years. A seven-year-old child cannot do much else of worth but pick stones from the fields, and this back-breaking work is what we did until the boys were old enough to labour and the girls old enough go into service. We never had new clothes or any clothes that fit us. Everything we owned was handed down, patched and worn. I never wore a pair of boots that did not leak nor a dress without a stain. I would like to say that we were happy despite our poverty, but it would be a lie. It was a hard, cruel life, and we were always hungry and often cold. Accidents and deaths were commonplace and became increasingly more so as we grew older. One of my brothers fell out of a cart, broke his head, and died. Another lost three fingers to a scythe when he was only ten. But those of us who lived eventually went our own ways and at least our father was well-regarded in the village despite our lack of money, which is more than can be said for most.

Anna Saunders was my friend from as long back as I can remember. I cannot recollect how we met – it was not at school because I never went, but we were always friends, and our friendship grew stronger as we approached the age that we would expect to leave our father's homes and be married. Anna's father was not rich, but he owned property and a store, and I always knew that she was better than me. I thought it would not matter, but it came to matter a great deal.

I was not quite twenty when I married James Cage. We had known each other before we married, and he agreed to make an honest woman of me. I loved him at the beginning which is why I let him bed me in the freezing stalls of the hayloft one frosty January when he was the worse for ale, and I, desperate to show him that I could love him like a grown woman. He was older than I and had other women before me, and there was much to prove.

After a short life as hard as mine, I ought to have known better than to think we would be happy, and life would be easy for it was not easy at all. But for the intervention of my father, I do not think in hindsight that James would have wed me at all. I birthed my first girl in my twentieth year and a boy two years after that. Those intervening years were hard, but not as hard as those that followed. If I knew then what I know now, I would have considered those years the easiest of times, for I had the support of family and friends even though I did not enjoy the respect of my husband, whose violence increased as his love of the grain grew ever stronger.

My boy, James, died before he reached the age of one. He had been small and frail from birth, and his death came almost as a relief, as it was wholly inevitable. I did not grieve and already carried his replacement, a boy we also named James. I did not love either of the children named James. Whether this was because I called them after their father, I could not say. I have loved some of my other children, though not all, so why not these first two boys? It made their deaths easier to bear, though, so perhaps it was as well.

The boy child I loved best of all was called Richard. I am sure it was because I loved his father the best for, he was the only of my children not fathered by James Cage. 1827 was the year I thought to be free of James and headed towards a newer, happier life. After the death of my father, James became progressively more violent whenever he returned from the alehouse. James controlled his temper at first, but it didn't last long. He started beating me in front of the children, and on one sickening occasion, while Anna was in the house. The pity in her eyes hurt more than the bruises. The beatings were bad enough, but James was often laid-off work because of his drinking. He became increasingly unreliable, so we had no money to eat or heat our rooms. Then James began to look for other ways to find beer money, indulging in poaching and burglary. He was caught and charged on more than one occasion, and when he was given a gaol sentence for larceny, I was part relieved and part concerned about how I would manage without going into the workhouse. I begged my mother to let us stay with her, even though she had no money either. But I reasoned that if she could mind the children for me, I could find work labouring in the fields and earn enough for all of us to eat.

I applied to Mr Last's farm where my friend Kitty was a dairymaid, and he gave me work. The labour was long and arduous, but it suited me well, particularly as George Thurlow had returned to the farm to finish some buildings for Mr Last. I was happy to reacquaint myself with him, now James was away.

I did not intend to cohabit with George Thurlow. I thought only to enjoy myself and have some freedom from the children and the grind of my daily life, but after only a few weeks, I fell in love.

George was kind to me; kind in a way that I had never known from James. Perhaps it was because he had steady work and no inclination towards excesses of alcohol. His industrious nature and sobriety gave him time to show me kindnesses that were only small but meant a great deal. He would not let me carry a load in his presence, and he stroked my hair and told me I looked pretty, even when I did not. After the beatings I had endured, these words and deeds warmed my heart, and I would have done anything he asked of me.

One day he called me to his lodgings, and I went, knowing full well what would happen. We lay together, but it was different because he asked me first, unlike my husband, who took it whether I offered it or not. And his breath was fresh and sweet; not rancid with the sour taste of stale alcohol and sweat. After that first time, I returned every night, leaving the children with my mother. She was angry, to begin with, and asked what I thought my father would have said, had he been alive to witness my disgrace. I countered this by asking her what he would have said if he'd seen the bruises James Cage caused, not to mention his recent arrest. Mother did not answer because she knew what he would have said and what he would have done. We did not speak of it again, and she turned a blind eye to my living arrangements if I gave her money for the children's keep and visited them every day, which I did.

I lived with George for six months, and for the first time in my life, I did not worry about food and shelter. My bruises healed, and instead of dreading the door opening, I welcomed it. I knew I was living on borrowed time and soon enough, James Cage returned from gaol and came to claim his possession. It was May of 1828, and I was returning from the top field with Sally when I saw him stalking towards me. I discovered later that he had come to Stonham Aspal by cart following his release from Ipswich gaol, and headed straight to the alehouse where he was greeted with catcalls and derision by his friends. They told him I was full of George Thurlow's child and that he was no man to have such a wife.

What he did and said to George Thurlow, I will never know, but I didn't see George again except once from afar. James dragged me by the arm and told me to return to Wetheringsett that night and forget about George or I would be the worst for it. I did not know he had spoken to George at that time and broke free from his grasp. I ran to George's lodgings. They were empty and cleared of his possessions, and I visited every one of his many kinfolks that evening. Some would not speak to me, and the others did not know where he was.

I returned to my mother's house and passed a troubled night there, but she would not let me stay any longer as she did not want repercussions from James. I took the children and left the next day, but just as I reached the front door of the house, Charlotte Thurlow appeared and told me that her husband, David, had seen George who said that he was going to Ipswich never to return and I should not think of him again. I had nowhere else to go, so heavily pregnant and with two small children in tow, I walked back across the fields to Wetheringsett and home to James.

The rooms stank when I returned. James had not set a fire or opened a window and the house, which had lain empty all winter, was heavy with damp and mildew and cold as the grave. James was sitting at the table, sharpening a knife when I returned. He got to his feet and, taking the children's hands, set them outside the door. Then he pushed me into the bedroom and threw me on the bed, stained and damp from the endless leaking. He claimed me right there, marking me as a dog scents his bitch, then climbed off and said he would keep the Thurlow bastard as a trophy. There was nothing I could do and nowhere to go

66

as I had no money and without it, no choices, so I stayed and spent the next months in fear for my unborn child. But when Richard arrived, James was at worst, ambivalent and sometimes kinder to Richard than to his own children. I never understood why. Perhaps he did indeed feel that the child was his reward for the slight George Thurlow had caused.

While James appeared to forget his time in gaol quickly, I did not. I tried to put George Thurlow far from my mind but missed him every day. When Richard was born, I was so low I could not rise to feed the children, nor care for them or myself. I missed him so much that I could not even cry. One day my mother visited and was so concerned she applied to the doctor in Debenham for some help. The doctor gave her some small, cream-coloured pills which I took with water. They made me feel a great deal better though tired and lethargic the next day, but they dulled the pain. I took them until the packet was empty, by which time the worst of it was over.

Anna Saunders married and left the village the year before my daughter, Sibella, was born. I had loved Anna for a long time, but the more she prospered, the worse my prospects became. I thought she was ashamed of me. Forgive me, Anna, but I still believe it although I forgive you now. I was never as clever as Anna, but even I am intelligent enough to notice the distance she kept from me. I met her husband for the first time this week in a condemned cell, twenty years after she married him. No, I do not think I have imagined the snub.

I wanted to be Anna Saunders. I wanted to read and write. I wanted to live in a proper house. There was only one child in the Saunders family, and there were thirteen of us: all those mouths to feed. I do not think Anna has ever gone hungry or understood what it was like to have no shoes. I think she would have helped me more if she had known how bad things were with James, but I did not want to be pitied by Anna. I loved her, and I wanted her respect and admiration, not her charity. I remember when Kitty told me that Anna was to be married. I was devastated to find out second-hand; so much I was almost doubled over with the pain of it. I was her best friend, yet I had no idea she was engaged. I thought I might, at least, meet her intended but it never happened. You will not have known this until this very moment, Anna, but I did come to your wedding. I walked through the Lychgate carrying a horseshoe decorated by my niece Sarah. I only wanted the chance to wish you luck and joy, but I was overwhelmed with jealousy and could not bring myself to enter. I hung the horseshoe in a tree and walked away. I wonder if you ever saw it. From that day to yesterday, we never met again. For what it is worth, I thought of you often.

I briefly forgot the loss of Anna when my favourite daughter, Sibella, was born. I know I shouldn't have favourites, but I did, and I make no apology for it. Her birth was quick and pain-free. She was an easy baby, cried little and fed contentedly from me. I loved this girl child very much. My life continued in the same vein; hard, grinding poverty, loveless copulation and the resumption of the beatings which had stopped for a while after Richard was born. By the time my son John arrived in 1833, I was weary to the bone. I could not eat, which is just as well as there was little food, and I could not feed John, who nearly died. We were both so unwell in the winter of that year that the vicar relented and agreed to baptise my three youngest children for fear we would die outside of God's grace. The vicar must have been well-disposed that month when he decided to baptise Richard. An ironic gesture considering that Richard's existence was the reason for refusing to christen my other children, as I had sinned in the eyes of the Lord.

I was so tired of life by then I cared nothing for baptisms and would happily have met my maker and sung at my funeral, but it was not to be. I rallied and recovered, but not before I had taken myself to the village pond at Stonham and thought to drown myself. I got as far as entering the freezing, fetid water but Mrs Tebbing saw me and took me to Ursula Rainor who gave me some pills like those I took when George left me. I felt much recovered after that and returned to her whenever I needed to replenish my supply. They bought me down hard the next day, but I could get through the worst of things, so long as I had my pills.

A few years later, we returned to Stonham Aspal never to leave again. James only worked sporadically at Wetheringsett, and we would have starved had we not moved. There was no improvement in our living conditions. We dwelled in a wooden house with rotting floorboards, one living room and one bedroom for all of us and a privy outside. It was a tiny space for so many, and not long after we returned another boy, William, was born and two years later a girl, Betsy Eliza, followed. They were both difficult children, but I had remembered the power of the pills, by then. When Richard was born,

68

and everything was so raw, I used the pills to quieten the children so that I might grieve my lost love in peace. When the pills were gone, as time went by, I forgot that use for them. But two nights with no sleep has a remembering effect, and I crushed the pills down, and the children lay torpid and quiet about me as Mary Ann and James had done those many years before. The same year Betsy was born, my mother died at last. She was a long way past seventy when she died, and it was time for her to go. Her mind wandered often, and she did not know me anymore, so I was not sorrowful at her departure. Besides, my days passed in a blur and I cared little for anything except my opium pills.

James died suddenly in 1842. Not James, my husband, unfortunately, for that would have been too much to hope for, but James, my son. Nobody could account for it. He just fell at home one day and was quite dead before he hit the ground. He was but 17 years old. His father James had continued his relentless taking of me, so I was heavily pregnant again and had Emma early, less than one week after my son James died. Although he was not a child of whom I was especially fond, neither was I glad about his death. A demanding baby in his place, before his body was cold in the ground, was a burden beyond my ability to cope. Do not judge me, Anna, for there are murders I can confess to, but I knew as I ground those pills up that I was using too many and I did it anyway. Emma lived but a week. And in early June, I did it again and buried little Betsy Eliza.

You may condemn me but don't until you have walked a mile in my shoes. What prospect did these children have? Emma was early and never likely to thrive. Betsy Eliza had no future but stone picking in fields only to marry a drunken wretch. I started with eight children and ended with five, all seven years and above and all able to support themselves and relieve us of the burden of filling so many mouths. I like to think of it as a sacrifice – the few for the many. Unfortunately, the rest of the village did not see it that way. The deaths of three children in as many months were never likely to be overlooked. I was the subject of relentless, cruel gossip lasting many months. They dug poor James from his grave and opened his coffin but did not find anything as I had not done anything to him. The gossip never went away, but the accusations did. I was well-used to being judged unkindly by the villagers, and their endless chatter did not concern me. I had hoped that would be the end of my child-bearing years, but as usual, James could not leave me in peace, and I bore another two girls in the following four years. I called them Betsy Eliza and Emma again as I could not find it in me to think up another two names.

~~~~~~~

Louisa turned the page, shocked at what she had read. Black ink turned to faded blue, which indicated the diary entries happened on different occasions and that it would be a suitable time to take a break. Besides, there was so much information to assimilate. Mary Emily, the hopeful young girl, starting a new life as a married woman, had become so embittered by circumstance that she freely admitted to killing her youngest two children, if not quite deliberately, then by extreme and calculated carelessness. Utterly shocked, Louisa's first thought was to tell Sophia. She ran down the wide stairs two at a time, tripping over her skirts as she fled into the hallway.

"Slow down, young lady," said her father, emerging from the study with a letter in his hand. "Where are you going in such a hurry?"

"I'm going to visit Sophia," she said breathlessly.

"Not without an invitation," he replied with a twinkle.

"Really father," Louisa said, "no invitation is likely to be forthcoming while that insufferable cousin of hers commands her every deed. What sort of independent woman is she?"

"Don't be too hard on her," Henry Russell replied. "She is torn between duty and friendship. If you are a true friend to her, you will go to London and give her time to attend to her family matters alone."

"Oh, have you heard from my uncle?" asked Louisa eagerly.

"I have," said her father. "You are invited to Kensington for two weeks and will travel Friday. We have planned a treat for you, Louisa. You will travel by motor carriage. Your uncle under-takes a business trip to Bury St Edmunds and will call for you on his return. How do you like that idea to take your mind off your friend?"

"It's a wonderful plan," she said. "And will do very well to distract me from Sophia. Thank you." Louisa kissed her father on the cheek, before walking downstairs to the kitchen.

"Maggie," she called from the foot of the stairs. Maggie emerged from the kitchen clutching a tureen which she was busy drying.

"Can you bring my cases up when you have a moment? I'm going to London in two days. Bring my hatbox too."

"Of course, Miss," said Maggie. "Will you need all of them?"

"Yes, please," said Louisa. "I might not take them all but bring them upstairs so I can look. Perhaps you will help me pack later?"

"Yes, Miss," said Maggie. "I'm not taking my half day today after all, and I'll be around to help."

"Sorry, Maggie, I forgot it was your day off," said Louisa. "Do you plan to take another day instead?" she asked.

"I don't know Miss," said Maggie. "I was going into town with Minnie Cole, but she can't come. Mr Drummond is sick again."

"I thought he was better," exclaimed Louisa.

"Far from it," said Maggie, gravely. "The doctor visited in the early hours of the morning. Mr Drummond hovers between life and death, and they are not sure he will recover at all."

Chapter Seven

An unexpected encounter

By the end of the week, Louisa was happily settled in her aunt and uncle's large townhouse in Harrington Gardens, Kensington. She occupied a generous bedroom on the second floor which looked across beautifully tended formal gardens, with a window seat perfect for watching the comings and goings to the front.

The park was frequented by smartly dressed nannies, each walking their charges or pushing perambulators if the children were too small to walk. They arrived at midday, like clockwork each day, exchanging stories and, no doubt, discussing the machinations of their employers. Occasionally, smart-looking gentlemen hurried by on their way to the city, but the park, by and large, was a relaxed area and made Louisa appreciate her privileged position. She was lucky to have a wealthy uncle who could afford to live in pleasant surroundings.

Within a few short days, Louisa had slipped into a routine of eating, shopping, and people-watching interspersed with the occasional visit to a theatre with her aunt. Aunt Beatrice was older than her father and had no children of her own. Married to a successful banker, she enjoyed a prosperous but sometimes lonely life seeming to take great joy at having Louisa at home and always treating her with kindness.

Immediately on her arrival in Kensington, Louisa wrote to Ada at The Empress Club. Ada replied by return of post and Louisa read the letter excitedly as she anticipated meeting her cousins at Caxton Hall in a few days. Try as she might, she could not remember her aunt's stance on suffragists. Her mother's family were mainly supportive, but her fathers were a different matter. As it happened, she need not have worried. As soon as she asked for leave to visit her cousins, her aunt made the connection.

"Aren't they the Ridley girls?" asked Aunt Beatrice, on hearing mention of their names.

"Yes," Louisa replied, biting her lip.

Aunt Beatrice put her hands upon Louisa's shoulders and scrutinised her face with a serious expression.

"I must tell you that your uncle does not approve of suffragists," she said, "and as much as he dislikes their mainly peaceful actions, he abhors the violence of the suffragettes."

Louisa sighed and lowered her head, but her aunt placed a gentle hand beneath her chin, lifting it until Louisa's eyes met her own green orbs.

"But what he doesn't know cannot hurt him," she said with a twinkle.

Louisa threw her arms around her aunt, beaming in gratitude.

When her aunt disentangled herself, she continued. "I, Louisa, admire them greatly but do be careful. The vastness of London magnifies problems. I hope you can assure me that you are a suffragist of the peaceful kind and that you won't get involved in anything that could bring trouble to my door."

"Of course," said Louisa. "I would never seek to hurt anyone or anything, and I am as opposed to violence as my uncle. I'm sure you've heard that my second cousin is Millicent Fawcett, and we follow her methods, not those of the Pankhurst's."

"Thank you for your reassurance," said Aunt Beatrice. "We will discuss it no further, except to make arrangements for your travel. Where do you intend to meet your cousins?"

"They've invited me to their club, but there's no need to go," said Louisa. "Ada has given me a contact number, and perhaps I can use your telephone to finalise the arrangements? That way I can go directly to Caxton Hall."

"Do that," replied her Aunt. "And I will arrange a hansom cab for your journey."

Louisa took leave of Aunt Beatrice and rang the Empress Club. Neither Ada nor Bessie were present to receive the call, but she left a message in the care of the receptionist for them, asking them to meet her outside Caxton Hall the following night. With her aunt having no further need of her that afternoon, Louisa decided to take a walk. In keeping her aunt company, she'd had little chance to explore since her arrival.

It was warm and breezy for April, and Louisa dressed in a light cream smocked and embroidered silk dress with a matching wide-brimmed hat. She set off for her walk wearing low-heeled, sensible shoes and hoped that her smart attire did her aunt and uncle justice. Louisa wandered down Collingham Gardens and through a pretty mews road, before finding herself on The Earls Court Road with its imposing brick houses and rows of bustling shops and banks. While lingering outside the post office, she noticed a railway arch and from there saw a sign for the underground. Intrigued, she entered, determined to catch sight of one of the new moving staircases but had not gone more than a few yards inside when she heard a voice. The voice was familiar but did not sound happy.

"What are you doing here?" asked Daniel Bannister, brusquely.

Louisa stood open-mouthed. For a moment, she did not recognise Sophia's cousin, out of the usual context.

"Never mind me, what are you doing here - and where is Sophia?"

"She is at home looking after her mother," said Daniel. "And I would be with her, but for this infernal problem with the electricity supply." He nodded vaguely in the direction of the doorway. "Why are you travelling alone in the underground railway system. It isn't safe. Are you lost?"

"No, I am not," protested Louisa. "I went for a walk and decided to explore the new moving walkways."

"Well, you shouldn't do it, unchaperoned," said Daniel. "Allow me to escort you home."

"I don't want you to," said Louisa churlishly. "I don't need chaperoning, and I wouldn't choose you if I did. You wouldn't let me see Sophia when I needed to. Why would I want your company now?"

"Because if Sophia were here, she would want me to," replied Daniel. "She would expect me to keep you safe."

"That is cruel," exclaimed Louisa, "you must know I could not refuse Sophia."

"Exactly," he smiled. "Now, where shall I take you? I need to go to the power station, but I have half an hour to spare."

"I'm staying in Harrington Gardens with my aunt and uncle.

"Good. I know exactly where that is," said Daniel. "Come along."

He escorted her from the station, and they walked back through a succession of small parks and gardens using a much prettier route than the one Louisa had taken on the outward journey.

"How is Sophia?" asked Louisa presently after the silence grew too stifling to bear.

Daniel sighed, stumbling on his words, and said, "if my visit wasn't necessary, I wouldn't have travelled today. Sophia's father has taken another turn. He is extremely sick, indeed. If I did not know better..." The words trailed away.

"What do you know?" asked Louisa in alarm.

"Nothing, it is not for me to speculate. Sophia is well. She is well. They all cope well with it." He stared into the distance momentarily, lost in thought. Louisa wished she knew him better so she could decipher the meaning behind the words he had not said.

"What is your occupation?" asked Louisa, trying to divert another bout of excruciating silence.

"I studied engineering," said Daniel, "and I now work with electricity. I learned my trade in London, before coming to Ipswich. Now there is a problem with my former electricity company, and they have asked for my assistance at this most inconvenient time."

"Will you be in London long?" asked Louisa.

"Not if I can avoid it," replied Daniel. "I must return to my aunt's house at the earliest opportunity. I expect to be here for no more than two days."

Louisa felt like little time had passed by the time they reached Harrington Gardens. They walked through the park, and then Daniel escorted Louisa up the steps of her uncle's house.

"What do you intend to do with your time in London?" he asked.

"I am going to Caxton Hall tomorrow," she said excitedly, the words flying from her mouth before she had time to think.

Daniel shook his head. "I've passed Caxton Hall and seen the notices. Clearly, you are indulging in more of this suffragette nonsense," he said. "What a pity. I am surprised that your father allows you to roam around London alone. It's not like the provinces, Louisa. There are parts of London where a young lady simply should not go."

"My aunt has arranged a carriage," said Louisa, "not that it is any concern of yours."

"At least one of your relatives has some sense," Daniel countered.

"Please, don't speak to my father of this," begged Louisa. "You will get back to Ipswich before me."

"So, your father doesn't know?" exclaimed Daniel. "At least he is not complicit in this."

"It's only a debate," cried Louisa. "'I'm going to meet my cousins at Caxton Hall, and I'll be perfectly safe."

"You are right. You will be safe if you stay close to your cousins and remain near the road. But please, for Sophia's sake, don't wander off on your own, Louisa. She has enough to worry about."

"I will be careful," said Louisa petulantly, "but not for your sake; only Sophia's."

"Very well," said Daniel, fleetingly touching the brim of his hat, before setting off with long, measured strides.

"Insufferable man," said Louisa aloud. "He is quite intolerable".

She stalked up to her room and sat down heavily on the window seat, watching over the park.

"I can look after myself without his help," she said aloud and watched the park for a while. A young boy and his sister were playing with a spinning top in the dry earth of the walkway. While she did not know why, it put her in mind of Mary Cage's children, and she thought of the diary carefully packed away at the bottom of her luggage. It seemed as good a way as any to distract herself from her annoyance at Daniel, even if she was reluctant to read on after the last, horrifying instalment. Nevertheless, she unclipped her case, extracted the diary and began to read.

Chapter Eight

The only way out

Elizabeth Lambert came to live with us in the summer of 1846. She was a simple girl and not the type I would usually befriend, but she was distant kin through a relative in Wetheringsett, and we already had a connection. Elizabeth had made an unfortunate marriage in Debenham and never lived with her husband, though she bore him a child. She couldn't abide him and quite why she married him, defeated me. Elizabeth was only twenty when our paths crossed. Her mother had turned her from the house and left Elizabeth and her young daughter without shelter. I was sympathetic to her situation, which was not dissimilar to my own, evoking memories of when I was young and hopeful and yearned for a better life. I took her in even though there were eight of us sharing two squalid rooms. But she was grateful, at least I thought so at the time.

Elizabeth minded the younger children, and it gave me a chance to get away from the house that I had come to hate. I grasped the opportunity and spent a great deal of time in the company of others like me; women and men hardened with despair, none of us careful in our conduct. It shames me now, how we behaved, but it is impossible to understand what it is like to live without hope unless you have experienced it.

I knew my time without responsibility would be limited, so I lived life hard. James had taken a liking to young Elizabeth, to which I turned a blind eye. Far be it from me to cast aspersions, but the year after she left us, she bore another child, and I cannot say who the father was; nor do I care. James insisted that she left, in the end. I don't know why, but within four short months, I'd lost my freedom again and came home.

I could never rest easy after that. The horror of domestic life with James Cage was enough to make me weep with despair. But for my pills, I would have tried to do away with myself again. I could see no end to it. Then after a year, I met a man who I did not love. But he was tolerable, and to his credit, he was not James, and that was good enough. Robert was younger than me. I never looked my age, though how I escaped looking haggard and careworn after the hardships I endured, I do not know. Though Robert had little money, he had secured lodgings, and after very little thought, I joined him. We did not live much of a life, but he was not free with his fists, and I thought well enough of him. Then Mary Ann sought me out, and everything changed.

Mary Ann married out of our hell-house in 1845 to a poor but kind man. She bore three little urchins of her own, and when she came to see me, it was evident that another was on the way. She told me that she was not the only one. Sibella was in the family way too. I don't know why Sibella did not tell me herself. I would have understood only too well. But I felt obliged to care for my girl and left Robert to return to Stonham Aspal before her father found out. I did not know whether he would be angry or ambivalent, and there was no telling with James Cage, but I could not risk his wrath.

Sibella had lain with one of the village lads and was not long gone, but far enough for Mary to notice. Poor naïve Sibella thought she was in love with the boy and continued to see him knowing full well that her father would disapprove. Inevitably James came to hear of it, and I returned in the nick of time intending to protect Sibella. I did not know how I was going to offer her the protection I had never found for myself, but I would try or die trying.

Naturally, James laid the blame at my door. He called me a harlot and a whore and said that I had corrupted my daughter and made her in my image. Then he beat me harder than he had ever done before. I could not walk for two days. My swollen tongue prevented any attempt to speak or eat, and the beating was so severe that Constable Whitehead reported James and held him at the station. I was still not up and about when they sentenced him to two months hard labour in Ipswich gaol for assaulting me. As I lay there in my damp blood-stained rags, hurt and angry, I swore I would have my revenge on him, the brute.

When I could finally walk, I took Sibella and her young man, who she would not leave, and we journeyed to Ipswich to find Robert. He took us in, and we all lived there together for a while. I imagined how the village gossips would enjoy this latest evidence of my misconduct, not to mention my daughter's corruption, but I did not care a fig for their prejudice. I had spent the last thirty years beaten by my pig of a husband, and not one of them ever lifted a hand to help me. They had no right to judge. Sibella thrived in the environment of shame, and her progress while living in proximity to her wicked mother and her mother's lover, confounded the gossips. Sibella flourished in an environment without violence or rage and grew large, round, and healthy. I cannot pretend these were happy times. I was not in love with Robert as I had been with George Thurlow, but although hunger was never far from me, I did not starve and was never in pain.

With all I had suffered, I expected that if anything finished me, it would be an act of violence; but instead, it was a glimpse of what might have been. Towards the end of the summer, Sibella and I hastened from our lodgings in Ipswich High Street to the Butter Market to purchase supper with our paltry allowance when I glanced at a familiar-looking man across the thoroughfare. Even though twenty-two years had passed, I recognised him at once. There was no mistaking George Thurlow, and he was still a handsome man with dark, wavy hair, peppered with grey. He was well-groomed, dressed in tidy apparel and the young woman to his side was clean and attractive. She held the hand of a boy of about six years old who looked just like George.

I stood on the opposite side of the road, invisible in middle age, poorly clothed with a pregnant daughter and ill-used by my husband, watching watched what my future could have been. I stood and stared until they were far in the distance, not saying a word until Sibella caught my arm and asked me, 'what in God's name was wrong.' I thrust the coins at her, stumbled back to our lodgings alone and cried and cried at the injustice of it.

My anger boiled for two days, and then, by chance, I discovered that James Cage was due for release from gaol, and I marched straight to the prison and waited for hours until he finally emerged. When I saw his callow face and sneering eyes, I launched at him and scratched him, biting his chest, and striking him over and over until the guards dragged me off and took me away. I was still screaming profanities inside the cell at the police station over an hour later. Never have I hated anyone as much as I hated James that day.

They confined me to the cell all day and into the evening until I calmed down. Even then, they made me wait until the next day. I pretended to be sorry, and they released me. By the time I returned to my lodgings, Sibella's boy and Robert Tricker had gone, and it was just the two of us again, with no money again, so we went back to Stonham again. Back home with our tails between our legs and any remnants of dignity long gone.

I remember walking back through the doors of that cesspit home I shared with Cage, hoping he would not be there, but he was. They were all there, every one of my children, except Mary Ann; the one who got away. James sat slumped on his usual chair, spindly legs splayed and his filthy boots, stinking and holed. His matted beard was mottled with grey and his lips, wet with beer. I almost vomited with hate and shame.

He did not say a word; just sat there sneering while my children stared passively. I hated being home, and could not bear it, not even for them. By then, the only child I had any time for, other than Sibella, was Richard; but even that was wearing thin. It wasn't enough to sustain me in Cage's presence and, I walked through to the bedroom, pulled up the floorboard where I had stashed a handful of opium pills, and took one. Within half an hour, life was almost bearable again.

I woke the next day to the noise of scratching in a bedroom full of sleeping bodies and winced as James Cage's rancid breath wafted towards me. His face was so close that I could see his blackened teeth and count the coarse hairs on his chin. His chest rose and fell, too regular to bear, and I wished his heart would stop. The mattress was rank with lice, and the scratching I'd heard belonged to a sickly, under-nourished brown rat, who was scrabbling against the floorboards in the corner of the bedroom. I could not summon up the will to shoo the rat away. It was more welcome in my bedroom than Cage ever was, and it put an idea in my head that would not go away. My plan was not impulsive. I thought about it for a few days before acting on it. I considered all the consequences and however bad they were, they did not fill me with the same dread as continuing my sorry existence.

I still had some of Robert Tricker's coins and ventured to the chemist in the village to put them to good use. Two other people were milling around inside with no discernible purpose, which delayed my purchase. Mr Smith's shop had always fascinated me, and I was not unhappy as I wasted time there looking at items I could never afford. I stared at the glass-fronted cabinets with their intriguing variety of bottles, wondering what they contained and what use I could make of it. Mr Smith's counter housed the biggest bottle I had ever seen. Fashioned to resemble a giant teardrop with a spear-shaped stopper, it dominated the store. I couldn't work out what it contained, but the liquid was viscous. Perhaps it was medicine, or maybe poison. I longed to know. Next to the bottle, was a set of scales, and Mr Smith's pock-marked assistant stood there, weighing quinine pills for Mrs Drew and her imagined ailments.

When Mrs Drew finally left the store, I got to business and, without small talk, asked the man for two candles and some poison. He drew himself up, fixed me with a stare and asked what I wanted with poison. I told him that I had a problem with rats. He shook his head and refused me. I argued, but he was unmoved. I was angry, but there was no point in persisting, as, clearly unwilling to debate the matter, he hastened to the side room and out of my sight. I snatched the two candles without paying for them and marched from the store.

I walked the streets considering my options and decided to pay a visit to my old friends at the farm. Kitty had long gone, married to a decent man. They all married decent men except me, though Alice remained - poor, spinster Alice, a fifty-year-old cowhand, with a life as sad as my own. So, I wandered over to the farm and engaged her in small talk. When I left, I stuck my head around the door of the barn to see if the rat poison kept there years ago, had gone. People are such creatures of habit, are they not? More than twenty years had passed since I last laboured for the farm, yet everything was exactly where it always had been. Better still, nobody was around, and I took a small pewter bowl and scooped what I hoped was rat poison. It was a risk. The substance looked just like flour and could have been harmless. Nevertheless, I placed it in my basket, walked out and left the farm, just like that.

The older children were all at work when I returned. Sibella, now big with child, was minding her sister Emma. I sent them out and put a scoop of powder down for the rat. I hid the rest under the floorboard near my pills. Next day, I woke to find a dead rat in the corner of the room and two dead mice beside it, so I knew I had been right, and it was poison.

The following morning, I sent James to work with bread and butter and a little extra for his dockey. I took care to use only a small amount of poison for I wanted him to suffer, but not to die. I wanted him to be ill, very ill for a very long time. He would know something of the agonies I had suffered. I cannot remember enjoying a day as much for a long time, revelling in anticipation of his pain, and it did not take long. James was brought back in a cart before noon, writhing in agony and complaining of a fire in his stomach. Two men carried him in, one my son Richard and another with whom I was unacquainted. I ushered them to the bedroom, and they laid him on the lice-ridden bed. When they left, I went to him and watched as he clutched his stomach and asking for water to quench an intolerable thirst. I did as he asked and he drank half of it, clutched his stomach and dropped the rest on the floor.

James, never a clean man, stank like a fetid old goat. He had messed himself, and it was all over his trousers and now on our bed. I removed his vomit-stained jacket, but it was as much assistance as I was prepared to give. "Help me, woman," he screamed, and I nearly gagged as the smell of vomit met the stink of human waste. James was a filthy human being and not worth my bother. Unable to spare a single drop of compassion for the loathsome man I had shared my life with, I shut the door on him, deaf to his screams.

Sibella, who disliked her father almost as much as I did, complained bitterly. She was due to give birth any time and should have taken the bed for her own. Sibella found her father's condition revolting and refused to enter the bedroom. She said she would make do with the parlour instead. I asked her if she was sure as her siblings slept there and there would be no privacy, then patted her hand and said I was sorry. I had not considered Sibella's comfort, a fact I deeply regretted in hindsight.

Richard, on the other hand, was sympathetic to his stepfather. Richard had always known he was a bastard, yet he was the only one of my children who tolerated James. I found his loyalty disappointing.

Richard insisted on telling me how his stepfather fell ill. James had clutched his belly shortly after eating his bread and complained of a sadly stomach. It got worse quickly and, when he fell to the floor and started grinding himself into the earth in his pain, the men thought it best to take him home. His symptoms were so severe that some feared cholera had returned to the village. Their anxiety made me happy. I was still profoundly resentful of their tolerance of Cage's mistreatment of me. Their anxious faces as they considered the consequences of a cholera epidemic filled me with gleeful pleasure.

By early evening, Cage's incessant screaming was starting to trouble the younger children, and I worried that they would pressure me into calling the doctor, which would be costly and risky. But by nightfall, James had stopped crying and seemed to be sleeping soundly. I thought it best to leave the powder where it lay beneath the floorboards for a few days.

James kept to his bed and appeared to rally. I feared he would mend too quickly and waited until they were all out and he was asleep in his room, then removed the powder from the bedroom and re-located it under a brick in the privy. The next morning, I fetched James some ale with a little of the powder inside which produced a new round of vomiting and diarrhoea. On the one occasion I looked in on him that day, James was curled in a foetal position on the bed, moaning. Though it was spring outside, the room was cold and dark, and the dead rat still occupied its space on the floor, a suitable companion for my odious husband.

The day after, James was making so much noise in his agonies that the two middle boys, William and John, mithered at me to go to the doctor and get him some medicine. I welcomed an excuse to get out of the noisy, filthy rooms and took the long walk across the fields to Debenham, where I visited Doctor Lock's establishment.

Several others were waiting to see him; two elderly women who I did not recognise and Mary Jane Durrant who was carrying a sickly-looking infant with a rasping cough. She prattled on in some distress, fearful that it would die as the child had been unwell for most of the year. Looking at its sallow, sunken face, I thought it might be better for all concerned if it did expire. I could not say this, of course. People shun the truth. Mary Jane was called through ahead of me and returned shortly after with a worried look on her pale face. She carried a poultice and a glass bottle, filled with a creamy liquid. The child flopped against her shoulder, staring at me through half-open eyes as they left the room, and it occurred to me that she would not have much longer left to worry.

Doctor Lock sat behind his solid, dark wood desk, peering at me over round-lensed glasses. He interviewed me at length about James' illness, with particular regard to the symptoms he displayed. I found it hard to concentrate at the sight of his bushy eyebrows which seemed to have a life of their own, moving above his owl-like glasses. It was all I could do not to laugh out loud. After considering James' symptoms, Doctor Lock concluded that he was suffering from a gastric ailment and poured a thick, creamy liquid from a large receptacle into a brown bottle which he sealed with a cork stopper and passed to me, charging me half a penny for the privilege. I reluctantly handed the over money and left the premises, choosing to walk the long route by the roadside in the hope of securing a ride back to my village along the way.

I did not meet anyone and arrived wearily back at Stonham Aspal mid-afternoon. My children worked in the fields, and Sibella was not at home, even though she was close to her confinement. James emitted a piteous moan as I reached the door of the bedroom, and I decided to take a handful of pills from my hiding place and wait for them to take effect.

When I was suitably numb, I opened the bedroom door. The assault on my nostrils from this stench was almost too much to bear, despite the opiates calming effect. I handed James a cup of water and the bottle of medicine from Doctor Lock as if I were a dutiful wife. He sat up in his vomit-stained, crumpled shirt and took a slug of medicine straight from the bottle.

He grimaced, and said, "I am in a great deal of pain, Mary," as if he hoped for sympathy from me. I could not help but laugh at him, and I told him he deserved it and that I hoped his illness would be of long duration. His yellowing, bloodshot eyes filled with tears as a fresh cramp assailed his guts, and I walked from the room, leaving him to his agonies.

The following evening, Richard interfered with my plans by sending word to Doctor Lock when the screams became too much for him to bear. The Doctor could not attend until the next morning, but the thought of his visit caused me so much concern that I dropped the remains of the powder down the privy and swilled out the pewter bowl. While Richard and Sibella waited at the house, the others being out in the fields, I went to Mrs Cooper's shop and asked how much she would pay for the pewter bowl. She gave me some coins which I concealed in my pockets, as it was rare for me to have money to myself.

By the time I returned, Doctor Lock had arrived by carriage and stood in my front room holding a well-worn Gladstone bag, bulging with medical paraphernalia. By now, James' screams had turned to low moans, but they were still loud enough for the doctor to find his patient without further direction. When Doctor Lock emerged from the room, he fixed me with a hostile glare and barked orders to "clean the man up." Then he turned to Richard and told him that his father was very sick indeed and needed better care. The household squalor was impeding his recovery and making him suffer more. He said James must continue to take his medicine, and Richard should contact him immediately if James's condition changed. Then he turned abruptly and left as quickly as he arrived. He could not have spent more than six or seven minutes during his visit, but who could blame him. If any of us could have left the hovel, we would have.

I did not clean James's bedsheets, his festering body, or the vomit-stained floor that day or any of the three days that followed. Perhaps others did, but I did not check and cared not a jot. On the fourth day, James rallied, briefly left his bed, and seemed somewhat improved. He cleaned himself and threw the filthy sheets in a pile on the floor, then called for me, and I fetched him water and a little food. He thanked me, then grabbed my arm and leered at me, thrusting his lips towards mine. I turned away, sickened.

That night I dreamed he was on top of me again, pinning me down while his bristled jaw scraped my face as he thrust deep inside. The horrific certainty of what would be if he recovered was enough for me to ensure that it could not happen. I excused myself from the house with the intent of fetching more medicine and walked briskly to Debenham, as fast as I could.

I returned to Doctor Lock, who glowered as he passed another bottle of medicine. He said he trusted his patient was residing in better conditions than previously, and I assured him that he was. I never lied when I was Mary Moise, yet Mary Cage was an accomplished liar with little conscience. The doctor dismissed me from his rooms with a flick of the wrist, wearing a pained expression on his weathered face, and I left clutching the bottle, which I placed inside the pocket of my apron. As I walked past the chemist shop, I imagined purchasing more poison to take him down for another week or two, then thought the better of it. It was too close to Doctor Lock and therefore too risky.

Then it came to mind that Elizabeth Lambert resided a short distance away and the whey-faced vixen owed me for treating me as a fool all those years ago. I sought her out and found her at Mrs Parker's crowded house where she resided with two adults, their four children, Mrs Parker, and Elizabeth's two girls. Unfortunately, they were all in, and Mrs Parker lay inconveniently on her bed in the corner of the room watching me through hawk eyes. She had been bed-bound for the last six years, and the comings and goings of the household were her entire world. I thought it imprudent to talk to Elizabeth in front of her and suggested that we go for a walk down the lane so the old woman could not hear us.

Elizabeth joined me and prattled about her tedious life and her profoundly uninteresting family, while I pretended to be fascinated. Not once did she ask me about my kin, which was useful as I did not want to bring the subject of James' illness and poison together in one conversation.

At the end of the lane, Elizabeth said how pleased she was to see me, but that she must go. I clutched my head and told her that I had forgotten an errand in Debenham and had promised to buy some rat poison for my daughter Mary Ann and would she mind fetching it for me. Elizabeth said no. I was shocked as I had not considered that a woman with her docile qualities would deny me and quickly feigned a malady. I slumped to the ground, fanning my face with my hand, and told Elizabeth that I had felt faint all morning and could only manage the walk home if I rested first. She was finally persuaded, took the money, and set off for the chemist. I had been right; she was sufficiently stupid.

Elizabeth could not have encountered any obstacles in her task as she returned far more quickly than expected, carrying a small package marked with a written label. I thanked her, then cautioned her not to mention the transaction to nosy Mrs Parker and headed for Stonham. Nobody was there when I arrived, and I secreted the poison in my hiding place beneath the brick and put my head around the door of the bedroom to see how James was faring. He had been sick again and was pale and drawn. His recovery had not continued unabated, as I feared. I placed a glass of water by him, but he grasped my wrist with his dirty, clawed hands and asked me what I had put in his food. I was so surprised that I sat down momentarily on the bed. Watching me through crusty lashes, he searched my face for clues. My discomfort must have been apparent, for he said he could see guilt etched into my features. He said I was trying to harm him, and he would refuse any more food or drink from me. I dashed his filthy hand away and told him he was hallucinating and that his illness had made him mad. I said I hated him but not enough to risk my life, and he lapsed into silence, considering my words. Then I left the room and perched upon the doorstep thinking about what he had said, and I resolved to give him another dose to keep his loose mouth quiet.

Next day, I could not find time to introduce the powder into his food or drink. Sibella had taken to her bed in the front room in the early stages of childbirth. Kezia Oxborrow was nigetting, coming in and out without a by-your-leave. Sibella's labour was long and hard. It was not until the next day that she finally birthed her daughter, Jane. Richard asked me to bring bread and butter to James and, while they all clucked around the new baby, I took the plate to the privy intending to sprinkle some of the powder over his meal.

I nearly dropped it such was my shock when I realised the brick had been moved. I lifted it, but there was only an empty indentation, and the powder had vanished. I slipped the plate back on the table and surveyed the room in disbelief. Richard, Sibella, Emma and Betsy were at home. John and William were out. I had not seen the powder for two days, and the privy was never locked. Anyone could have had it, but I could not risk asking after it.

I passed the plate to Richard in stunned silence, and he took it to the bedroom. Seconds later, the tin plate rattled to the floor as James spewed a stream of profanities. I opened the door and told him to quiet his filthy mouth. Bread and butter were strewn over the bedroom floor, too dirty for anyone else to eat. I asked Richard what happened, and he said James refused to eat anything I had prepared, now or ever. He told Richard that I was an evil bitch, bent on his destruction. I said, in my defence, that James was losing his mind and Richard should not heed the ramblings of a daft old man. Richard scraped the bread and butter from the floor and passed it to me, and I gave it to the cat, who licked the butter with relish. Afterwards, I left the house and wandered the street of Stonham, contemplating the missing poison.

I was out for several hours, and by the time I returned, James had eaten and was resting quietly. Sibella and her daughter slept, and the room enjoyed a peaceful calm I hardly recognised. Even when John and William returned, peace reigned for a while. Then, in the dark of the night, James screamed as if a thousand devils were torturing his soul. The noise was as penetrating as the cry of an animal in the abattoir and the whole house roused, beginning with the squalling baby.

I hastened to the bedroom, not to help but to try to quieten him. He clutched at his throat, scraping his skin with filthy nails. Then he sat up and vomited over himself, over the floor; green, viscous vomit, spewing from his mouth in bloody lumps. The wailing continued through the small hours turning, into moaning as the dawn broke. The children had gone back to sleep but Sibella, Richard and I could not.

A return to the doctor the next day was unavoidable. James had taken a turn for the worst, and it would have excited too much attention not to have seemed, at least publicly, to be tending to him as a devoted wife should. So, I trudged the long walk to Debenham again, using the last of my coins to purchase more medicine as James was swigging it from the bottle as if it were ale.

Doctor Lock said he would visit James the next day. I thanked him although I did not care one way or the other, but uncommonly met with good fortune when I encountered William Gunn in his cart. I knew William by sight and thought I might prevail upon him to take me to Stonham Aspal. As it turned out, he was occupied in fitting windows at Mr Sparrow's building in Stonham, every detail of which he subjected me to on the ride home. William was evidently not a man comfortable with silence. When he was not talking about himself, he was prying about matters that did not concern him. The village gossips had been out in force, and William Gunn was not only possessed of the information that James was extremely sick but was also aware of my recent relationship with Robert Tricker. He offered his sympathies on the one hand while trying to glean information about Robert, on the other. Gunn had the bad manners to ask me how I would manage if my husband died, and I squirmed with pent up rage at his nerve. I was so irritated that I told him to mind his own business, which annoyed him in turn, but not enough to stop him asking a succession of increasingly intrusive questions.

We finally reached Stonham, and I departed with a brusque thank you before delivering the medicine to James, who was twisting from side to side in agony when I entered. I shoved the bottle towards him, and he eyed it with suspicion, then dashed it to the floor. I knelt and took a handful of the sticky glass, not caring about the fragments that cut my palm. I hurled them onto the bed and told him that was the end of it. There would be no more medicine for we had no money. James could scarcely speak but swallowed, then with considerable effort, said that he would refuse anything I touched, so it did not matter. I raised my eyes heavenwards and left the room.

Kezia Oxborrow was in my parlour by then, checking on Sibella and baby Jane. She told me that James had been calling for Samuel Oxborrow all day and that Samuel would visit tomorrow when he returned to the village. I told her Samuel could do as he pleased. I did not tell her I would much have preferred it if he did not. I did not like any friend of James, and they had long since despaired of me.

By the time Doctor Lock arrived the next day, there had been a sudden change in James. He was much worse, and his mind had wandered irrevocably. He clutched at his stomach, complaining of creatures inside him. There was also a marked change in my attitude. I began to realise, for the first time, that James, who should have been recovering from his illness having received no further poison from me for several days, had deteriorated beyond all reason. I did not understand science, but his worsened condition seemed inconsistent with the doses I had given. A creeping dread gnawed at the pit of my stomach. James' dramatic deterioration meant that he could easily die. The poison I had persuaded Elizabeth Lambert to purchase was missing. All at once, the prospect of James becoming sicker was terrifying.

I joined the Doctor in the bedroom, as he examined James, who was thrashing around the bed, screaming incoherently. The Doctor scowled and ordered me out of the room. When he returned a few moments later, he gave me another lecture about the state of the room and the lack of bedding. Then he scribbled some words onto a sheet of paper and instructed me to present it to his assistant, without delay.

I left our rooms and rested on the stile in the field behind the house where I could watch to see when he left. There was no point in going to the doctor's rooms, for I had not a farthing left. I could not pay for the medicine, and I could not see the purpose of trying to explain this to the doctor. He had eyes. He must have been able to see there was no food or drink in the house, no soap, no water and barely a stick of furniture. I had purchased as much medicine as I could afford, and if I had any money left, I would have used it for opium pills before I fed myself or the children. No doubt that sounds selfish, but Richard made my choice easier. He was a good son and used his earnings to support the other children.

No sooner had the doctor removed himself from the house, Samuel Oxborrow arrived and let himself in. I hastened back as I wanted to be around to hear their conversation. I was beginning to worry and did not want James to have the opportunity to accuse me of interfering with his food if he unexpectedly became coherent.

I stood at the door of the bedroom, watching over Samuel's shoulder as he approached James. As much as I disliked my husband, what I saw in that room haunts me to this day. Blood dripped from James' face. It dribbled from his mouth in slavering, gobs of sputum. He screamed again and put most of his right hand in his mouth, scratching at his gums until the blood spurted down his chin. His left hand clawed at his stomach, shredding the skin in bloody lesions. In between his fingers were slivers of flesh.

Samuel grabbed James' hands and held them away from his body. He turned to me, words spilling out of his mouth in a torrent of horror as he explained that the shreds were strips of flesh that James had wrenched from his stomach. While Samuel spoke, James, in his delirium, screamed of rats and ferrets. In one sickening spasm, he pulled his hand away and tore a strip of flesh as big as a fist from his stomach and thrust it down upon the mattress, claiming he had discovered the creatures that tormented him.

I don't know how Samuel stayed in there. It finished me. I exited the room, shocked, and stood trembling in the doorway. Kezia glared at me and asked what was wrong. She said it was no secret that I hated James, so why did I look upset now that he was dying?

I answered that he was a wicked man and had ill-treated me the whole of our marriage, but for what it once had been I hoped he would die and die quickly, for no man should suffer as he did. She sneered at me and told me I was the wicked one and would burn in hell for what I had done. Sibella admonished her, but the words were out. Kezia tended to all birthing women in the village and was a gibble-gabble. I did not doubt there would be talk, as there was when my children died ten years before. There was some justice in that, just as there was in this, but it was not the whole story. Yes, I had given him poison. Yes,

I had made him sick, but who had removed the poison? Had someone given him more? They must have.

James lingered another two days. Doctor Lock visited one of the days, but James had stopped screaming by then and lay quietly. By the time I rose and looked in on him the next day, James was dead; his body cold, bloody and ravaged. I knew they would hold me to account. It was only a matter of when.

Chapter Nine

A clash with the law

Louisa arrived at Caxton Hall by hansom cab, excited and happy. It had taken several days to recover from reading the contents of Mary's journal, and she was contemplating whether to dispose of it altogether. Louisa had encountered little unpleasantness in her life, and the grotesque descriptions laid bare in the diary were too graphic to leave her unmoved by the experience. On the one hand, she thought Mary Emily Cage was an inhumane monster comparable with Jack the Ripper and his recent reign of terror in the streets of Whitechapel. But another part of her sympathised with the young girl who started her life full of hope. Unendurable hardships and cruelty had moulded Mary into the cruel, selfish woman she became. But would anyone have survived such trials unchanged? There but for the grace of God, thought Louisa. Still, tonight was the wrong time to dwell on Mary Cage, and Louisa had other, more exciting plans to consider.

Louisa alighted from the cab just before six o'clock and was thrilled to see the familiar forms of Ada and Bessie Ridley waiting on the pavement in front of the arched entrance to Caxton Hall.

"Hello cousins," she cried jovially and reached to them, taking each of their hands in turn and kissing their cheeks.

"It's good to see you," said Bessie. "Have you enjoyed London?"

"Very much," replied Louisa. "I've been to the theatre twice and watched an opera already. I've been shopping almost every day and have got to know Kensington very well. I'll be sorry to go home next week."

"I'm sure you miss your family," said Ada. "You will be glad to leave by the time it comes around. London is too tiring after a while. Come inside. Meet some friends."

Louisa needed no introduction to Millicent Fawcett and recognised her as soon as she stepped into the large hall. Millicent was surrounded by crowds of eager women, preventing easy movement and Louisa waved across the room instead. Ada gently guided her towards a stern-looking woman wearing a high collared lace shirt with navy blue satin dress over. She sported an impervious expression.

"I would like to introduce you to Emmeline Pankhurst," said Ada.

"Pleased to meet you," said Louisa, exchanging pleasantries for a few minutes, until Emmeline made her excuses and joined Millicent Fawcett on the stage. A younger, shorter version of Emmeline, who Bessie identified as Christabel Pankhurst, climbed the stairs to join them. Moments later, a solidly built woman dressed in a dark, high-necked brocade dress in stark contrast to her white hair, edged in between Millicent and her companions, completing the four speakers.

"Charlotte Despard," said Ada reverently. "Poor Millicent is rather outnumbered tonight."

"What do you mean?" whispered Louisa as a rotund woman in high stiletto heels, joined the stage and began to introduce the speakers.

"They are all militants, and she is not," explained Ada. "This debate could be very one-sided."

The large woman finished her introduction and beckoned Christabel Pankhurst to come over. She stepped forward confidently and launched into a strident attack on the government.

"As you all know, we ceased militant action at the end of last year on the promise that the Conciliation Bill would go through. While Prime Minister Asquith is making all the right assurances, I have it on exceedingly good authority that this bill won't pass through parliament. He hasn't got the smallest intention of granting us the vote and rumour has it that his priority will be to enfranchise all men first."

"You don't know this," protested Millicent Fawcett from her podium. "And I don't profess to know what machinations occur within the government, but we can't take the position that they are liars before they have had the opportunity to debate the bill, which we know can't happen until May."

Emmeline joined her daughter on the opposite side of the stage.

"But we do know," she said. "It is openly discussed in parliament. We have a few male politicians sympathetic to the cause who have reported otherwise. The Liberals think their secrets will be safe, but we have heard that this bill will not go through, despite their promises. We say act now and lose no time."

"Hear, hear," the hall filled with a roar of encouragement as a substantial part of the audience expressed their approval. The debate continued, and Louisa listened enthralled, empathising with both points of view. But as the Pankhurst's continued their impassioned plea, the atmosphere in the hall grew ever more febrile. Tempers frayed and some of the women became so agitated that Louisa witnessed language that she hadn't heard before from the coarsest of men. It was a markedly different atmosphere to the quiet, dignified night of the census evasion.

By the time the debate ended, passions were high. Ada, recognising the change in atmosphere took Louisa's hand and began to propel her to the front of the hall. It was time to say goodbye and commiserate with Millicent Fawcett, who had been on the less popular side of the argument. But in the excitable crowd of women, Louisa dropped her hand and became separated from her cousins.

Feeling faint in the stifling, crowded hall, she squeezed past a gap in the crowd and through a side door. She gulped the cold air in deep staccato breaths, panting audibly.

"What's wrong," asked a well-spoken woman in a black evening dress and a tailored coat. She drew deeply from a cigarette, and the smoke hung in the air as she exhaled.

"I was feeling a little faint, but I'm better now," said Louisa. "It was stifling in there for a while."

The woman opened an elegant silver cigarette case. "Would you like one?" she asked.

"No, thanks. I don't smoke," Louisa replied.

"More fool you," said her companion. "Cigarettes and alcohol make it all so much more bearable."

She held out her hand. "I am Clara," she said.

"Pleased to meet you," said Louisa introducing herself. "I don't live in London and have travelled from Ipswich to stay with relatives in Kensington."

"How very provincial," said Clara, "have you been one of us for long?"

"One of you?" asked Louisa, confused.

"A suffragette, you silly ass," said Clara.

"Not really," said Louisa. "I joined the Ipswich census evasion though."

Clara laughed. "How militant of you," she said. "Have you been on a demonstration yet?"

"I don't know if my father would allow it."

Clara snorted. "Really," she exclaimed, "my father has no idea what I do, and I don't consider it to be any of his business."

"You're very brave," said Louisa uncertainly, the words trailing away.

"I'm not brave," said Clara curling her lip. "The whole point about being a suffragette is to try to change the patriarchal system under which we are living. And that means we don't ask men for permission. Haven't you ever broken the rules or fallen foul of the law?"

"No, never," said Louisa.

The side door banged open behind her, and another two young women in long dresses and feather boas emerged, giggling.

"There you are," said Clara.

"Cynthia, Laura, I would like to introduce you to Louisa. She has never attended a demonstration nor challenged the lawmakers."

"Pleased to meet you, "said Louisa, inching towards the door, "but I must go now. My cousins are waiting inside."

"You can spare five minutes, can't you?" asked Clara taking Louisa by the hand and dragging her towards the side street.

"I really can't," said Louisa pulling away.

"Come on, quickly," said Laura. "Just up here."

"But…"

"Come on," cried Clara pulling Louisa by the hand and running towards a small crowd of about twenty women at the top of the narrow street.

Louisa opened her mouth again to protest but was propelled along by Clara. There was no mistaking that the crowd of women were suffragettes. They wore purple and green badges and carried large placards with "Votes for Women" in bold black writing, just readable in the fading light.

"What are they doing?" asked Louisa.

"You will see," replied Clara darkly, reaching into her bag.

One of the women in the group, notably taller than her peers, clapped her hands, "quickly now girls," she said. "We don't want Millicent getting wind of this."

They hurried down a wide road, into a warren of alleyways, and presently found themselves at a street corner. The tall woman beckoned them to stop, and they stood quietly in the shadow of the wall.

"The police station is over there," she whispered. "As soon as you have let loose run as quickly as you can in different directions like you did before. Are you ready?"

"Ready for what?" asked Louisa, but a sea of noise drowned her voice as the women ran towards the red-brick station, hurling a volley of stones into the windows of the building. They cracked like gunshots in the night.

"Run," cried Clara as the front door of the police station slammed open, and a whiskered policeman ran out brandishing a stick.

"Oi, you little witches; stop at once" he commanded, as the women fled up the street. He ran behind them as several of his colleagues emerged behind him, joining in pursuit.

Louisa ran instinctively. She did not know where she was running to until she saw Laura ahead, feather boa trailing from her neck. Louisa ran towards her, but she was not shod for fleetness of foot. She stumbled and wrenched her ankle as she stepped into a pothole in the road. Louisa collapsed in a heap and was scrabbling to her feet when one of the younger constables caught up and grabbed her roughly by the coat.

"I've got one of the bitches," he shouted up the street.

"Get off me," Louisa cried. "This has nothing to do with me."

The constable dragged her coat open, and her buttons pinged into the gutter. "What is this?" he asked, pointing to the purple and green badge given to her by Constance Andrews on the evasion night protest.

Louisa groaned inwardly, wishing she had not decided to wear it beneath her coat that night in support of the movement.

"You are coming with me," said the policeman, grabbing her roughly by the wrist. He dragged her behind him as he walked in strides too long for Louisa to match.

As they neared the police station, Louisa crunched through glass laying scattered across the street. Every window in the station was cracked and broken. A policeman appeared from the dark of an alleyway pulling a woman behind him. She spat and snarled like a wild cat as she struggled to escape his grasp. "I am not coming with you," she screamed and sat down mutinously in the road.

The policeman hauled her to her feet by her hair and slapped her twice in the face. "That is where you are wrong, he snarled. You walk, or I will drag you."

"You pig," screamed the woman who Louisa now recognised as Clara. "I will have your badge for this."

The policeman laughed at her and spat on the ground close to her feet. "Get through that door now," he said. "We will see what my sergeant has to say about your behaviour."

He pushed the girls unceremoniously through the entrance of the station where a second policeman joined them. Together, they marched them down a corridor and into a small room with bars across the window, and a hatchway in the door then pushed them roughly into the cell. Louisa fell onto the floor, sobbing dramatically.

"Pull yourself together you silly woman," hissed Clara. "Don't give them the satisfaction."

"I didn't ask for any of this," snapped Louisa. "How has this happened?

Why did you force me into joining you?"

"Nobody made you do anything," said Clara. "Either you are one of us or you are not."

She sat down on the metal bed and lit a cigarette from the bag she still carried, took a long drag, and blew the smoke in Louisa's direction. Louisa flinched and turned away. "What happens now?" she asked.

"How should I know," said Clara. "I have never been caught before."

"I need to speak to my aunt," said Louisa. "She will be wondering what has happened to me."

"You will be lucky," said Clara. "We won't be released tonight."

Louisa put her head in her hands, cursing her stupidity at getting caught up in the demonstration. She should have had the strength of character to refuse, especially as she didn't know the women and owed them no allegiance. Louisa sat in silence while Clara smoked her cigarette. The cell was deathly cold, and the only place to sit was on the bed, so she perched next to Clara shivering as Clara glared disdainfully.

Louisa jumped as the hatch on the door slammed back unexpectedly, and a face appeared through the bars. A voice rumbled in the background.

"Two of them," he said gruffly and a few seconds later, "glad to."

Keys clattered against the metal door which opened to reveal a sharp-faced man wearing a dusty cape over his suit and sporting a neatly clipped moustache.

"What have we here?" he asked, peering at the two women.

"Please, I need to telephone my aunt," said Louisa.

The man looked down his nose towards the young woman sitting on the bed, head bowed and staring at the floor.

He laughed a deep, unsympathetic laugh. "Well, you can't," he sneered. "There are no windows left in my police station, and you are going to pay dearly for what you have done."

"But I didn't do anything," cried Louisa jumping to her feet. "Honestly. I didn't throw stones. I was just there at the wrong time."

Clara took another cigarette from her bag and placed it carelessly in the side of her mouth. "She never did a thing, the little mouse," she said. "She's not a suffragette - she's a child."

The sergeant snatched the cigarette from her mouth and ground it into the floor with an unpolished boot.

"No smoking in here," he said, removing her bag. "I'll have yours too," he continued, reaching towards Louisa.

"Please, no", she said, but he took her bag roughly from her hand.

"You are up in front of the magistrate tomorrow," he said to Louisa, before pointing at Clara. "And you can come with me."

He dragged Clara from the cell, leaving Louisa alone. A door clanged down the corridor, and Louisa heard Clara shouting from a nearby room. Ten minutes later, the strains of the suffragette anthem were ringing loudly. "From the daughters of the nation, bursts a cry of indignation…" Clara was singing discordantly at the top of her voice. She kept it up for several hours, and when Louisa finally fell asleep, huddled on a thin bolster on the wooden bed in the freezing cell with no blankets, she could still hear the faint, tired strains of singing.

Louisa was woken in the early dawn by the clang of the door bolt. A whiskered constable, who she had not encountered the previous night thrust a bowl of thick porridge towards her.

"Eat," he commanded, dropping a spoon into the bowl. Porridge splattered across the floor, landing on Louisa's skirt. She was about to speak when the sound of metal clattering onto the stone floor distracted the constable, who darted into the corridor.

A roar came from the distance. "You filthy, little bitch," yelled a deep voice. "She has thrown her breakfast on the floor."

The door of Clara's cell opened, and Louisa heard a slap followed by a high-pitched scream. She covered her ears and wept.

Chapter Ten

Trapped

The experience of standing in the dock of the Magistrate's Court, next to a sullen Clara while trembling from head to foot, was one Louisa hoped never to repeat. The reprimand from the judge, followed by a two-week custodial sentence, brought Louisa to the lowest point of her young life.

After the judge rapped his gavel and dismissed the court, two female warders removed Louisa from the dock and marched her through a white-washed corridor to the holding cells. She stood in disbelief, wondering how she had got to this point, before spotting Laura and one of the Pankhurst women as they rushed towards her.

"Clara, Clara," shouted Laura. "Do not worry. We are trying to secure your release."

"A good thing too," snapped Clara.

"Can't you help me?" cried Louisa.

"Who are you?" asked Laura.

"I am Louisa Russell. Tell Ada or Bessie Ridley that I am here," she said, "or Millicent Fawcett. They will wonder what has happened." Her voice faltered as she spoke, and tears pricked her eyes.

"Don't worry, I will," assured Laura.

The warders lead them past noisy cells and through a door at the end of the corridor, before herding them into a large, black automated cab. For one moment, Louisa hoped they might be going home; but after an uncomfortable ride, they arrived outside the iron-railed gates of Holloway prison.

Louisa gasped at the size of the building as she emerged from the cab, horrified at the prospect of incarceration. As if on cue, it started to rain. Large droplets splashed onto her face, dripping from her nose. Louisa wiped the rainy tears from her face, hands over her mouth, trying to stifle the sob that threatened to overwhelm her.

Louisa reached for Clara's hand as the warders escorted them through a side gate and into the black and white squared corridor of the woman's prison. She wanted to offer solidarity and receive sisterly comfort, but Clara pushed her away. After registration, in a bleak, unheated reception room, they found themselves the occupants of single cells opposite each other, barred doors allowing a partial view into each other's cell.

Louisa placed her face against the metal bars." I want to go home," she whispered.

"Darling, this cell is your home for the next few weeks," said Clara harshly, seemingly recovered from her ordeal.

"Can your friends secure our release?" asked Louisa.

"They will try but whether they will succeed is an entirely different matter," said Clara.

"Aren't you worried?" asked Louisa.

"Not at all," Clara replied. "I am not afraid of anyone."

At midday, a dour prison wardress placed a tin plate of unappetising, congealed meat through the cell door. She handed over a spoon, and Louisa picked through the mess, eating only a tiny portion. Clara took her meal with a smirk, refusing the cutlery. She waited until the wardress turned her back to leave the cell and hurled the plate against the barred window, laughing as it dripped down the brick walls.

"And don't bring anymore because I won't eat it," she screamed at the prison wardress. True to her word, she deposited her evening meal on the floor of the cell, and by the next day news of her misdemeanours had spread among the prison staff. At breakfast time, the wardress thrust a thin bowl of porridge towards Clara hissing, "this is your last chance."

Clara picked up the bowl and spoon as if she intended to eat but walked straight in front of the prison wardress before deliberately upending the unappetising gruel over the warder's shoes.

"You have done it now," snarled the woman as she pushed Clara onto the bed and pinned her down while she blew a whistle. Clara shook her head, pushed her away and glared as she started to sing.

"Stop it," shouted Louisa from her cell. "You will be in terrible trouble."

Clara pressed her face to the bars. "I – do – not – care," she said slowly and precisely. Then shouted, "I do not care" over and over until her voice cracked from the strain.

As Clara continued her vocal protest, footsteps clattered on the floor further up the corridor. As they came closer, Louisa could hear the creaking of wheels, and through the grille in the door, she watched two men in white coats pushing a gurney containing tubes and a jug of dark green liquid. Even from a distance, the rancid odour of rotting cabbage assailed her nostrils, making her retch. A hard-faced female warder and a well-dressed man in a smart suit and polished shoes walked alongside the gurney.

The warder unlocked the door to Clara's cell, and the men wheeled the trolley to the far end. The warder reached below and produced a bowl of cold porridge.

"You have one more chance to eat this," she said, "otherwise you will be made to eat it."

"Never," snapped Clara.

"Please eat it," called Louisa, "please Clara."

"I will not," said Clara shaking her head stubbornly.

The suited man nodded while the white-coated men pushed Clara onto a wooden chair by the side of her bed. She screamed and thrashed, trying to free her arms before two men pinned her to the chair and secured her arms with leather straps. The men worked in silence, placing a metal gag over her face with fearsome efficiency. The contraption jammed her mouth open, and Clara struggled and moaned, red-faced with exertion as she tried to escape, but for all the effort, she remained trapped.

"Hold her head," barked the man, nodding to the wardress.

"Yes, doctor."

The men stood either side of Clara holding her shoulders until she was motionless. Then the doctor grabbed a dirty length of hose from the gurney and snapped it straight. Taking Clara's chin in his hand, he tipped her head backwards and rammed the tube into her gullet. Clara instinctively gagged causing lumps of vomit to stream either side of the metal gag, which spewed down her face.

"Stop it," screamed Louisa.

The doctor raised the tube high over Clara's head, inserted a funnel and poured the evil-looking green liquid into the pipe where it gushed into Clara's stomach.

But for a small part of grille blocked by the warder, Louisa could see everything. She forced herself to watch as Clara repeatedly vomited, while the green liquid spurted from gaps between her mouth and the metal gag. When the jug was empty, the spectacle ceased. The doctor removed the restraints before lecturing Clara on the stupidity of refusing food. He said he hoped she had learned her lesson and that he would never see her again, then gestured to the men to remove the gurney. They left the cell without a backward glance at Clara, sitting broken on the chair staring wordlessly at the mess on the cell floor.

"Talk to me, Clara," said Louisa. "Can you speak?"

Clara stared with hate-filled eyes. "They will pay" she whispered, through swollen, battered lips. Vomit coated her smart, black dress and her matted, loosened hair stuck to her shoulders. Sweat and liquid feed covered her skin and clothes.

"I am so sorry," said Louisa. "The utter brutes. How dare they treat you so unkindly. I can't believe their cruelty."

"Then you are naïve," said Clara hoarsely. "Lots of us have endured force-feeding for the cause."

Louisa opened her mouth to sympathise, but Clara said, "I cannot talk any longer." She hauled herself to her feet and limped around the chair, clinging to the back for stability, then crawled onto the bed and laid face-down, immobile except for her shaking shoulders.

Louisa watched silently from her cell. Every so often she pressed her nose to the door bars, checking on Clara who was still lying prone on the bed. Louisa was shocked and angry at the scene she had witnessed, numbing her to the routine prison noises. The sound of footsteps coming down the corridor failed to register in her consciousness. When a wardress unlocked her cell in the early afternoon, Louisa was taken by surprise, oblivious to her presence and deaf to her footsteps.

The door clanged making Louisa jump. The wardress entered her cell and beckoned. "Come with me," she said.

Louisa meekly followed until they reached a small room, containing only a table and two wooden chairs.

"Wait here."

She waited an anxious five minutes, drumming her fingers on the table, until she heard more footsteps, and watched as the door swung open. Standing next to the prison wardress was Daniel.

A mixture of relief at a familiar face, and shame at her circumstances, overwhelmed Louisa. She dropped her head in her hands and sobbed.

"Come now," said Daniel, patting her shoulder awkwardly.

"Have you come to help me?" asked Louisa between sobs. Daniel nodded.

"I am sorry," she sniffed, "but I didn't do it. I was in the wrong place at the wrong time and caught up in something I didn't understand."

"They know," said Daniel. "Some of the other women you were with that night came forward and volunteered an explanation. They insisted you were not part of the demonstration and didn't engage in any violence. The authorities were unconvinced at first, but your uncle intervened and persuaded them of your innocence."

"My uncle," gasped Louisa. "I will be in so much trouble. How are you involved?"

"Mrs Fawcett heard of your predicament," said Daniel. "She contacted your cousins, who informed your aunt and uncle. I happened to be visiting Harrington Gardens because," he looked at his feet, "because I felt it necessary to ensure you had returned safely from Caxton Hall following the debate. I called the next day and found your aunt and uncle recovering from their visit by the Misses Ridley."

"Was my uncle furious?" asked Louisa.

"He was less than impressed," said Daniel, "but I explained our connection and asked if I could be of help. They spoke with me more openly than they might have done in other circumstances. You are fortunate that your uncle is such a highly regarded surgeon, for it was his influence that precipitated your release. He does not think it appropriate for a man in his position to visit Holloway Prison, so they agreed I should come, and I am here now to escort you home."

"I am grateful," murmured Louisa. "Thank you for your kindness to my aunt and uncle, and also towards me."

"I did it for Sophia," said Daniel curtly. "Had she known of your predicament she would have insisted we help. It's time to leave now," he continued, turning to the wardress.

The hook-nosed woman grimaced as she led them out and glared at Louisa through narrowed eyes before opening the heavy doors into the reception area where Louisa's bag was waiting.

Louisa followed Daniel towards the exterior prison door, then grasped his arm and pulled him back. "I cannot leave Clara", she said.

"Then stay," said Daniel, "Clara's fate is in the hands of the Pankhurst's. I believe they are trying to secure her release, but it is not your problem, and it's certainly not mine."

"They hurt her terribly," cried Louisa. "She is alone and in pain."

"I am sorry," said Daniel, "but I can do nothing for her. I am responsible for your recovery, and that is all."

Louisa stood still, looking back towards the reception area through haunted eyes.

"I will not waste precious time trying to convince you to leave," said Daniel with his hand on the door. "I am going now. Join me if you want, or not as the case may be." He strode towards the carriage without looking back.

Louisa took a final glance before rushing to catch him and joined him by a carriage parked outside the driveway of the prison grounds. Daniel opened the carriage door just long enough for Louisa to enter, then slammed it shut. She sat down, chest heaving with the exertion of trying to reach him. He did not look her way.

Louisa remembered little of the journey from the prison to her aunt and uncle's house. She was tired, relieved and above all concerned about the likely reaction from her uncle. The journey barely registered before Louisa found herself alighting from the carriage outside Harrington Gardens. Daniel, silent through the journey, opened the door of the cab and helped Louisa down. He guided her into the house where her aunt and uncle were waiting in the drawing-room.

Louisa opened her mouth to apologise, but her uncle ignored her. Shaking Daniel with a firm grip, he said, "thank you for returning my niece. Please join me in the study?"

"Thank you, sir," replied Daniel, and the two men left the room.

Louisa turned to her aunt, lowering her head, "Is uncle very angry?" she asked.

Her aunt sighed, "Yes, he is Louisa. I wish it were not so. It was all I could do to prevent him from sending word to your father. In this, I have succeeded, but he wants you to leave the house at once."

"I am so sorry," cried Louisa. "I did not set out with the intention of any wrong-doing. I was naïve and stupid, perhaps even weak. I take full responsibility for that, but please believe me when I tell you that I never intended any harm."

"I do believe you," said her aunt, "but reputation is everything to your uncle. The slightest hint of a scandal and he is outraged. You know he deplores the idea of suffrage and sees your attendance at the rally as no less serious a misdemeanour than your detention in Holloway. I cannot convince him that this escapade was unplanned. Much as I will miss you, it is best if you return to Ipswich. I will have a better chance of smoothing matters when you are not here."

"But my father doesn't expect me back until next week," said Louisa. "He will ask why you don't want me."

"While I hate to conceal anything from my brother, I can see no benefit in telling him what has happened," said Aunt Beatrice. Not only will you be in trouble, but there will be a question over our guardianship while you were in our care. Ada and Bessie have convinced me of your innocence, and I would not see you punished any further for your naivety. I believe you have suffered quite enough. I will write to Henry today and tell him that I have been unwell, and you are returning to Ipswich to avoid catching my illness. You will travel back tomorrow. The letter will be with him by the time you arrive."

"Thank you," said Louisa, "and thank you for believing in me. I am so sorry I let you down, but I promise I will never place myself in such a position again. As strongly as I feel about our cause, I am more convinced than ever that Millicent's position is the right one. We will only succeed in our endeavours through peaceful protest."

Aunt Beatrice smiled, "a useful lesson learned," she said as the door opened, and Louisa's uncle entered alone.

"I am truly sorry, sir", said Louisa before he could speak. "I would not wish to bring embarrassment to your house for all the world."

"No doubt," said her uncle curtly, "but the fact remains, that you have. Your foolishness has given rise to unanticipated consequences. You have precisely demonstrated those reasons why women should not be allowed to vote. Women lack the wisdom and rationality to make sensible choices."

Louisa bit her lip, trying not to let her uncle goad her into an argument over his unreasonable views. She managed to control herself. "I am sorry, sir," she said again.

"Indeed," continued her uncle. "But I think it is best if you return to the care of your father, so there is no future temptation to involve yourself in this senseless cause. Mr Bannister is travelling to Ipswich by coach tomorrow and has offered to escort you home. I have agreed."

"Thank you, uncle," said Louisa, "but I do not need a chaperone."

"Nevertheless, you will have one," said her uncle firmly. "You can leave after breakfast tomorrow."

Chapter Eleven

To death with dignity

From the moment Louisa boarded the carriage the following day, her expectations were low. She anticipated little pleasantness from her travelling companion, and this assessment proved correct. Daniel was dour and wore a constant frown, barely uttering a word as they travelled in uncomfortable silence.

After half an hour, Louisa felt so awkward that she tried to start a conversation. "How is Sophia?" she asked.

"I do not know," Daniel replied. "It has been several days since my last contact with her. My recent concerns have been with other matters, and I've neglected the family too much considering the Charles parlous health when I left."

"I am sorry if I have been one of the other matters to which you refer," said Louisa." I appear to have, unwittingly, taken up too much of your time - time that you no doubt would have preferred to spend in your duty to your family."

Daniel sighed. "Do you ever think of anyone but yourself, Louisa?" he asked. "I have been occupied, in the most, with business. The electrical consultation did not conclude satisfactorily."

Louisa blushed. "I'm sorry I offended you," she snapped. "I was trying to apologise. And I am sure Mr Drummond will be quite well by the time you return."

"I will be greatly relieved if that is the case," replied Daniel, drifting off into another brooding silence.

Louisa sighed. She had packed the diary in her bag in anticipation of any awkwardness on the journey, knowing that conversation could be politely avoided by reading. As Louisa held the journal in her hand, the repulsion she felt towards Mary Cage left her unsure whether she could bear to read to the end. Given that the alternative was a stilted conversation and an uncomfortable journey, she decided it was the worst of two evils and opened the diary at the place marked with a purple ribbon.

The village gossips finished me in the end. We almost buried James. I thought it was over until Constables Grimwood and Whitehead strode through the Lychgate while we waited to toss the final sod into his grave. We surrounded the coffin-like black-clad crows while Reverend Shorting read the litany. Before the last words were uttered, Constable Grimwood raised his hand towards the Reverend and beckoned him over. A whispered conversation ensued, then Reverend Shorting announced that the funeral would not take place today and there would be a coroner's inquest instead. The crows took flight, cackling together, filled with gleeful pleasure at my misfortune. Then Constable Whitehead asked me to follow him back to his house, which was also the village police station.

Kezia Oxborrow watched as I left the churchyard, looking down her long nose with an air of satisfaction. "Now you will hang," she said.

I stayed the night at the police house with Constable Whitehead, which was not at all uncomfortable, considering the conditions I usually endured. They gave me three meals a day during my time there, which was two more than usual.

I returned home only once again. It was the following day, and the doctors had finished picking over James, returning his body to the church for a decent burial. Constable Whitehead escorted me to the graveside, and I watched my husband interred for the second time. Then Mr Grimwade told me they knew about the rat poison that Elizabeth Lambert purchased for me and asked me where it was now.

He escorted me back to the house, and I told him he could look around to his heart's content, but that he would find no poison. He located a packet of orange-coloured powder in one of the cupboards which caused him no end of excitement, and he passed it to another policeman who took it away. Quite how he found anything at all is a miracle. We had nothing. There was never any food or drink in the house.

Then he told me to follow him, and he walked to the privy, opening the door with the edges of his fingers, curling his lips in disgust. I joined him, disinterestedly watching as he kicked the loose brick away from the floor with his foot. There, in the hollow, was the missing packet of powder; but a lot less of it. I sat, before I fell, with the shock of it. How the poison came to be there, and from where, I could not imagine. The rest of the day passed in a blur.

I remained with Constable Whitehead and his family until the inquest which was held about a week after James died. Phoebe Whitehead, an old acquaintance of mine for many years, kept me apprised of the tattle in the village during my confinement. It was she who told me when they removed James' bodily organs to test for poison, and I knew it would not end well for me. Poor James could not sleep quietly in death any more than he had in the last weeks of his life, for they dug him up once again to remove his brain, so Phoebe said.

The inquest took place at the Ten Bells public house over the weekend. They called upon my two children, Mary Ann and Richard, to give evidence. Richard, a good, loyal son, would not speak ill of me but Mary Ann went against me. It was not entirely unexpected. After all, I implicated Mary in my lie to Elizabeth, and Mary was the type of woman to value the truth above her own mother's life.

I did not comprehend most of the evidence given at the inquest. There was much talk of tests and medical matters and a drawn-out discussion over the presence of poison in James' stomach and bowel. After much debate, they concluded that James had died from ingesting arsenic. Then the Coroner pursed his lips and told me in a hushed voice that I would be remanded in custody to await the Ipswich summer assizes.

After the inquest, they moved me from my comfortable quarters in the prison room at Stonham to the cold, crowded cells of Ipswich Gaol. They placed me in a cell with three other women and set me to work in the prison laundry. The work was hard, but I did not mind as I still received three meals a day. Breakfast was a paltry affair of bread and tea, but we received meat and potatoes every day for dinner, without the worry of having to pay for it. Working in the laundry bought the additional reward of a small piece of cheese with the supper meal. Some women complained of the hard, heavy labour, but it kept me warm, and the food kept me full. It made my time in prison bearable, and while it was not the best, neither was it the worst time of my life.

I thought I would be a pariah in prison, but unexpectedly made friendships. A particular friend was Polly, a girl in her third decade, slim and pretty but with only one arm, having lost the other in a childhood accident. Polly was smart and made up for the loss of her arm with tricks and wiles. She had a reputation for being able to procure anything, and there was always a ready supply of gin and tobacco for those who wanted it. Polly became a faithful, loyal friend who did not judge me as others had, choosing to disregard gossip in favour of finding out information by asking. Though there were two decades between us, we got along well, having led similar lives. Before gaol, she lived with a cruel man who beat her so severely that she lost a child and never conceived another. It bonded us.

I must have mentioned my fondness for opium pills during our time in prison because she presented me with a small packet before supper one night. I was delighted, not just because I desired them but because it was the first time in memory that anyone had been good to me, for no personal gain. Opiates were cheap, of course. How could poor women afford them *otherwise? But it was still a rare kindness, and I will never forget it.*

Ipswich Gaol was not built to provide prisoners with views of the outside. Some cells had windows, but mine did not, however, there was a window on the way to the laundry room, so I noticed as the days became lighter and, before long, I felt them getting warmer too. Summer was on its way and along with it the Summer Assizes, at which I would be judged. As the time drew closer, I received the first of two visits from my attorney Mr Gudgeon, a pock-faced man of about forty summers. Gudgeon spoke in a deep, monotone voice, and sported a poorly trimmed beard and a full handlebar moustache, both of which obscured his features. His natural air of gloom and despondency sapped my confidence during our first meeting and destroyed it entirely by the second. Finally, the day of the assizes arrived, and I was called to the bar to face the judge with my attorney by my side, like a grounded albatross.

I was permitted to dress in my own clothes for the trial. Someone took it upon themselves to launder them during my confinement in prison, and they retrieved and mended my black bonnet too. I looked quite respectable for once; ironic given the circumstances. Court orderlies guided me to the dock, built for others taller than I. It was a challenge to see over. The jury, composed of stern-looking, middle-aged men, were sworn in. There was not a kind face amongst them. Proceedings began when the judge banged a gavel.

The prosecution started by summarising the last days of my husband, James, beginning with his breakdown in the field through to a graphic description of his final, agonising injuries. Then they introduced Elizabeth Lambert and called her to give evidence.

She stood, trembling on the stand, unfamiliar with the formality of the situation, and I felt shame that my actions had bought her to this. They asked Elizabeth to recount her story, which she did in a faltering voice. I leaned forward to hear better and as I did, my legs buckled, and the wardress behind me shoved a wooden chair behind my legs, There I sat looking through the dock as Elizabeth continued to give her evidence.

On the day I visited her, it transpired that Elizabeth had returned hotfoot to her lodgings to tell the bed-bound Mrs Parker all about the errand. Half of Debenham would have been aware of it by the end of that day if Mrs Parker had the opportunity to see anyone else. As it happened, Elizabeth's mother was the next visitor, having travelled from Wetheringsett for the day. Mrs Parker lost no time in relaying the gossip, and Elizabeth's mother took it upon herself to tell Mr Grimwade.

Mr Smith, the chemist, was next to the stand. He fixed me with a cold stare as he gave his evidence, describing Elizabeth's visit dispassionately and stating that he had, at first, refused to serve her. The prosecutor cross-examined him and implied that he should have stuck with this course of action. Even I noticed his discomfort at the notion that he might have saved a life had he shown more resolve. It is curious how crime causes so many casualties other than the criminal and the victim.

After Mr Smith sat down, he continued to stare at me. I was hypnotised by the hatred manifested upon his face and could not wrest my eyes from his countenance until my eldest, Mary Ann, was bought to the bar. Her red-rimmed eyes peered through swollen slits in her face, and she could barely stand. I leaned forward, looking straight at her, silently mouthing my apologies. She did not look in my direction and stared at her feet as she spoke. Her voice trembled, and the judge asked her to speak up on more than one occasion. Her ordeal lasted but a short time, there being nothing much to say except to refute the story given to Elizabeth Lambert. She denied ever having spoken of rats, mice or poison and said it had been three months or more since she visited Stonham Aspal and was not aware of her father's illness, as the news had not travelled to her village, some three and a half miles away.

William Gunn was called next. He took a long look at me and then purposely misquoted some of my words. Although I had long reconciled myself to the deceit and folly of my former life, I *was unprepared for downright lies from another about my conduct on that fateful day. Gunn claimed I told him James was 'so ill he could keep nothing down and that it would soon go one way or the other'. That was indeed true, but I never told him that 'the other man was not far off,' yet that is how he quoted me in court, under oath. We parted on bad terms that day, and it is clear he has neither forgiven nor forgotten. His evidence served me ill. Perhaps I should have been more tolerant of him; after all, he did me kindness in providing a ride without expectation of payment.*

I was relieved to see my son, Richard, on the stand after Gunn. I knew he would be loyal as he had already proved at the inquest. He told the truth, as he saw it, but when he confirmed that I was the only one who waited on James during his illness, I knew it to be another nail in my coffin. Somebody else waited on him. Somebody gave him at least one dose, if not several, from that poison I had off Elizabeth Lambert. I wish I could go back in time and re-live that day. It was a senseless waste, procuring poison without having the use of it.

Richard was kept at the stand for a long time and questioned relentlessly. He called me attentive, kind, and affectionate in his evidence, although I was none of those things. I realise now what a selfish, uncaring monster I had been. I wish the same bitter feelings towards James that motivated me before still drove me now. Having had the benefit of shelter and nourishment even in these difficult circumstances, I no longer feel the same hatred of the world. I will never forget how cruelly James treated me or how my life might have been different if he were a kinder man, but the disgust that fuelled my every callous action no longer fires me. My selfish anger has dissolved, replaced with sadness and shame.

Indeed, my shame was made public in court when Mr Power, the Prosecutor, asked Richard about Robert Tricker. Despite his loyalty, Richard had no choice but to confirm I had gone away with Tricker on more than one occasion. An unfamiliar feeling of embarrassment covered me until the colour rose in my cheeks, and I was hot and flustered. For the first time, I understood why the faces of the jurors displayed puzzled disgust as they tried to comprehend how a mother could desert her young children for her lover, leaving them to fend for themselves. There were no poor people on the jury, though. How could they know what it is to have no money and no choice?

There was a moment of hope when Mr Cooper, the defence, asked Richard about the cat. A cat may seem unimportant, but on the Wednesday before he died, I handed Richard some bread and butter to take to James. By then, mistrust of me had consumed James, and he would not eat anything I prepared even if given to him by another. James dashed the dish to the floor and refused to eat it, so Richard picked it up and returned it to me. The food was too spoiled for anyone else, so we gave it to the cat. Richard explained that the cat ate the food and remained healthy, suffering no ill effects from its repast. The jury would surely realise that poison could not have been added to the bread and butter, which might cast doubt on some of the other allegations.

The witness I dreaded most of all, took the stand next. Samuel Oxborrow was a life-long friend of James. He attended our wedding and James attended his. I knew Samuel would not hold back, but he gave a more balanced account than I expected. Samuel did at least tell the jury that James had been gaoled for misusing me, but talked about Robert Tricker again, reminding the jury of my faithlessness.

As Samuel began to speak, I remembered the horror of the last days of James' life, which I had managed to keep suppressed until now. A wave of nausea flooded my gullet, and goose-bumps stood cold upon my skin. In answer to careful questioning by the defence, Samuel described the moment James tore strips of flesh from his stomach and mouth in his mania, under the illusion he was curing himself of the ravaging pain. An elderly, corpulent man on the jury put his hand to his mouth and visibly wretched. The judge asked if the man would like to be excused, but the juror declined, although he remained ashen

115

grey for the rest of the testimony. As I slumped further down in my hard wooden chair, I wished the judge would excuse me for a few moments as the guilt and shame threatened to overwhelm me.

While Samuel was unexpectedly fair in his account, his wife Kezia manipulated my words until she was as close to a mistruth, as is possible, without perjuring herself in court. She was asked about the events of the night before James died and told the jury that I said James was an evil man and prayed God would take him before morning. My actual words were that I hoped he would die that night because he was in so much pain. But what right do I have to argue the point when I introduced the poison into his system in the first place?

The next witness, Mr Image, puffed his chest out, resplendent with self-importance while relaying a barrage of scientific language, that meant nothing to me. I could not comprehend the meaning of his evidence in the courtroom any more than I had at the inquest. The little I understood revealed that arsenic was present in James' stomach, though why it took quite so many words to say so, I will never know. Perhaps if I had benefitted from an education, I would have understood the evidence that would ultimately condemn me.

I wonder, Anna, as I recite this, whether it would have made any difference if I had been as honest with the defence as I have been with you. I had no confidence that Mr Cooper would succeed in defending me from the gallows. Yet, he fought valiantly on my behalf, giving the jury severe misgivings about my motivation for murder. After all, I had come and gone from the home freely during my marriage, whether my husband wished it or not, and James had no money, so there was no financial gain. What might he have been able to do, had I confessed to purchasing the poison and admitted someone took it from me?

Not much, probably, as there is no excuse for using poison in the first place, but the real reason that I did not volunteer the truth is that any of my children could have poisoned James.

Richard had never shown anything but kindness to his stepfather, but appearances can deceive. He was, after all, a bastard and there was a stigma attached. Indeed, he may have blamed James for the loss of his birth father who never returned to the village again. It was no secret that Sibella disliked her father intensely. She was dear to me, and I dear to her. Every time he abused me, she felt it keenly. I cannot think of a reason why the younger boys would have poisoned him, but both John and William were old enough to have done so, had they found the powder and realised what it was. James was a disagreeable man and John had fallen foul of the law on several occasions. His lack of conscience was troubling, but the reality is that anyone could have taken the poison. It was no accident. The powder was wilfully removed and replaced. Who is to say whether it was one of my family or another unrelated individual, but I have been a poor excuse for a mother, and if there is a chance that one of my children did this terrible thing, I must pay for it for making them that way.

Louisa looked up from the book, eyes filled with sudden tears. She felt a wholly unexpected sympathy for this woman who she had despised during her last reading of the diary.

Daniel noticed her head move as he watched the passing scenery. He turned his gaze towards her. "Are you well, Louisa?" he asked softly.

"Quite well," she said, blinking away her tears.

"It is over," said Daniel, misunderstanding her concern. Your uncle will not discuss the matter with your father, and you have nothing more to worry about as long as you don't get into any further trouble."

"Thank you, but that is not it," said Louisa. She was about to try to explain the diary and her unexpected surge of compassion for Mary when there was a sudden jolt, and the cab lurched forward. The impact threw Louisa towards Daniel, who was sitting in the opposite seat. She fell, kneeling in front of him and he grasped her hands instinctively as he moved forward. He held her close, her face just a few inches from his. Their eyes locked and they remained there for several seconds as if hypnotised, then the carriage halted and righted itself. Daniel gently pushed her back onto the seat and dropped her hands.

"Are you hurt?" he asked.

"Not at all," she said, looking at the floor.

Daniel opened the door. "What happened?" he asked the cabman.

"Nothing to worry about, Sir" the driver replied. "The wheel ran right over a branch in the road. No harm done."

"Carry on then," said Daniel. The cabman checked the wheels, looked over the horse and took his position at the front of the carriage. In a few moments, they began to move, and the silence inside was punctuated with squeaking and grinding as the wheels ran over the uneven road surface.

Daniel sat down and picked up a newspaper. He looked towards Louisa, opening his mouth as if he were about to speak, but changed his mind. He folded the paper and resumed his examination of the Essex countryside.

Louisa's heart was beating so quickly that she struggled to catch her breath. She could not look at Daniel for fear of blushing. Those few seconds where he held her hand and her gaze had provoked a flurry of emotions, she neither anticipated nor desired. She felt awkward and uncomfortable, glad of the opportunity to retrieve the diary from the floor of the carriage where it had fallen; grateful to distance herself from the discomfort of the moment. There were only a few paragraphs of Mary's entries left to read.

I sat through the summing-up of both prosecution and defence with my head in my hands, weary of the words that would decide my future, crossing back and forth between educated men in a blur of incomprehension. Finally, the judge dismissed the jury, and they set off to consider their verdict and released me from the dock. I rested some twenty minutes and drank a cup of water. The prison wardresses were kinder than usual, and it felt like no time passed before I was called back again and made to stand in front of the judge. The clerk asked the jury if I was guilty or not guilty, and the foreman got to his feet, standing straight-backed and unflinching. He looked me in the face and said "guilty" in a firm voice.

I was not shocked. Indeed, if it had gone any other way, then I would have been. The verdict was as I had expected, and nothing less than I deserved. Other women are beaten and do not use poison to try to teach their errant husbands a lesson.

The judge fixed me with sorrowful eyes, peering through thick-lensed glasses. He said I was a dissolute, licentious woman. I did not understand what those words meant, but they sounded wicked, so he was probably right in his assessment of my character. Then he placed a black cap over his wig and told me that I would be hanged by my neck until I was dead, and he asked the Lord God Almighty to have mercy on my soul. I clasped the rails by the dock, using them to stand upright, wobbly from the long day and the expanse of time that had passed since breakfast. I plodded wearily back to the cell and collapsed on the bed, with something closer to relief than distress. I never had any doubt it would end this way.

Chapter Twelve

The return

It was early evening before the cab reached the outskirts of Ipswich and Louisa was subjected to two stops at coaching inns to change the horses, and two meals eaten in awkward silence with Daniel. She was relieved to see the familiar sight of Ipswich and positively joyful when Christchurch Park loomed into view, and she knew she was only a few short minutes from home. Her joyfulness turned to concern as they approached the upper part of Ivry Street, to see an unfamiliar motor vehicle and a windowless horse-drawn carriage parked by the front of her house.

She hung out of the window on one side while Daniel opened the opposite window, both watching at first with interest, then fearfully as they closed the distance.

"Dear God" exclaimed Daniel rapping loudly on the front of the cab. "Stop here," he commanded, throwing the door open before striding up the road. Louisa took another look and understood what Daniel had seen that she had not. The horse in front of the second vehicle wore a black plume; the colour of death.

Louisa remained in the carriage while the cab driver trotted the horses the remaining twenty yards. He stopped the carriage opposite the unfamiliar vehicles, and she opened the door and alighted without delay. It was now apparent that the vehicles were directly outside The Rowans. A wave of relief, tempered with guilt, washed over Louisa as she realised it was Sophia's family problem and not her own.

Without waiting for the cab driver to remove her luggage, Louisa raced up the driveway to Sophia's house in time to see the door closing on Daniel. She was about to ring the bell but reconsidered when she noticed a freshly made laurel wreath tied with a black ribbon hanging from a hook on the front door. Louisa watched in silence. Every curtain in the house was drawn, bringing the inescapable conclusion that someone in the household had died.

Leaving her bags at the side of the road, Louisa flew into her own house. "Mother, Father – what has happened next door?" she called frantically opening doors as she sought out her family. Presently her mother descended downstairs.

"Thank the Lord you are home," she said, embracing Louisa. "I fear Sophia will need your friendship more than ever."

"What has happened?" repeated Louisa. "Has somebody died?"

Marianne gestured towards the drawing-room. "Sit down," she said, settling next to Louisa on the couch. She took her daughter's hands.

"It is Sophia's father," she said. "He passed away yesterday afternoon, thank God."

Louisa gasped. "Poor Sophia," she said. "Her father was ill when I left for London, but no one expected him to die."

"No, dear, they did not," said Marianne. "Charles was extremely unwell but rallied after a few days. Then five days ago, he was taken ill again with agonising stomach pains. His suffering was excruciating."

"What caused this change in his health?" asked Louisa.

"They think it was dysentery or some other condition of the bowel. Doctor Hill has been here every few days with medicines and potions of one kind or another, but he could not make him better."

"How is Sophia?" asked Louisa. "Have you seen her?"

"She kept to her room yesterday," said Marianne, "at least that is what Maggie tells me. The household is at sixes and sevens. Jane Piggott cooks, but nobody eats; Harold cannot get near the garden for running errands to the doctor, and Minnie spends more time keeping our servants informed than at her work."

Louisa smiled despite the sadness she felt for her friend. "Trust Maggie to arrange things, so she does not miss out on any of the household intelligence," she said. "I am truly sorry for the Drummonds though, especially for Sophia and poor Mrs Drummond. They must be heartbroken."

"I have not seen them," said Marianne. "I should call to pay my respects. Perhaps you would care to join me?"

"I would," said Louisa. "Has my father visited yet?"

"He cannot. He is in Cambridge on business for a few days. He is not even aware of this death. We will both represent him tomorrow."

When Louisa woke the next morning, she realised with relief that her return from London had barely registered and her exploits would probably never come to light. Guilt tarnished her relief as she realised that another's misfortune had concealed her misdeeds. Louisa felt a quiet dread for Sophia and was nervous at the thought of seeing Daniel again, assuming he permitted the visit at all. She was relieved to be attending with her mother as it was unlikely that Daniel would turn the two of them away.

She breakfasted with her mother and sister, pacing the back of the house until mid-morning when her mother deemed it an acceptable time to visit. They walked to the neighbouring house, clad in dark apparel.

Jane Piggott answered the door, acknowledging them with a nod and showed them into the drawing-room to wait. The long, velvet curtains barred daylight from the room, which would have been entirely dark but for a small side window, through which a chink of light fell. The gloomy room with its dark, mahogany furniture made them feel claustrophobic, and they stood quietly, watching the door for signs of movement. After a few minutes, it opened, and Daniel entered the room.

"Mrs Russell, Miss Russell," he said nodding politely.

"We are so sorry to hear the sad news about your uncle," said Marianne, "and have come to pay our condolences to Mrs Drummond."

"Thank you," said Daniel. "She saw you walking up the driveway and asked me to tell you that she will come through shortly. May I trouble you to wait here while I escort Miss Louisa to the morning room? Sophia is greatly distressed by her father's death and will appreciate a friendly face at this difficult time."

"Of course," smiled Marianne Russell.

"Thank you," said Louisa, as she followed Daniel down the tiled hallway into the morning room.

"Louisa," cried Sophia, jumping to her feet. "Oh, Louisa," her red-rimmed eyes peered from a tear-streaked face framed by tousled hair hanging loosely about her shoulders.

"Come here," said Louisa reaching out. She hugged Sophia tightly, stroking her hair as her distraught friend cried into her shoulder. Sophia sobbed for several minutes, then stopped shaking, and pulled away. Louisa guided her to a chair, drawing it close to her own. Holding her hand out tow Sophia, she said. "I am so sorry about your father. What can I do to help?"

"There is nothing you can do," sniffed Sophia. "It is my poor mother who concerns me."

"Yes," murmured Louisa, "she will miss your father dreadfully, and I know it will not be easy. These things take time to mend".

The silent look that passed between Sophia and Daniel as he glanced across the Morning Room did not escape Louisa. It was a look she was familiar with, reflecting an understanding of a situation to which she was not privy.

"My mother will offer any help she can," said Louisa uncertainly. "Ask anything of us; we only want to help."

Sophia gazed at Daniel as if looking for permission to speak, but did not utter a word, and the moment passed, leaving Louisa floundering for something else to say.

"Would you like to take a walk in the Park?" she asked.

"I would like that very much," replied Sophia, "but tomorrow would be better. Forgive me, but I do not think I could face being among strangers today."

"I quite understand," sympathised Louisa. "I will call for you tomorrow," she said. "I can see how upset you are, and I won't take up any more of your time today but do send Minnie to us if there is anything at all that we can do." She embraced Sophia again and joined her mother in the drawing-room.

Mrs Elizabeth Drummond was a gentle, elegant woman with violet eyes and dark hair, streaked with the barest trace of grey. Her face was pale, and her cheekbones high. Clad in black, she sat quietly by Marianne Russell in the drawing-room talking softly in delicate tones. She projected an air of sophistication that Louisa had not anticipated in an inhabitant of rural Wiltshire. She did not know Mrs Drummond well and had only exchanged a few words with her before today but sensed an air of fragility and understood why Sophia showed more concern for her mother's well-being than distress at her father's sudden death.

"We must not keep you any longer," said Marianne. "Thank you for seeing us at this difficult time, and please ask if we can help in any way."

"Thank you for coming," said Elizabeth politely. "I appreciate it very much. I wish we had become acquainted in more favourable circumstances."

She escorted them to the door of the drawing-room, where Daniel was waiting. He took over her duty, accompanying them through the front door and to the end of the driveway.

"Thank you for seeing my aunt," he said to Marianne Russell. "She is delicate, and your visit will mean a great deal to her."

Smiling, he took his leave.

"What a nice young man," said Marianne.

"He would not let me see Sophia last week," protested Louisa. "He is not usually this accommodating."

"He may have had a good reason for denying your visit," said Marianne. "Not everything revolves around your needs," she teased.

"I can't see why not," laughed Louisa, relieved at having left the tension of a bereaved household. "My needs are extremely important."

"Of course, they are, my darling," said Marianne as they returned home.

The postman had been while they visited The Rowans and Louisa noticed a stack of letters on the hall table as soon as she came through the door. She flicked through them, finding nothing addressed to her, and went to her room to look for a book. Maggie knocked on her bedroom door to see whether she had finished unpacking.

"Can I take the cases back to the storage room? "she asked.

"There are a few things left to put away," replied Louisa. "But come in and help me, and then you can take the cases when you go."

"What was London like?" asked Maggie, shaking the creases from a jacket.

"It was big, very noisy but pretty in places," said Louisa. "I was impressed with the underground railway system."

"Underground?" asked Maggie.

"Yes, deep beneath the streets of London. You descend using a moving staircase called an escalator, board a train and return up another set of moving stairs until you reach your destination."

Maggie frowned. "I don't like the sound of that," she said. "I would rather walk."

Maggie took a dress from Louisa and hung it in the second of the dark, wooden wardrobes.

"Mother and I went to The Rowans this morning," said Louisa.

"Is Miss Sophia any better?" asked Maggie. "She was very low yesterday."

"She is still distressed," replied Louisa, "but bearing up. She is more concerned about Mrs Drummond."

"As well she might be," said Maggie.

"What do you mean by that?"

"Minnie saw the doctor take some of Mr Drummond's vomit away. He asked her for the sheet too," she said darkly.

Louisa gasped. "No," she exclaimed.

"I would not lie about such a thing," said Maggie indignantly, snatching a hanger from the bed".

"No, I know you wouldn't, Maggie. I didn't mean to imply that you lied. But I know what it means for a doctor to test bodily fluids. If they have taken samples, they must suspect poison."

"Lawks, Miss Louisa," said Maggie. "They think he had dysentery. That is why they are testing, but it must be horrid for Mrs Drummond, all the same. I can't imagine they suspect us of putting things in his dinner." She chuckled to herself, "the very notion of poison in the soup."

Louisa blushed, angry at herself for speculating in front of Maggie.

"Mind you," Maggie continued in full flow, "he wanted poisoning that one, the way he treated poor Mrs Drummond. A proper brute, he was."

"Maggie," said Louisa disapprovingly, "what a thing to say. What can you mean?"

"Well, she said, putting her finger to her lips conspiratorially. "Mr Drummond gave her a black eye once."

"Really, Maggie; that is enough," said Louisa.

"He did too, Minnie saw it. She tried to help Mrs Drummond after it happened, but Mrs Drummond sent her away. Next day she told Minnie she walked into a door, but it wasn't true. Mr Drummond hit her across the face, and I believe Minnie."

"Thank you, Maggie," said Louisa shaking her head in exasperation. "You can take the cases now."

125

Louisa sat on the bed with a bump, angry at herself for speaking out in front of Maggie and cross with Maggie for her indiscretion. The Drummond's housemaid, Minnie enjoyed more gossip than was good for her and seemed unable to separate the truth from fiction. Louisa considered the matter a moment longer trying to decide whether she ought to do something about Minnie's tattling. The last thing the Drummonds needed, at this challenging time, was a housemaid with an overactive imagination. She wondered whether to discuss it with her mother or Charlotte. Eventually, Louisa opted for the wise counsel of Janet McGowan. Louisa sat at the table in the morning room, embroidering while she waited until Janet bustled in to set the lunch table, as was her routine.

"Can I talk to you about Maggie," she asked without explanation.

"Of course, you can," Janet replied. "What has the silly, young thing done now?"

"It is not what she has done," said Louisa, "it is what she has said."

Janet listened while Louisa explained. When she was sure Louisa had finished, she took a deep breath.

"There are two things you should know," said Janet. "Maggie is much too fond of talking for my liking, but she is generally quite truthful. If she says Minnie has told her this, then she has. Now whether Minnie is a stranger to the truth is anyone's guess. I cannot tell you myself as I have only ever spoken a few words to her. The other thing you should know is that I spoke briefly with Jane Piggott yesterday to enquire how Mrs Drummond fared. Mrs Piggott was concerned, fearing for Mrs Drummond's health. She told me that Mrs Drummond did not fare well at all and was very distressed. Then she continued to say, that at least, now, Mrs Drummond would know some peace. Make of that what you will, Miss Louisa."

"It could mean anything," said Louisa doubtfully.

"Yes, it could," Janet agreed, "but it was the way she said it, you know, the intonation. I got the impression that the importance lay in what she did not say."

"I too," exclaimed Louisa, "I had that exact feeling when Daniel Bannister spoke to me - as if he were not telling me something of great magnitude."

"Would you like me to have a word with Maggie about her behaviour today?"

"No," said Louisa, "if you think Maggie is truthful, it may be useful to hear what she has to say in the coming days."

Janet raised an eyebrow.

"Well, I won't encourage her to gossip, of course," said Louisa. "But neither will I deter her by unfairly remonstrating if she does."

Louisa retired to bed that evening, mulling over the matter and spent a restless night battling with rational and irrational thoughts. There was nothing of great significance that made her anxious about the death of Mr Drummond, but there was an air of secrecy in The Rowans. The atmosphere was heavy with unspoken words. She was glad when dawn broke, and she had the distraction of breakfast. She ate a little and then spent some time in the garden cutting fresh flowers and arranging them in her mother's heavy, cut-crystal vases.

By the time she was ready to call on Sophia, Louisa was in turmoil, desperate for someone to talk to about her fears. She realised that Sophia was the wrong choice and elected to bite her lip and speak of other things.

She rang the doorbell and Sophia emerged immediately, dressed in a light coat and hat. She had evidently been waiting by the door.

"I am glad you are here," she said as soon as they left the house. "It is unbearable at home."

"It must be dreadful," sympathised Louisa. "I feel for you all."

"Everyone behaves so strangely," Sophia continued. "Mother is anxious, Daniel is like a cat on hot coals, and Minnie has turned the house upside down looking for something but will not say what it is."

"I am sorry," murmured Louisa.

"And a policeman arrived unannounced last night," continued Sophia. "Daniel received him and said it was nothing to worry about, but he would not tell me what the policeman wanted. Anyone would think it is his house and not my mother's."

"What could a policeman possibly want?" asked Louisa.

"I don't know," said Sophia tersely. "That is the point. Daniel will not tell me."

"Can I ask you an indelicate question?" asked Louisa, "You must not reply if it upsets you, and you think it is too soon to ask."

"You may ask of me what you will," replied Sophia, "although there is every chance I will not know."

"Will you tell me more about your father's illness, if you feel you can talk about it? I was away, you see, and know nothing of his medical condition and how his health deteriorated so rapidly."

"I see," sighed Sophia. "Father became unwell in the weeks before you left but recovered somewhat after. Then he was almost better for a whole week before becoming ill again. The second time was worse. He was in so much pain it was unbearable to hear. He did not recover."

"And what were his symptoms?"

Sophia frowned. "He had a raging fever from the very first," she said, "and the most awful vomiting and diarrhoea. I cannot tell you any more than that. I heard him but did not see him."

"You did not see him?" asked Louisa. "Not at all?"

"Not at all," confirmed Sophia.

"My goodness," said Louisa. "If my father was ill, I would have visited every day."

"Good for you," snapped Sophia. "But I did not."

"I am sorry," said Louisa. "I didn't mean to offend you. Every family is different, of course."

Sophia stared at the ground and continued to walk. They were in Christchurch Park now. The cloudy sky broke momentarily, allowing slivers of sunlight through and then just as quickly closed over to block it out again.

Sophia shivered. "We should return," she said.

"Of course," said Louisa, then, "what was the doctor's opinion of your father's illness?"

"He thought it was a stomach ailment," Sophia replied. "Probably dysentery or food-poisoning, although mother said he expressed some concern over father's low spirits. He told her that he thought Father was depressed. She told him she thought it was most unlikely."

"Do you remember that diary I read?" asked Louisa.

"I shall never forget it," said Sophia. "You were glued to the wretched thing while we were all jolly and singing."

"Well, it put me in mind of something, but I don't know if I should speak of it."

"Do not play with me," said Sophia. "If you wish to speak, then do so."

"It is sensitive," said Louisa.

128

"Have I not demonstrated sufficient fortitude as a suffragist?" asked Sophia. "Do you not think I can bear what you have to say?"

"I know you are resilient. You demonstrated it amply at the census evasion, but this requires more mental fortitude than physical."

"I don't see what this has got to do with the diary. You mentioned the diary. What of it?"

"It recounted the last days of a woman accused of poisoning her husband," said Louisa.

Sophia stopped suddenly. "I hope you are not implying what I think you might be," she said open-mouthed.

"No, Sophia. Not your mother. I did not mean that. I merely wondered whether poison could have caused your father's symptoms, but of course, it could not…"

"Louisa, I thought you were my friend, but I tell you now, I do not like the way this conversation is going between us, and I think it better if we part company."

Sophia stood pale and trembling. She stole a tearful glance towards Louisa, then shook her head and hurried away.

"Sophia, I am sorry," called Louisa. "Wait."

"Please go," shouted Sophia over her shoulder, walking briskly now. "Leave me alone."

Louisa sat on a nearby bench holding her head in her hands, wondering what had possessed her to speak so frankly about the diary at this most inappropriate time. How would she be able to repair the friendship?

She sat anxiously for ten minutes, then rose unsteadily to her feet, and retraced her route back to The Poplars.

Louisa had not quite reached the driveway to her house when she heard heavy footsteps behind her and turned to see who the footfall belonged to.

"What the devil have you done to Sophia?" Daniel thundered. "What have you said to her?"

"I am sorry," said Louisa in a faltering voice. "I was stupid. I did not think…"

"She is distraught," said Daniel. "I thought you were her friend. Why is she so upset?"

Louisa stared at her feet, blinking away tears. "I read a diary about a poisoner. I should not have mentioned it in context with her father's illness, but I did. I am sorrier than you can know."

"You silly woman," barked Daniel. "What were you thinking? I have tried to keep this from her. How could you possibly have known?"

"I did not know," said Louisa. "But I read an account of something like it very recently."

"I have done everything in my power to keep Sophia and her mother protected," said Daniel tossing a cigarette to the ground and grinding it to powder. "Then you come along and reverse all my attempts to keep this family's business out of the public domain. You should not have interfered. Do not visit The Rowans and stay away from Sophia. I will not tell you again."

He strode angrily back up the street.

Louisa burst through the doors of her house, ran upstairs, and threw herself onto the bed sobbing. She must have cried herself to sleep for she awoke a few hours later with red-rimmed eyes and a tear-stained face, heart heavy with the loss of her friend and the injustice of Daniel's words. His tirade seemed especially harsh considering he obviously suspected the same thing himself.

Louisa washed her face, changed her dress, and walked downstairs and into the hallway. A cacophony of excited voices emanated from below stairs, the volume suggesting they were oblivious to her presence. Louisa could only hear snippets of conversation, but the tone implied news of great importance. She rushed downstairs to find out what was going on.

"They are there now," said Maggie gesturing towards the front of the house. "There are two of them."

"Two of who?" asked Janet.

"Two motor vehicles," said Maggie, "parked next door. There are policemen everywhere, but I do not know why."

Louisa's eyes widened, "It cannot be true," she said.

"It is true," scowled Maggie. "I saw them."

"Can you find out why they are here?"

"I don't think so," said Maggie, "not yet. I will see Minnie later, but I have no wish to go near a house full of policemen. My father says not to talk to coppers."

By the time Louisa returned upstairs, her mother and sister had reached the drawing-room and were watching discreetly through the window as the scene unfolded. The rear of the second vehicle was visible behind the gated driveway with its doors hanging open. A policeman stood motionless beside the vehicle. The tension in the air was palpable.

As they watched, Maggie emerged from the side of the house and sidled towards the front gate.

"What is Margaret doing out there?" asked Marianne.

"I think she is seeking information," said Louisa.

"Well. I wish she would try to be a little less conspicuous," said Charlotte. "She will never make a spy."

Maggie came to a halt, loitering at the end of the driveway. She stared into the house next door with a total lack of discretion. The three women watched her gesture towards the policeman before engaging him in conversation."

"Oh, dear," sighed Marianne. "Not only does she make our household look terribly nosy, but the laundry will not wash itself."

Maggie remained outside for half an hour as Marianne began to lose her patience. "I don't pay her for this," she complained, as the clock chimed the hour.

Just when Louisa was on the verge of going outside to retrieve the housemaid, Maggie turned and ran up the driveway at speed.

Showing a lack of propriety, even by her usual lax standards, Maggie flung open the front door, slamming it against the inner doorstop.

"Margaret," admonished Marianne. "You will break something."

"I'm sorry Ma'am, cried Maggie, "but they have taken her away. She is gone."

"Who is gone?" asked Louisa.

"Mrs Drummond. They have put her in a black cab and taken her to the police station."

Louisa looked speechlessly towards her mother.

"Why?" asked Charlotte.

"They've accused her of murdering Mr Drummond," said Maggie dramatically. She turned to Louisa, "He was poisoned - just like you said, Miss."

Chapter Thirteen

A friendship mends

Breakfast the next day was a trial for Louisa. She was still sitting at the table pushing a congealed slice of bacon around her plate, long after the rest of the family had finished, and was relieved when the door opened, and Janet entered.

"Cheer up, Miss Louisa," she said with a broad smile. "You have a visitor."

"Who is it?" asked Louisa, gazing over the lawn.

"Miss Sophia," said Janet. "Shall I show her through?"

"Sophia, oh thank goodness. Yes, please tell her to come in."

Louisa jumped to her feet as Sophia came through the door, clasping her hands nervously.

"Thank you for seeing me," she whispered. "I didn't know if you would."

"I always want to see you," cried Louisa. "The argument was my fault. I should not have spoken quite so directly. It was not my place to speculate."

"On the contrary," said Sophia. "You had every right. I was awake most of the night, considering your words. You gave me much to think about, but there are things you do not know - things I should have confronted before and chose to ignore instead."

"You must not feel obliged to delve into any distressing matters because of my ill-considered opinions," said Louisa. "Please, forget I said any of those things."

"May I sit," asked Sophia. "I have hardly eaten these last few days, and I am feeling quite faint."

"Of course, I will ring for some tea and toast," Louisa said, summoning Maggie. "Now, what can I do to make things better?"

"You can listen," said Sophia, "which you excel at. I think you would have heard me a long time ago, had I been ready to speak."

Louisa nodded, waiting for Sophia to begin.

Sophia opened her mouth, took a breath, and stopped. She composed herself and tried again.

"They...they came for mother last night," she said, faltering. "It was not wholly unexpected, at least not by Daniel, though I was not aware of it."

"Does Daniel know you are here?" asked Louisa, despite her determined intent to listen without interrupting.

"No, he does not," admitted Sophia. "There is something about you that brings out the worst in Daniel. It must be hard for you to appreciate what a kind man he truly is."

"Quite unfathomable," said Louisa bluntly.

"Anyway, it appears that Daniel possessed information that I did not know. He was aware that Minnie had watched the doctor remove bed sheets from my father's room and saw the doctor scraping vomit samples from the rug. But that is not the worst of it."

Sophia took a deep breath and stared at the back of her hands. She spun a delicate gold ring round her finger as she considered her words.

"Minnie saw my mother take a small vial from the bedroom before the doctor arrived. She does not know what was in it, and she has not seen it since."

"That is not so very odd," said Louisa. "It could have contained any useful medicine or tincture. Why would Minnie assume a problem?"

Sophia covered her face with her hands, and it was several moments before she spoke again. Louisa waited, not sure whether to comment or remain silent.

"Minnie would assume a problem because she knows our family is riven with them," said Sophia eventually, raising her head and looking directly at Louisa. "Daniel has also known for a long time. He watched over us from the moment he first arrived, dismayed to be called away to London during the onset of my father's illness at the most inconvenient of times. He would have remained here had his work with the electricity company not been of such vital importance."

"I suppose my conduct in London could not have helped matters," sighed Louisa.

"I do not know anything of your conduct in London," said Sophia. "Only that you returned in the same carriage as Daniel."

"I will tell you another time," said Louisa, making a mental note to thank Daniel for his discretion, "but I still don't understand why the police took your mother away."

"It's been brewing for a few days," said Sophia. "Earlier this week, a policeman called at the house, spoke with Daniel and took a short statement about those present during the last days of my father's life. They told Daniel that they were testing samples taken from my father's bedroom after he died. As Daniel is fully conversant with our unfortunate domestic situation, he suspected the worst."

"Your situation?" asked Louisa.

Sophia exhaled, fixing her gaze on the garden in the distance. "My father was not a pleasant man," she said finally, "and hid behind a demeanour of respectability. He was hard-working and wealthy, bringing much comfort to our physical living conditions, but he was cruel, bad-tempered, and unkind, particularly to my mother. He was quick to temper and when in a rage, he would, he would…," Sophia faltered, and her eyes filled with tears. "This is not easy," she said. "I am ashamed."

Louisa reached out and took Sophia's hand, who rallied and continued.

"My father was violent," said Sophia. "There, I have said it now. My father would hit my mother, quite deliberately and often."

Louisa bit her lip. "I cannot pretend I am not shocked," she said. "One hears these things, but normally from families driven to despair through poverty. How you must have suffered, Sophia."

"We did not suffer any physical pain. Our hurt came from watching our mother endure constant humiliation."

"Couldn't she leave him?" asked Louisa.

"Yes, in principle", said Sophia. "Mother had an inheritance of her own, and the law allows her to retain it in her own right. But it is the disgrace of it, Louisa, and the certain loss of her family. Father would have fought her for John Edward, and Mother could not contemplate parting with her youngest child. She has borne my father's violence for such a long time, for the sake of her children, that I simply cannot believe she would act now. Why? What gain would there be?"

"I don't know," said Louisa, "but I agree it sounds unlikely after all she has endured. Still, it does not explain why the police have taken her away."

"It is because the doctor was suspicious of my father's symptoms in his final days. That is why he took samples. We would not have known it without Minnie, but Minnie saw it, and what Minnie sees, she says, however unwise. They tested it, Louisa, and found a poisonous substance called Antimony."

"That is precisely what I feared," said Louisa, casting caution aside, now that Sophia appeared willing to talk openly. "It must be fate that I found the diary. It educated me in the ways of the poisoner, and the effects poison has on a human being. Although it was a different substance, in the case of Mary Cage, it produced similar effects. And Sophia, I hardly dare tell you this next thing."

"You must, interrupted Sophia. You can and must tell me everything you know."

"My reluctance to speak of it is because of the reason for the poisoning. It happened because of the abuse Mary suffered from her husband."

Sophia's face fell. "I cannot believe my mother did this. I will not," she declared.

"It is an odd thing that Mary Cage was convicted of the murder but denied it to the very end, even when she confessed to other equally disgusting crimes."

"You must tell me how it ended for her," said Sophia, face pale and anxious.

"It ended on the gallows," whispered Louisa. "I am sorry."

"That will not happen to my mother," declared Sophia. "Daniel has secured a barrister, well-known to his father. She will have the best legal representation."

"I still cannot understand why they fix this crime upon her."

"It is the vial Minnie saw. As usual, she could not keep her tongue still and gossiped to half the household before somebody passed the information to the police. They questioned Minnie and, of course, she told them all about it and a lot more besides. That is the problem with new servants. They lack the loyalty of those who have been with the family for a long time. Both Harold and Jane have served us for many years, and their discretion is exemplary. Minnie has only been with us for a few months and has no care for the consequences of her chatter."

"Housemaids are all the same, in my experience," said Louisa wryly. "We have the same problems with Maggie."

"We have always been lucky," said Sophia. "Jane was a housemaid at my mother's home before she met my father and accompanied them to Wiltshire when they married. My parents employed Harold soon after, and though he is close to retirement, we have never needed to take on another gardener. He does the work of two men."

"How does your mother explain the vial?" asked Louisa.

"She does not. She refuses to talk of it. Daniel has asked her on several occasions, and she won't even discuss it with the barrister."

"Will she explain if you ask her?"

"I do not think so."

"Perhaps she feels a responsibility to you and Daniel because you are younger. I wonder..."

"What?"

"I wonder if she would speak to my mother?"

"She does not know her," said Sophia doubtfully.

"Precisely," said Louisa. "She owes my mother no duty of care, as they are so little acquainted. I could ask her to visit. My mother excels at putting people at their ease."

"I doubt it will help," said Sophia. "If she is unwilling to confide in her counsel, then what is the point of having the information even if she shared it with your mother?"

"It could not worsen her position, though."

"No, it could hardly be any worse than it already is. In that case, please ask your mother to visit her. You have my permission to tell your mother anything you think she ought to know in advance of her visit."

"Thank you," said Louisa, "and thank you for forgiving my clumsiness yesterday."

"It is all forgotten," said Sophia. "I am indebted to you for making me confront our secrets. There is no shame in being a victim of violence, only in concealing it. I grieve for my poor mother, but I feel so relieved at lifting this cloak of secrecy."

"I will seek you out as soon as I have some news."

"Come to Ethel's house then," said Sophia. "I will be there for the next few days. Two of Ethel's children are poorly with influenza, and I have promised to help her. It will take our minds off poor mother."

They embraced and said goodbye. Louisa hurried to locate her mother and found her writing letters in the drawing-room. Marianne quietly listened as Louisa recounted all the necessary details of Sophia's story.

"I must visit at once," she said when Louisa finished. "That poor woman should feel she has some support after the difficulties she has endured."

"Do you think she did it?" asked Louisa.

"She has suffered great provocation, but I am inclined to agree with Sophia. What would she gain from taking action now?"

"I knew you would understand," said Louisa hugging Marianne "I am lucky to have such a wise mother."

Marianne smiled. "I feel sorry for poor Sophia. She must have felt powerless watching her mother suffer, unable to offer any practical help. No wonder she embraces suffrage. She must yearn to have some control over her life. There is no point in delaying this mission. Where can I find Mrs Drummond?"

"She was at the police station," said Louisa. "She may still be there, but Daniel will know."

"I shall call on him before I leave," said Marianne. "And we will talk later." Folding her letter and placing it on the hallstand, she swept upstairs to get ready.

Chapter Fourteen

The Visit

By the time Marianne located Daniel and discovered that Elizabeth Drummond was ensconced in Ipswich gaol, it was too late in the day to arrange a visit by the usual means. Fortunately, Henry Russell returned home in time to use his influence and secure Marianne a private audience with Elizabeth the following day.

Daniel collected Marianne Russell and escorted her to the prison, leaving her with a wardress at the entrance to the gaol. Between them, they had decided that he should not go any further, allowing Marianne the opportunity to speak freely with his aunt.

Marianne was guided to the holding cell, where Elizabeth Drummond sat quietly on a wooden chair leaning over a writing desk while penning a letter in small, precise strokes.

"Good morning," said Marianne. "Are you willing to receive a visitor?"

Elizabeth Drummond looked up. "Good morning Mrs Russell," she said. "I am surprised to see you."

"I hope I'm not intruding upon your task," said Marianne.

"I did not expect you, but you are very welcome," replied Elizabeth. She snapped the lid onto her fountain pen and placed it on the desk. "Please sit," she said, gesturing to a plain wooden chair on the opposite side of the table.

Marianne turned to face the wardress positioned in the corner of the cell. "Please leave us," she said. The wardress pursed her lips but did not move.

"The Governor promised privacy," said Marianne, raising an eyebrow.

The wardress shook her head and left without speaking.

"How are my children?" asked Elizabeth.

"They are well, but missing you," said Marianne. "Sophia is looking after John Edward and Ethel has returned to manage the house in your absence. Daniel is keeping a careful watch over them."

Elizabeth smiled weakly. "He is a good boy," she murmured.

"I agree," said Marianne.

The two women smiled at each other, both uncertain of what to say next. Marianne spoke first. "I have been charged with a task," she said, "and I do not know how best to fulfil it, save by asking you an indelicate question, which you may find offensive. If so, I apologise in advance."

Elizabeth nodded her head, imperceptibly. "And I apologise to you if I choose not to answer," she said, "but I will hear your question."

"Before I ask it, I must tell you for better or worse that I know what you have endured, and I sympathise."

Elizabeth sighed. "It is shameful," she said. "How do you know? Who told you?"

"It does not matter," said Marianne, "suffice to say that it is not in the least bit shameful. You have suffered enough, through matters not of your own making and you shouldn't feel worse because others now know what you have endured."

"It won't help me in court," said Elizabeth bitterly. "It gives me all the more motive in their eyes."

"The police are already aware of the violence, and there is little you could now disclose that would be harmful," said Marianne.

Elizabeth sighed. "It's not that simple, but what do you want to know?"

"What was in the vial?" asked Marianne, seeing no reason to prevaricate.

"Do you know everything about my life?" asked Elizabeth.

"Not everything, but it might help to know more if you feel able to tell me."

"You are very blunt, Mrs Russell."

"I want only to help you, Mrs Drummond."

Elizabeth's violet eyes sparkled. "I believe you do," she said, "but I don't know if you will feel the same way when I tell you what I have done."

"There is only one way to find out," said Marianne, smiling.

"Very well if you insist. The substance in the glass vial was potassium bromide."

"What use was that to Charles?"

Elizabeth blushed. "I didn't use it to help Charles. It was there to make my life easier," said Elizabeth. "To give me peace."

"I may be married to a chemist," said Marianne, "but I don't know anything about medicine, and I don't understand what you mean."

Elizabeth sighed. "This is so embarrassing," she said. "Thank goodness we are at the start of a friendship and not better acquainted. I could not bear the shame."

"I am glad to hear you speak of a friendship at all after my impertinent questions," said Marianne. "Please continue."

"You know enough of our troubles to be aware that Charles ill-used me. I won't mince my words. He beat me badly and sometimes in front of the children."

"I know," said Marianne sympathetically, "it must have been dreadful."

"Charles took my self-respect and my confidence. He also took other things that married men think they have a right to whether or not they are given freely."

"Ah, I understand," said Marianne. "Charles enforced his spousal rights regardless of your wishes."

Elizabeth nodded. "I came from a wealthy family, but we were encouraged to work and make ourselves useful. Before I married Charles, I spent many years in nursing, and I still have medical contacts to this day. One of these colleagues helped me obtain a bottle of Bromide a few years ago. When I was a nurse, we used Bromide to treat epilepsy and to calm certain male urges. I have given it to Charles regularly since then and have known, if not perfect peace, then much less disturbance."

"I see," said Marianne. "The bottle that you removed contained a drug to stop your husband from becoming aroused?"

"Exactly. But how can I confess to this? They will think if I can add one thing to his drink without his knowledge, then I can easily add another."

"It is a dilemma," agreed Marianne, "but surely all you need to do is present the bottle for testing. The police can then establish whether there is poison in it."

"They could and perhaps it would help, but I repeat, how much more likely is it that they will think I gave him something else?"

"You should allow them the chance to find the bottle and test it."

"I cannot. I will not, and you are not authorised to speak to anyone about this."

Marianne considered the matter for a few moments.

"Elizabeth, my dear, if you did not poison your husband and somebody else did, that person could be in your house with your family, even as we speak."

There was a long silence.

"I haven't considered this prospect," whispered Elizabeth. "I have been absorbed in how it affects me. When the doctor first expressed his concerns over Charles, I panicked and assumed something had contaminated the bromide dose. I thought that I might have been responsible for his symptoms. I haven't given a thought to the possibility that somebody else could have done it."

"Well, I think you should consider it now," said Marianne.

"The glass vial is in the linen cupboard," said Elizabeth. "I did not have time to dispose of it, just to hide it. If you can find it, I will confess to administering the substance, if you think it will help."

"It couldn't make matters worse," said Marianne. "I will speak to Daniel and call again tomorrow to tell you of our progress."

"I am grateful for your help," said Elizabeth.

"Until tomorrow, then," said Marianne patting Elizabeth's hand.

She called the wardress, and after a few moments, she appeared wearing a sullen expression. She escorted Marianne back through the prison and into the entrance hall where Daniel waited impatiently.

"Well?" he asked.

"We can talk in the cab," said Marianne.

They walked to the bottom of the drive and hailed a carriage at the gate.

As soon as they had settled into their seats, Marianne spoke. "I talked with your aunt," she said, "and I am sure she is innocent."

"I think so too," said Daniel, "but there is the small matter of the vial."

"If I tell you that there was no poison in that glass bottle, will you refrain from asking me about the contents?"

"If I must, although I would prefer to know."

"I would prefer not to tell you unless it becomes absolutely necessary. Trust me when I tell you that you don't need to know what was inside to prove your aunt's innocence."

"Very well, then I agree."

"Your aunt tells me the vial is in the laundry cupboard on the upstairs landing of your house. If you can retrieve it, get Minnie to identify it and give it to the police for testing, your aunt's innocence should be established in no time."

"Thank you," said Daniel. "That is excellent news. I will look it out immediately."

The cab alighted outside their respective properties, and Daniel said goodbye, running up the driveway with undue haste.

Marianne opened the door to The Poplars as Louisa was coming downstairs.

"Did you see her?" she asked before Marianne had taken two steps over the threshold.

"I did but let me remove my coat and shoes before I tell you more."

Louisa paced the hallway waiting for her mother.

"Sit down," said Marianne beckoning her into the drawing-room. She moved the Times from where it was carelessly discarded on the couch and set it beneath the coffee table.

"Did she confide in you," asked Louisa.

"She spoke openly," Marianne replied.

"What did you discover?"

"I am certain she did not poison her husband," said Marianne.

"Did she admit to having the bottle?"

"She did but…"

There was a rapid knock at the door, a ring of the bell, followed by another succession of loud raps.

Louisa jumped up and ran to the window.

"It's Daniel," she said.

"Let him in," replied Marianne.

Louisa opened the door, and Daniel strode through. "Good day," he said. "Where is Mrs Russell?"

Louisa gestured to the drawing-room.

"It's not there," he said when he saw Marianne.

142

"It's not in the laundry cupboard?"

"No. I have searched it from top to bottom."

"What isn't there?" asked Louisa, "what are you talking about?"

"The bottle that Elizabeth disposed of," said Marianne. "She said she hid it in the laundry cupboard. Is there another similar cupboard?"

"I don't believe so," said Daniel. "There is a washing room, but it is near the servant's quarters. It's not my house, and I don't go down there. I have no idea whether there is another cupboard somewhere else."

"Can't you ask one of the servants?" asked Louisa.

"I wouldn't advise it," Marianne interrupted. "There is no doubt that Charles Drummond was poisoned, and as we all believe in Elizabeth's innocence, the poisoner must be someone else, quite possibly an occupant of your household."

She turned to Daniel, "Don't you agree?"

"It is what I most fear," he replied.

"You should not alert any other person, and we must use the utmost discretion in our attempts to prove that Elizabeth did not poison her husband. Demonstrating her innocence will not suit everyone."

"But surely, I must tell my cousins?" asked Daniel.

"You should limit the information as far as you can," counselled Marianne. "It is all too easy to let a secret slip."

"Then I must return and search the house at once. There is no time to lose."

"And be discreet", said Louisa. "It might be difficult to search the house without drawing attention to yourself. To be thorough, you must check every single room."

"I suppose so," said Daniel. "Although its unseemly to rummage through my cousins' possessions and those of the live-in servants."

"I can help if you want," said Louisa.

"I do want," replied Daniel. "It would feel less of an impropriety."

"When do your servants take their half days?" asked Marianne.

"Minnie's is today. No doubt, she will already have left," said Daniel. "Harold works outside, and I could send Mrs Piggott out on an errand."

"A good plan," said Marianne. "So, you will deal with Mrs Piggott and then search the rooms occupied by men while Louisa checks your cousins' rooms and those of the servants."

"I am not comfortable with the thought of checking my cousin's rooms," said Daniel. "It is an invasion of their privacy."

"Anybody could have removed the bottle with the most innocent of motives," said Marianne. "Search your cousin's bedrooms but do it last. With any luck, you will find what you are looking for elsewhere. But don't omit a search for the sake of good manners. Nothing could be worse than losing the opportunity to help Elizabeth."

"You are right," agreed Daniel. "And fortune favours a search today with Sophia and John Edward at Ethel's house and usefully absent from home. Louisa, allow me half an hour to send Mrs Piggott to Ipswich on an errand, then join me for the search if you are still willing to assist?"

"Of course," said Louisa. "I will do all I can to help."

"Thank you," said Daniel as he left.

Louisa wandered aimlessly, killing time until the half-hour had passed. When the clock hand finally dragged itself to the appointed hour, she departed to The Rowans and tapped on the door. Daniel was standing by the study window at the front and noticed her immediately.

He let her in. "Where would you like to start?" he asked.

"We should be methodical," said Louisa. "The rubbish cart has not been here for three days, so it would seem logical to start at the bin store."

Daniel pulled a face. "I should change out of these clothes then," he said.

"You should," Louisa agreed. "That suit is too nice to ruin. If you cannot find the bottle in the rubbish, check all the basement rooms and the family rooms up here. I will check the bedrooms and the servant's quarters in the attic."

"That sounds sensible," he said. "Thank you, Louisa. I am grateful."

Louisa smiled as she ascended the stairs, pleased to be the recipient of a few kind words, at last.

A large picture of a racehorse filled an entire wall at the top of the stairs. The bedrooms surrounded a galleried landing, and Louisa turned left into the nearest bedroom, which appeared to belong to a man. The square room contained sparse furnishings and a dark, wooden bookcase running from floor to ceiling. A polished mahogany desk faced it, upon which a trio of ivory elephants had been

144

carefully placed, arranged from largest to smallest. A double-posted bed stripped bare of linen, stood incongruously in the centre of the room near a rug upon which several discolouration's were still visible, despite evidence of recent cleaning.

Louisa grimaced, then systematically began her search of the room, starting with the bookcase. There were few personal effects in the room, but sufficient clues to identify it as Charles Drummond's bedchamber.

When Louisa opened the heavy wooden doors of the wardrobe, she baulked at the thought of searching through a dead man's clothes, but she did it anyway. Louisa tried to open the top drawer of Mr Drummond's desk, but it was firmly locked. She made a lucky guess and located the key beneath a plant pot on the window ledge without expending undue energy in a fruitless search. The contents of the desk were disappointing. Louisa pulled out drawer after drawer but found only paperwork relating to Charles Drummond's trade as a corn merchant. She sighed. It would have been unlikely to locate the bottle in the first room they searched, but she was nevertheless disappointed.

The feeling of frustration continued as she searched the remaining rooms on the first floor, finding nothing of note. She avoided Daniel's bedroom, deeming a search unnecessary but located the laundry cupboard, removed every piece of linen, and searched again. The bottle remained stubbornly absent.

Louisa found the staircase to the servant's quarters through a narrow door near to the main staircase. She climbed the steps, treading on a squeaky board mid-way up the stairs where the steps bowed. At the top of the house were three rooms and a bathroom. Louisa performed a meticulous search of the bathroom and the empty bedroom, before moving on to the smaller of the remaining bedrooms.

A yellow counterpane covered the bed, and a small vase of matching daffodils graced the windowsill. Pots of nail polish and laundered handkerchiefs sat on top of the desk, making it likely that the room belonged to Minnie. Louisa's guess was confirmed when she discovered an unsent letter addressed to a young man in Minnie's spidery handwriting. Minnie, showing a typical lack of caution and propriety, had written urging him to meet her the following week. Her fountain pen lay in a pool of ink next to the letter.

"My goodness," exclaimed Louisa, opening Minnie's wardrobe. There were many more outfits than Louisa expected a housemaid to own, and they were all well made. Although there was no evidence of a bottle, Louisa made a mental note to mention the outfits to Daniel, as they implied that Minnie had access to more money than she ought to. Closing the door, Louisa entered the final bedroom which, by process of elimination, must belong to Jane Piggott.

The dark green curtains in the housekeeper's room were closed. Not quite wide enough for the window, they left a gap just large enough to allow a chink of light which fell across a tidily made single bed, illuminating a wooden cross on the wall above. The room contained an identical desk to Minnie's, positioned against the opposite wall. Several reading books, a newspaper, and an old bible, lay upon it. Louisa opened the desk draw containing a few dog-eared letters and some writing paper, a tin of buttons and a half-full bottle of ink. She picked up the books, two by Jane Austen and opened the bible lovingly inscribed, "the dying gift of my dear mother." She was about to open the wardrobe when she heard a voice down the corridor.

"Come, Louisa, I have found it."

She hurried from the room to find Daniel at the end of the corridor holding his finger to his lips. "Don't say anything. Jane Piggott is back," he whispered, "and I don't want her to see you up here."

Daniel peered round the door. The coast seemed clear, and he beckoned Louisa to follow.

As they descended the stairs, a squeak burst from the bottom step before they had a chance to reach the landing. They stood stock-still, waiting for Mrs Piggott to hear them but nobody came. They tip-toed quietly through the landing and made their way downstairs just as Mrs Piggott emerged from through the kitchen door.

"Good day, sir," she said before looking straight into Louisa's eyes. "I have taken the box of fruit to Mrs Lucas as you asked."

"Good, thank you," said Daniel watching Louisa blush to the roots of her hair. "Are they well?"

"Mrs Lucas and Miss Sophia are quite well," said the housekeeper, "but the children are still sadly. The littlest one has a shocking cough."

"The fruit will help, I am sure," he murmured. "Thank you."

Jane Piggott returned to the kitchen while Daniel escorted Louisa to the study.

"What must she think of me?" asked Louisa. "She saw us coming down the stairs together. She will assume the worst."

146

"I am sorry," said Daniel. "I don't know what to say to make this better."

"It is too humiliating," said Louisa burying her face in her hands.

"I will speak to her."

"You will not," said Louisa. "It will only make matters worse. Never mind. She will have to think of me what she will. Do you have the bottle or not?"

"I think so," said Daniel. "I must ask Minnie to identify it. He put his hand in his pocket and retrieved a bottle from a brown paper bag. The bottle, manufactured from clear glass, was sealed with a glass stopper and droplets of clear liquid were just visible inside."

"That must be it," said Louisa. "Where did you find it?"

"On the floor of the pantry," said Daniel. "I nearly missed it as there were so many other bottles. It was behind the jam jars."

"Oh, well done," said Louisa. "What will you do now?"

"I'll speak to Minnie and make sure it is the same vial, then take it to the police station and demand that they test it."

"Please give me the news as soon as you can," asked Louisa.

"I will," promised Daniel. "I am grateful, Louisa. Thank you." He took her hand and brushed his lips lightly against her fingers."

Louisa shivered as a sensation like mothwings shimmered along her spine. She did not speak; she could not. Daniel held her gaze, and neither moved. Then Jane Piggott's footsteps advanced along the tiled hallway, and the moment was lost.

Murmuring goodbye, Louisa left the house and returned to The Poplars to tell Marianne the good news.

The days dragged by as they waited for news of the tests. Neither Daniel nor Sophia visited The Poplars, but Maggie and Minnie saw each other daily. Maggie passed on any gossip with great alacrity, notifying them as soon as Daniel summoned Police Sergeant Gordon to the house to witness Minnie's identification of the bottle. The Sergeant, to his credit, was cooperative and understanding, although he was not prepared to accept Daniels' word that there was no poison in the bottle. He insisted on visiting The Poplars where he interviewed Marianne Russell at length.

She told him everything she knew, and at the end of the interview, she asked, "Will they release Elizabeth?"

"If they don't find any poison and if it were up to me, I would release her," said the Sergeant, "but I am not in charge. We will have to see what the Inspector decides".

After two days of waiting for news and receiving none, Daniel took matters into his own hands. He strode down to the Police Station in Prince's Street, passing several "Wanted" posters pasted to the stone block walls and became increasingly irritated at their presence. The thought of his innocent aunt imprisoned in gaol, while fugitives of the most callous nature were at large, angered him. Daniel entered the Police station, approached the front desk, and demanded to see the Chief Inspector in charge. A tired-looking constable directed him to a hard, wooden bench upon which Daniel sat drumming his fingers as he watched the occupants of the busy Police Station. After a short, but frustrating wait, he spied the familiar figure of Sergeant Gordon.

"Good day, sir," said the Sergeant tipping his helmet.

"Good day Gordon," said Daniel. "Do you have any news about the tests."

"No, sir," said Gordon, "The tests are complete, but the results are under consideration."

"Under consideration, by whom?" asked Daniel.

Gordon pulled a face. "Chief Inspector Briggs, I'm afraid," he said.

"I have asked to see the man in charge," said Daniel. "I dare say it will be Briggs."

Eventually, a half-glazed door opened in front of him, and a whiskered Police Constable emerged.

"Come through, sir," he said, ushering Daniel down the corridor into a comfortably furnished room at the end.

Daniel entered the room to find the corpulent figure of Chief Inspector Briggs, squeezed into a well-padded leather chair. Above him, a clock with a large, round pendulum ticked sonorously from its position on the wall. The air was heavy with tobacco smoke, which Briggs drew rhythmically from a battered, wooden pipe. The Chief Inspector stared at Daniel through heavy-lidded eyes.

"Take a seat," he said gesturing to the left of a pair of red leather chairs.

Daniel sat. The Chief Inspector smiled and flipped open the lid of a long, narrow box which he offered to Daniel. "Cigar?" he asked.

Daniel waved a hand to decline and reached for his cigarette case. He extracted a cigarette and snapped the lid closed.

148

Daniel waited, watching the Chief inspector intently while he marshalled his thoughts.

"Why is Elizabeth Drummond still in prison?" he asked curtly. "You have new evidence to hand. She should have been returned to her home by now, not left languishing in gaol with common criminals. What is the delay? I anticipated her release long before now."

The Chief Inspector exhaled a puff of smoke and spoke in measured tones.

"We have tested the bottle, and it is, indeed, potassium bromide just as Mrs Russell advised," confirmed the Inspector. "Clearly, this did not cause Mr Drummond's death."

"That's excellent news," said Daniel. "When will my aunt be released?"

"Slow down," said the Chief Inspector. "It is not as simple as that."

"I can't see why."

"There is a distinct lack of motive for anyone other than your aunt," Briggs replied.

"My aunt had no motive," said Daniel leaning forward, raising his voice a notch.

"On the contrary, she had a compelling motive, as you are well aware."

"No, she did not." Daniel declared. "If you are referring to my Uncle's appalling treatment of her, you should know that he has always behaved in that way and she has never retaliated. She only needed to wait for her youngest son to reach maturity, and she could have left him."

"Not without a scandal," said Chief Inspector Briggs.

"So, you are holding her purely on circumstantial evidence?" asked Daniel.

"She was present at the crime scene and lived with the victim for the duration of his illness. She was in the habit of doctoring his food, had ample motivation for the crime and most of all, there are no other suspects; not one."

"This is shocking," Daniel shouted, slamming his hand on the Inspector's desk. "There is a poisoner loose about our residence, and you have locked up an innocent woman, putting other lives in peril."

"Other lives will be in peril if she is allowed to return," said the Chief Inspector. "That is the decision that we have made. Now, I am sorry it is not what you wanted to hear, but there it is."

149

Daniel marched from the room and left the Police Station, striding angrily up Princes Street, clods of dry earth billowing beneath his feet. A half-full tram stood outside the chemist, and he jumped aboard, making his way to the quieter top deck. There he sat watching horses trot by, lost in thought. Daniel flexed his fingers together contemplating the horrible lack of progress made so far. The efforts of the barrister supplied by his father had come to nothing, despite his vast experience. An infrequent visitor to Ipswich, the barrister was likely unaware of this latest development, so Daniel decided to give him one last chance by informing him of Elizabeth's continued detainment without delay.

He left the upper level and loitered at the rear of the tram which soon juddered to a halt. Daniel pushed past the waiting travellers and doubled back to his club in Church Lane. The red, yellow, and blue of the tiled flag-bearer marked his way as he hastened up the narrow alley and into the Conservative Club. Daniel passed his hat and coat to the attendant, purchased a whisky from the bar and asked for the club telephone. Standing in the foyer with his hand in his pocket, he dialled the exchange and asked for Sir Roderick Yates.

The ensuing conversation did not improve Daniel's faith in the legal system. Although the barrister was confident of procuring a not guilty verdict in court, he thought it considerably less likely that he would be able to influence the release of his client without her first standing trial. Daniel mulled over the matter smoking a cigarette, imbibed another whisky then walked off his frustrations during his return to Ivry Street.

Back at The Rowans, Sophia and John Edward had returned from her sister's house. She saw Daniel from her bedroom window and was in the hallway catching her breath by the time he reached the front door.

"What news do you have, Daniel? I saw mother this morning, and she is so thin and frail. Louisa tells me you have hopes of her release."

"It appears my hopes were premature," he frowned. "Inspector Briggs will not countenance her release until they find another viable suspect."

"That's outrageous," cried Sophia. "They have no reason to keep her now. It's not her fault they can't find someone else with a motive."

"It is as Elizabeth feared," he sighed. "They believe her predisposition for doctoring her husband's water gives her the means and motive to poison him. In the absence of any other suspect, they have pinned their hopes of resolving the murder entirely upon her. But there is some small reason for hope. I have spoken to her barrister. Although he thinks it is unlikely that he will be able to secure her release before trial, he will nonetheless make his approaches to the constabulary tomorrow."

"She is so frail, Daniel. I fear for her if she remains in gaol for much longer. She has no experience of living so poorly. She shivers all the time and does not eat."

"She is much stronger than you give her credit for," said Daniel. Marianne Russell thought her quite indomitable and was much impressed with her resilience."

"She is my mother, and she is suffering," insisted Sophia. "She was wracked with coughing this morning, Daniel. She is truly sickening for something."

"I know it's inadequate, but I can't do any more than this," said Daniel. "I wish it were not so."

"It's so unfair," cried Sophia. "She wouldn't be in that cell if she were a man. There is no reason to confine her, no evidence against her. They have done it because they can."

"I am sorry, Sophia."

"I am even sorrier." Sophia left the room, pushing the door so hard behind her that it slammed into the frame, and without a hat or coat, she ran up the driveway of The Poplars and hammered on the door.

"Hello, Maggie," she said when she saw the housemaid. "I need to see Louisa."

Maggie did not have time to open her mouth, much less respond, when Sophia strode towards the drawing-room and flung open the door.

She stopped, looking around the room in embarrassment, as she realised that it was full of women, many of whom she did not know.

"I am so sorry," she whispered, putting her hands to her mouth. "I have interrupted you, please forgive me."

Louisa set down her coffee cup and walked across the room. She put her hand around her friend's shoulders.

"Whatever is the matter, Sophia?" she said.

The room fell silent, and Marianne Russell looked up. "Do tell, us Sophia," she said gently. "You are among friends."

As Sophia took a closer look, she spotted Ada and Bessie Ridley in the room, and their presence gave her the confidence to talk freely.

"They have refused to release my mother," she said.

"Even with the new evidence?" asked Louisa.

"Not even with that," Sophia replied. Daniel has done everything he can, and my mother still languishes inside Ipswich gaol like a common criminal. She began to cry in gulping sobs.

"Oh Sophia," said Louisa, guiding her to the armchair she had previously occupied. She gestured to Sophia to sit down.

"Disgraceful," said Ada Ridley. "Tell me all about it."

Sophia recounted the tale through sobs. She spoke angrily in parts, lost her composure at times and most especially when she described her father's cruelty to her mother.

"Now she is in gaol, and we know she is innocent. They would not treat her so harshly if she were a man," she finished.

Bessie Ridley spoke. "Does a barrister represent her?" she asked.

"Yes, and Daniel says he is confident that it will come to a successful conclusion, but he does not think that he can influence her release before trial," said Sophia.

"Is there nothing we can do?" asked Louisa, turning to Ada Ridley.

"We can draw attention to the injustice," said Ada. "We can use the oxygen of publicity to promote the unfairness of this confinement. It may help Sophia's poor mother." Her eyes shone with enthusiasm.

"Mother knows few people of influence," said Sophia, "Daniel's father, perhaps, but no others."

"She might not," smiled Ada, "but you know women of influence, don't you?"

Sophia frowned. Ada and Bessie exchanged glances. "What do you think, Bessie?"

Bessie smiled. "Your mother has been badly treated, and if women had more power, she might not have felt compelled to tolerate the cruelty for so long. Where there are outrages against women, you can depend upon your suffragist sisters. We will help if you want us to."

"My mother is not a suffragist," said Sophia.

"But you are, and your mother is a victim of inequality. We are not without influence, Sophia. Would you like our help?"

"Of course, if you can, but I don't know how it would change the situation."

152

"I cannot make any promises," said Ada, "but we can speak to our sisters about your dilemma and see what they suggest."

"And any help they give will be peaceful?" said Sophia.

"Of course," Ada replied.

"Then, by all means, do so."

Chapter Fifteen

A Time for Action

Ada was a driven woman, working tirelessly over the week to promote public awareness of the injustice perpetrated towards Elizabeth Drummond. She contacted Constance Andrews and Grace Roe who found time to break away from their arrangements for the Coronation procession, just three weeks away, to lobby at the police station.

Ada wrote to Millicent Fawcett to seek her intervention and support together with other suffragists she had come to know over the years. All this she found time for while working with the WSPU to finish their Coronation banner.

Louisa watched her with boundless respect. She had long admired Ada's exquisite artistry, as she painted and sewed with equal competence. The more time Louisa spent with Ada, the more she came to regard her.

Bessie, too, was determined to spread the word, visiting her club in Dover Street without Ada who could not leave Ipswich. Several prominent suffragettes were living at The Empress, and she consulted with them to see what they could suggest to aid Elizabeth's plight.

The women worked quickly using all their local contacts. The initial publicity from the murder had subsided, but after renewed interest from the suffragist's intervention, the Suffolk Free Press soon took an interest in Elizabeth's story and ran the first of several articles criticising the local police force. As militant suffragette activity was quieter than usual while they awaited the outcome of the Conciliation Bill, the press seized any opportunity to report on the subject. The London newspapers rapidly picked up the story, guided by some of

Bessie's colleagues, and within a few days, it made the front page of the Times.

Soon after, Daniel, Sophia and Louisa were sitting in the morning room of The Rowans poring through the latest edition of the paper. Sophia jumped at a series of staccato raps at the door, and a subdued Jane Piggott entered, accompanied by Chief Inspector Briggs.

Daniel stood to greet him.

"May I sit?" asked Briggs as a bead of sweat dripped from his temple to his cheek and wobbled precariously, threatening further descent.

"Please do," said Daniel gesturing to the fireside chair. "Have you got any news?" he asked.

"I'm afraid not," said the Chief Inspector. "May we talk privately?"

"No, we may not," said Daniel. "My cousin," he said, gestured to Sophia, "is the daughter of the accused and has, if anything, a greater right to hear the news than I do."

"Very well," said Briggs, adjusting his tie around his portly neck. "I am here today charged with the task of telling you to cease harassing my police force at once. Your association with the publicity-hungry Suffragettes has not advanced your cause at all and will inevitably damage your aunt's prospects of release."

"I beg to differ," said Daniel coldly. "My aunt still lingers inside a gaol, charged on the flimsiest of evidence and becoming frailer with each passing day. If the case goes to trial, it will be after August, if my aunt survives that long. Her health is poor, and her spirits are low, so don't come to my house and demand that we turn away the only offer of hope left unless you have an alternative to offer."

"I don't think you understand the seriousness of this situation," said Chief Inspector Briggs. "I have just returned from Winston Churchill's office in Westminster where his aide summoned me last night, and it was not a pleasant interview, let me tell you. These blasted suffragettes are pillorying the liberal party from all positions and the last thing the government needs is a high-profile poisoning case linked to the Suffragette cause. I warn you it will not end well."

"Chief Inspector, you are badly informed if you believe the Suffragettes have hijacked this case. Any action taken has been eminently peaceful. My cousins and their friends are suffragists, not suffragettes, and even when militant members have joined in promoting my aunt's cause, they have behaved impeccably. They have broken no laws or public order disturbances, and I fail to see how we could have conducted ourselves with more decency."

"Nevertheless," said Briggs, "it is not politically expedient, and you must desist at once."

"Will you release my aunt, if we agree?"

"You know I cannot."

"Then not only do I refuse, but I give you fair warning that there is a demonstration planned later in the week, during which you will most certainly see a very public association between suffragists and my aunt's unwarranted imprisonment. So, I suggest you communicate that to your ministers and start looking at another suspect for this crime."

"You will regret this Mr Bannister," said Briggs, heaving himself to his feet. "Good day," he said through thin lips, then turned to the ladies and doffed his hat. Briggs shuffled up the hallway and left the house, slamming the door behind him.

"Daniel, you were simply marvellous," said Sophia. "I thought you were against women having the vote, and suddenly you are supporting suffragists in the face of the establishment."

"I have reconsidered my opinion during the last few weeks," said Daniel, looking directly at Louisa. "All the kindnesses shown to my aunt have come from women. The most skilled barrister of my acquaintance is unable to free her and yet women who do not even know my aunt, are working tirelessly for her release while highlighting the injustice that she faces. It has given me much room for thought."

"I'm delighted to hear it," laughed Louisa, a broad smile across her pretty face. "It is good to know you we have converted you to the cause."

"I wouldn't go that far," smiled Daniel. "Anyway, back to it. Did you say that the demonstration at the gaol is on Thursday?" he asked.

Louisa nodded.

"I'll be coming too," said Daniel.

"And join all the other men devoted to our cause?" laughed Louisa.

"Only on this occasion. I can make no promises for future events," said Daniel, blue eyes twinkling.

Louisa blushed while Sophia smiled. "You have changed so much, cousin," she said. "I remember the first week you arrived with us and caught me leaving for the census evasion. You were furious at my conduct, and look at you now, practically one of us!"

156

"Yes, my behaviour left much to be desired" admitted Daniel. "Too patriarchal. I suppose I was trying to do the right thing by Charles." Louisa frowned at the mention of Charles Drummond. She turned to Sophia. "Do you ever miss your father?" she asked.

Sophia sighed. "I feel like I ought to, but he was not a kind man. He mistreated our mother, and we often saw her suffer even when we were very young. Father employed a nursemaid in the early years, and we barely saw him except in the afternoon. He would come home, have his dinner, and send us away. It was then that Father would take out his temper on Mother, especially if he'd had a difficult day. I can't remember a time when he showed any interest in us or displayed any affection. He was a little kinder to John Edward but had to suffer three girls before his son arrived. I never felt loved; none of us did - not even John Edward."

"I am sorry," said Louisa simply.

Sophia continued. "Father was an unpleasant man, but I might have been more upset at his death had he not been in such an awful mood the week he died. Any little thing could set him off, but that week he was particularly angry with the servants and that, of course, meant trouble for Mother."

"Poor Sophia," Louisa took her hand. "I shouldn't have asked."

"You were right to," said Sophia. "We have hidden our family secrets for quite long enough."

Daniel, who was patiently watching a Nuthatch do battle with a caterpillar on the wall of the kitchen garden, turned to face Sophia.

"Why was Charles angry?" he asked.

"When?" asked Sophia. "He was always angry."

"You said that one of the servants had upset him."

"Yes, he was in a frightful rage. One of them had disturbed some papers, perhaps even taken something. He mentioned dismissing them several times."

"Who was he talking about?"

"I don't know. Father never mentioned who it was. He just ranted about a lack of trust and said that he could do perfectly well without them."

"Does Elizabeth know who upset him?" asked Daniel.

"She probably doesn't know anything about it," said Sophia. "Mother was quite poorly that last week, if you remember, and kept to her room most of the time."

"That changes everything," said Louisa.

"Doesn't it," agreed Daniel.

"What are you talking about?" asked Sophia, furrowing her brow.

"It's the first time we have heard of another motive for the murder," said Daniel. "Now think, are you certain that he didn't name the servant?"

"I'm sorry," Sophia signed. "I'm trying to remember, but I don't think he mentioned a name. Father was furious and spoke only in broad terms about the deceitfulness of servants in general. I'm surprised that you didn't hear him complaining. Did he speak to you?"

"Not that I can remember," Daniel admitted. "I gave him something of a wide berth. Though your mother didn't speak of his cruel treatment towards her, my family were aware. My mother was relieved when I told her that I was boarding with you and asked me to look out for her sister. She swore me to secrecy before disclosing details of the wretched treatment Elizabeth endured at the hands of her husband. I was polite to Charles but could not bring myself to make a friend of him."

"Should we inform the police?" asked Louisa.

"Ordinarily, yes," said Daniel, "but I am wary of sharing information while they continue to threaten us. Police Inspector Brigg's behaviour today is almost unprecedented. The government have nothing to fear from us, and surely can't be concerned about further publicity for the suffrage cause because of Elizabeth's confinement."

"Oh, but they can," said Louisa. "When I went to the meeting at Caxton Hall, Emily Pankhurst said that she'd received intelligence from inside the government. Contrary to their previous assurances, they were about to renege on their promise to advance the enfranchisement bill. Emily was certain of this. If the government are about to make such a declaration, they can expect a great deal more trouble from the suffragettes. It is clear why they would prefer to avoid publicity of any kind where inequality could be perceived as a factor."

"Now I understand," said Daniel. "This matter is more sensitive than I realised, and we should discuss it away from the house." He nodded towards the door. "We need to get away from the servants and anyone else who might be able to listen."

"You are welcome to come to The Poplars," said Louisa.

"Better not," said Daniel in a low voice. "If there is one thing I have learned since my arrival, it is that the servants seem to know a great deal more about household matters than the householders themselves."

"You are quite right," agreed Louisa, "Minnie and Maggie share everything. Where shall we go then?"

"It is a beautiful day," said Daniel. "We can walk to the park, and I'll buy you both an ice cream."

"That would be a guilty treat with mother shut away in such an awful place," said Sophia sadly.

"Your mother would want you to carry on as best you can," said Daniel. "Don't punish yourself on her behalf."

The trio left The Rowans, pausing only for Sophia to collect a parasol to protect her pale skin. They walked down Ivry Street and left into Henley Road where they entered Christchurch Park, stopping to purchase ice-creams from the vendor near the gate. The area around Brett fountain was alive with cosmos and larkspurs providing a pleasing palette of pastel colours with which to enjoy their walk.

They strolled along the pathway going south through the park and crossed the well-mown lawns to the shelter in the lower arboretum, where they sat beneath its sharply pitched roof. The park was busy with people enjoying the spring sunshine, but shade covered the gazebo, and they enjoyed complete privacy.

"So," said Daniel, taking charge. "Charles was angry with one of the servants. Which servants should we consider as suspects?"

"All of ours," said Sophia.

"And ours?" asked Louisa.

"I can't see how your servants could have upset Uncle Charles," said Daniel.

"No, I suppose not," said Louisa, then turned pale at the thought that next entered her mind. "But the poison would have been readily accessible to our servants."

"How?" asked Daniel.

"My father is a chemist," Louisa replied. "An industrial chemist. He keeps a small laboratory in the house so that he can conduct experiments away from the factory, and naturally has many chemicals on the premises."

"Surely he locks them away?" asked Sophia.

"Of course," nodded Louisa. "Father keeps a key about his person and a spare in the house, but anyone could gain access if they were sufficiently determined."

"I accept that your servants could have acquired the poison, but why would they want to harm my father."

"Someone had a reason," said Louisa. "And we know that your father intended to dismiss one of the servants."

"Those are not quite the words he used. He said he would have one of the servants dismissed."

"So, it might not have been one of your servants?"

"Quite," said Sophia.

"We are going around in circles," grumbled Daniel. "Surely Charles would not have been in a position to dismiss another householder's servants.

"Well," Louisa mulled over the statement. "He could, you know."

"How?"

"Maggie is in and out of your property, most days. Janet pays the occasional visit to Jane, and I know that Minnie has made several friends of other local housemaids. If somebody else's servant had taken something, your uncle could have threatened to have them dismissed by their employer."

"That's true," sighed Daniel. "And it complicates matters. Just when I thought we had a concise list of possible suspects."

"Your servants are at the top of the list," said Louisa, "I've written down Minnie, Jane Piggott and Harold Turner. I suppose I ought to put Maggie on too."

"What about your cook?"

"Janet McGowan? She is as straight, as the day is long," exclaimed Louisa, "and it is hard to imagine any of our servants committing such a crime after knowing your family so little time."

Daniel raised an eyebrow, "As you say, your servants had easier access to the poison so they should go on the list too. Are there any others?"

"You had better add Joan Bradley and Sarah Simmonds to the list," said Sophia. "I often find those two waiting in the house when Minnie has a half day. They could have gone into my father's study, although for what reason I cannot imagine."

"Well we now have a list to work from, but the idea of dismissal as a motive is s a tenuous proposition. I doubt that it's substantial enough to offer to the authorities. What can we do to improve our prospects of finding the culprit? How do we find out what they did to Uncle Charles?"

"We have searched the house already," said Louisa, "and there is nothing left to find."

"I don't think we are looking for an object so much as information," said Daniel. "Perhaps it would be better to question the domestics?"

"They may be reluctant to answer," said Sophia.

"Probably," agreed Daniel, "but we can be subtle. Shall I speak with Harold?"

"Yes, you will get a better response as one man to another," said Sophia. "I suppose that means that I will have to talk to Minnie and Mrs Piggott; two conversations which don't fill me with pleasure."

"Minnie will be easy to get information from," said Louisa.

"It is not getting her to talk, that worries me," smiled Sophia, "it is getting her to stop. And I shall be dreary for the rest of the day if I have to spend too long with the dour Mrs Piggott."

"I will speak with Janet and Maggie, for all the good it will do," said Louisa. But I am not convinced that we should include them."

"Good, now we are properly organised, we can make a start," said Sophia looking anxiously at an ominous grey cloud drifting across the sky.

"Yes," agreed Louisa, getting to her feet. "We will find opportunities for questioning today and tomorrow. We will be too busy after that with Thursday's demonstration. At least it feels as if we are finally doing something constructive."

They walked briskly back to Ivry Street, hoping that the cloud would burst and returned to their respective homes. Marianne Russell was leaving The Poplars just as Louisa arrived.

"Where are you going, Mother?" asked Louisa.

"I'm visiting Elizabeth," said Marianne.

"Good, Sophia is anxious about her."

"Understandably," said Marianne, "I am concerned too. Elizabeth's spirits are much lower than the first few times I saw her. She is too polite to say, but I can't help feeling guilty that giving up the vial has worked against her. I am fortunate that she is still prepared to see me."

161

"She is lucky that you are taking an active interest," said Louisa. "It must be frustrating for her hopes to have been dashed so cruelly. Does she take any comfort from the proposed march?"

"Elizabeth has allowed it, but she is far from enthusiastic, " said Marianne. "Everything about this experience is humiliating for her. She cannot bear a long stay in gaol and is willing to take a chance, even though she only wants to be left in peace."

"Chief Inspector Briggs visited earlier. He asked Daniel to call off the suffragettes," said Louisa. "Can you believe it? He says we have angered the parliamentarians."

"Oh, dear. I will have to tell Elizabeth," said Marianne. "I am obliged to, though whether she will respond favourably, I don't know. Perhaps this news will strengthen her resolve."

Louisa waved her mother off and, deciding there was no time like the present, sought out Maggie, who she thought would be an easier prospect than Janet McGowan.

Louisa was descending the stairs when the study door creaked open, and her father emerged with a pained expression across his face.

"What's wrong, Father?" asked Louisa.

"Where is your Mother? Something has happened that I can't account for," he said.

"She has gone to the gaol to visit Mrs Drummond. What is the problem?"

"Come in, and I will tell you."

Louisa entered the study and shut the door. Henry Russell pulled back the chair at the front of his desk, and Louisa sat down, waiting while he took the opposite seat. Henry Russell opened his desk drawer, removed a pencil, and scribbled nervously on a notepad while he considered his thoughts. His face was pale and drawn.

"When I heard that Charles Drummond had died from the effects of poison, I checked my supplies - every one of them," he said eventually. He tore the scribbled page from the notebook which he crumpled and tossed into a waste bin, then rolled the pencil across the desk with his finger. "I keep quite a lot of compounds here, as you know," he continued. "Quite frankly, I was beginning to wonder whether someone had tampered with them. I have never been concerned about the safety of my laboratory before. Why would I be? It is always locked. But since this blasted affair with Drummond, I have been a great deal more vigilant." He stopped, picked up the pencil and tapped the end against the desk. "This morning, I needed some Sodium Sulphate for an experiment and carried out a quick visual inventory of my chemicals while I was about it. I am missing a quantity of tartar emetic."

"Are you sure?" asked Louisa.

"Quite certain," said Henry Russell. "I have a habit of tapping the bottles on the counter after use so that the contents are uniformly spread. The tartar emetic has been tipped out but not evened. There is an obvious powder mark on the neck of the bottle, and the contents are irregularly spread."

"Perhaps you forgot to tap the bottle."

"I never forget. It is a habit, Louisa; quite besides which there is less substance in the bottle than there was when I last looked."

"What will you do?"

"I must tell the authorities. This is a serious matter," said Henry getting to his feet and reaching towards the hat stand.

"Are you leaving now?"

"Yes. I was going to speak to your mother first, but I cannot delay."

"Then tell me, when did you last check the laboratory? Was it before or after Elizabeth Drummond was arrested?"

"I don't know. I was away on business when the police arrived." Henry Russell strode to the door and then turned back. "If I haven't made my concerns crystal clear to you Louisa, I must spell them out. Tartar emetic is extremely poisonous. If somebody is trying to harm your friends next door, then you ought to warn them this substance is missing."

"I will go at once," said Louisa, alarmed, running around to The Rowans in unseemly haste, almost knocking Harold off his feet as she rushed up the driveway.

"Careful Miss," he grumbled.

She knocked at the door, gasping with exertion. Minnie answered.

"Can I speak to Mr Daniel or Miss Sophia?" she asked and waited in the hallway until the handsome form of Daniel appeared seconds later. "What is it?" he asked.

"I need to talk to you urgently," she said, surreptitiously pointing to the study while she watched Minnie clean a non-existent mark from the oak hall stand.

"Oh, I see," said Daniel. "Come inside." He ushered her in and closed the door. They walked to the front of the room and looked out across the front garden, where Harold was busy pulling weeds.

"My father has just set off for the police station," whispered Louisa.

"Good Lord, why?"

"A small quantity of tartar emetic is missing from his store cupboard."

"Is he sure," asked Daniel.

"Completely certain."

"Did you know that tartar emetic contains antimony?" asked Daniel.

Louisa shook her head. "No, I didn't."

"Well it does, and it might be the substance that poisoned Charles," said Daniel. "We must also consider the possibility that the culprit took this chemical to facilitate another poisoning."

"I know. My father fears this is the case. We must be vigilant," said Louisa.

"Chief Inspector Briggs can't ignore this evidence," said Daniel. "Surely, Aunt Elizabeth will be released now."

"It's not that simple," said Louisa. "Father doesn't know when the poison went missing, so it doesn't help at all."

"Then we should question as many of the staff as possible before the police arrive," said Daniel. "I have no faith in the police force and even less in the government."

"I will go and speak to them now."

"And Louisa," he said, grabbing her wrist and pulling her close. He paused and looked directly into her eyes. "Be careful."

Daniel walked away without another word as Louisa touched her scarlet, burning cheek, embarrassed at her unbidden reaction.

She left The Rowans in a trance then meandered down the hallway and downstairs to the basement kitchen.

Janet was stirring the contents of a large ceramic bowl while Maggie poured boiling water into jam jars.

"Hello, Miss Louisa," smiled Janet, "what can we do for you?"

"Can I borrow Maggie for a moment?" she asked.

"Where are we going?" asked Maggie.

"Just outside into the garden. I want to cut some flowers, but I have hurt my wrist. Can you get the secateurs from the shed and cut them for me?"

"Of course, Miss," said Maggie. "I'll be glad to get away from the kitchen for a few minutes. It is much too hot down here today."

Louisa and Maggie walked down the garden to the bottom flower bed where white roses bloomed against a trellis. They opened the shed door at the foot of the path, collecting secateurs and gardening gloves.

"Maggie, do you remember the week leading up to Mr Drummond's death?" asked Louisa, rubbing her wrists while she feigned soreness.

"I should, Miss, it was my birthday. It was a lovely week. Mrs McGowan helped with my chores, and my half-day fell on my birthday, so I went to my mother's house for tea. Fairly pushed the boat out, she did. She made me a seedy cake, and we had hot, buttered toast and jam."

"It sounds lovely," said Louisa, "and did you see Minnie that day?"

"Oh yes, she bought me a pretty little keepsake box as a birthday present, and even Jane Piggott put in some ribbons and a book."

"That was nice," said Louisa, "You haven't known them long. It is kind that they gave you presents."

"I haven't really, have I?" agreed Maggie," but Minnie and I get along so well that I was not at all surprised. It was very thoughtful of her, considering she was having such a horrid week."

"Why was that?"

"She knocked a vase over, I think. Something like that anyway," said Maggie, pulling her hand away with a start. She removed her gardening glove and examined her hands mournfully. A scarlet teardrop swelled across her thumb.

"Spiteful things, roses," she said, "I have never liked them."

"And everyone else was in good spirits?" asked Louisa.

"I suppose so," said Maggie. "Why are you asking all these questions?"

"No reason," murmured Louisa. "I was away in London that week, and I wondered what it was like in the days leading up to Charles Drummond's death."

Maggie frowned. "It was like any other day; perhaps a bit tenser, I suppose. I know you don't like me talking about my betters, but

165

Minnie said that Mr Drummond was even nastier to Mrs Drummond than usual."

"I asked you the question, and you must feel free to answer frankly," said Louisa.

"Well," said Maggie conspiratorially, "there was a big argument because some of Mr Drummond's papers went missing, and he blamed Mrs Drummond because he blamed her for everything. Minnie said he struck Mrs Drummond so hard that she hit her head and took to her bed for the rest of the day, but Minnie didn't actually see it. She only heard about it."

"Who told her?" asked Louisa.

"I don't know," said Maggie. "Perhaps Mrs Piggott. She is devoted to Mrs Drummond, but then again, perhaps not. I can't imagine her sharing anything with Minnie. Much as I like Minnie, she is a shocking gossip."

Louisa raised an eyebrow and restrained herself from saying "pots and kettles."

"Who do you think poisoned Mr Drummond?" she asked.

"I am sorry to say it," said Maggie, "but I think it must have been Mrs Drummond. Why would anyone else want to poison him?"

"I don't know," replied Louisa, "but I don't believe that she did it."

Maggie shrugged. "I hope you are right. Just because they haven't hung a woman in sixty years, doesn't mean that they never will," she said darkly.

"Maggie," exclaimed Louisa. "That's enough of that kind of talk. Miss Sophia or John Edward might hear you."

"I wouldn't say it in front of them," said Maggie sulkily.

"I know," said Louisa trying to coax Maggie for future cooperation. "Of course, you wouldn't, and you've been very helpful. Thank you."

Maggie brightened. "Can I go inside now," she asked. "I really must help Janet."

"Yes, of course," replied Louisa, taking the wicker trug full of sweet-smelling rose stems into the house.

She arranged the flowers across several vases and sat down in the morning room, thinking about how best to tackle Janet McGowan.

The opportunity did not present itself until the next day. Louisa breakfasted with Marianne and Charlotte. Even Albert made an

166

unexpected appearance, having caught the overnight train from London.

"Bessie Ridley told me about your march tomorrow," he said when asked why he was present, "I had a few days off due and decided to come and lend my support."

"Thank you, darling," said Louisa squeezing her brother's hand. "They will appreciate it, and I will introduce you to Daniel Bannister later today. I think you have already met Sophia. He is her cousin."

"Oh yes, I have met the lovely Sophia, and it is my great pleasure to know any relative of hers," grinned Albert. "But first, I must drag myself away from your company and visit my tailor in town. I had a little accident on the train," he said ruefully, unrolling a double-breasted jacket and pointing to a pocket curling away from the suit.

One by one, Louisa's relatives left the room until Louisa sat alone. Eventually, Janet McGowan appeared, and Louisa took a breath in preparation for a question, exhaling deeply when a volley of knocks at the front door shattered the silence. Henry Russell's study door swung open almost immediately as he uncharacteristically answered the door.

"Come in," he said beckoning a trio of policemen to his study; two in uniform and one in plain clothes. By the time Louisa turned back to talk to Janet McGowan, she had disappeared.

Annoyed at the missed opportunity and frustrated at the door barrier between her and what was going on in her father's study, she decided to visit Sophia and report her conversation with Maggie. She was also keen to tell her that the police were at the house.

Daniel and Sophia had managed to speak with all three of their domestics and were sharing information when Louisa arrived. They showed her into the library and closed the door. Daniel pulled up an armchair, and the two women settled on a leather couch where they whispered, in anxious voices.

"The police are with my father," said Louisa. "We may not have much time."

"Who have you spoken to?" asked Sophia.

"Only Maggie, I haven't been able to see Janet alone."

"What did you learn?" asked Daniel.

"Not a great deal," sighed Louisa, "and some of it is difficult to talk about."

"You must tell us everything," said Sophia placing her hand over Louisa's.

"Maggie said Minnie was upset that week. She had knocked a vase over. She also said Minnie told her that," she paused. "This is awkward."

"Please Louisa,"

"She said your father struck your mother so hard that she banged her head and took to her bed for the rest of the day."

Sophia sighed and looked at her feet. "I don't doubt it," she said. "I can't confirm her story as my mother took pains to conceal these things from us."

"Did Maggie say anything else?" asked Daniel.

"Only that she received gifts from Minnie and Jane Piggott for her birthday and that Jane Piggott was devoted to your mother."

"We know," smiled Sophia. "Jane is a treasure, for all her dour exterior. She has been with my mother for decades."

"What information did you acquire?" asked Louisa.

"Similar stories from Minnie, who I ended up interviewing in the end," said Daniel. "She mentioned the problems between Sophia's mother and father. She said that there was a previous incident a few weeks before. She was dusting in my aunt's room and saw bruises over her arms."

Sophia sighed, "My poor mother. If only we could have done something to make her life easier."

"You are not responsible for any of this," said Daniel gently and continued. "Minnie gave quite a graphic account of both Charles' bouts of illness, which were similar in nature. The first was of markedly shorter duration and less intense than the second. I did not press her for details, as the police already have this information."

"Did she tell you anything more?" asked Louisa.

"Nothing useful," said Daniel.

Louisa turned to Sophia, "and Jane Piggott?"

"She didn't say much," replied Sophia, "it was hard getting her to talk without asking a direct question. Perhaps Daniel should have tackled her. She might have been more receptive to a man."

"What did she say?"

"She confirmed that Mr Drummond was in a disagreeable mood before becoming unwell, and he asked her if she had removed any papers from his study. She was aggrieved that he felt the need to ask but answered politely confirming that she had not. Then I asked Jane if she had an opinion on who may have poisoned Mr Drummond. She said she didn't know but could personally guarantee that it was not Mrs Drummond. Jane was upset at the idea of it. She loves my mother and became tearful at the mention of her. It was very touching......"

Sophia was interrupted in full flow, as the door to the house flew open and Maggie ran through the hallway without knocking, yelling Louisa's name.

Louisa rushed to the study door and threw it open, "Maggie," she thundered. "How dare you."

"They have taken her," cried Maggie, trembling from head to foot.

"Calm down, girl," said Daniel, taking control. "Who have they taken?"

"Mrs McGowan," she replied and burst into tears.

Chapter Sixteen

Another Arrest

Sophia rang the bell and summoned Minnie.

"Get her some water," she said, then watching Maggie's trembling hand changed her mind. "No, get her brandy instead."

Maggie cupped the glass, breathing in the fumes. The glass wobbled in her shaking hands.

"Now Maggie, tell us exactly what happened," said Louisa squeezing the housemaid's hand.

Maggie took a deep breath and composed herself. In a faltering voice, she began to explain.

"Three policemen came to the house," she said.

"I know," replied Louisa. "They arrived before I left."

"Well not long after they came, Mr Russell summoned Janet and me to his office. The three men were with him and said that they were policemen and were going to search the house. They asked us if we had anything to say before they started. I asked what they were looking for and they said that Mr Russell had reported that some of his chemicals were missing. I said I had nothing to tell them, and Janet said likewise."

"What happened next?" asked Louisa.

"Mr Russell told us to stay in the study while they searched the house."

"All of you?" asked Daniel.

"Yes, Janet and I, Miss Charlotte and Mrs Russell stayed in the study too, and one of the policemen kept watch on us while the others searched the house. Everyone else was out, you see. We were only there for about a quarter of an hour when one of the policemen returned. He called Mr Russell outside then came back to the study. They asked me to leave, but I waited in the hallway. Then, Miss Charlotte and Mrs Russell departed, leaving Janet alone with Mr Russell and the policeman.

I sat on the stairs until the door opened again. The policemen came outside, holding Janet by the arm. I asked what was happening and Mr Russell said they had arrested Janet." Maggie covered her face with her hands, her silent crying only evident by her shaking shoulders.

"Why was she arrested?" asked Daniel.

"They found the missing chemicals in her cupboard in the kitchen."

"Well, that doesn't look good for her," said Sophia. "Was the cupboard locked?"

"Yes, it is always locked, and she is the only one with the key, except that I know where she keeps it, but I didn't tell them that in case they took me away too," stammered Maggie. "Will I go to prison?" she continued plaintively.

"No, Maggie," reassured Daniel. "You will not, and neither should Janet. Once again, they have made an arrest based on purely circumstantial evidence. What possible motive could a housekeeper have for murdering someone who was not even her employer?"

"Minnie, take Maggie into the kitchen and give her a cup of cocoa," said Sophia walking to the door.

"Thank you, Miss," said Maggie, glad to leave the room. Her eyes were still watering, and she bit her lip, trying to stem the tears.

When the two housemaids were safely out of earshot, Sophia spoke," Will they release Mother now?"

"One would hope so," replied Daniel. "But based on what we have witnessed so far, I have my doubts."

"The march is tomorrow," said Louisa. "A great deal of organisation has gone into it. We are expecting women from as far away as Colchester and Norwich. Bessie is even bringing a delegation from London. Ada suggested that there might be some well-known suffragettes among them."

"Then the march should still continue," said Daniel. "Even if Aunt Elizabeth is released, it is not right that your housekeeper is in custody on so little evidence. She has far less influence as a servant, and I am sure the women will be equally supportive of her cause."

"They will be," nodded Louisa. "Sylvia Pankhurst works tirelessly for the working-class women in the East End and would certainly want to set right an injustice for a woman unable to defend herself."

"That's settled then," said Daniel. "You go to the march as planned tomorrow, and I," he said, eyes twinkling, "will come along and supervise".

Louisa left the Rowans and hurried up Henley Road to Ada Ridley's home. She spent half an hour apprising her of the changed situation and was relieved to hear that Ada was as supportive of Mrs McGowan, in principle, as she was of Mrs Drummond.

Before Louisa left, Ada cautioned her. "Like you, dear Louisa, I am inclined to believe both women are innocent. The evidence against them is flimsy, at best. But you should prepare yourself for the possibility that one or the other could be guilty. Just because the evidence is circumstantial does not make it wrong, but we fight because on its own the evidence is not good enough. For your own sake, Louisa, keep an open mind."

Louisa thought about this all the way home. She considered Ada's words while Charlotte gave her details about the police visit and the dramatic moment the constable made Janet get the key to the locked cupboard, producing the bottle of tartar emetic from its hiding place in the salt cellar. Louisa thought about Ada's words as her father told her how sad he had been to identify the bottle of powder as his missing poison and how he had tried to prevent the police taking Janet away for questioning. Even though her father had promised to send legal help for Janet, Ada's words remained with Louisa, and by the time she retired for the night, she began to question Janet McGowan's innocence.

Louisa liked Janet. Their relationship had evolved in the six months since Janet joined the family and Louisa considered her much more than an employee and someone she could turn to for counsel. Louisa wracked her brain, trying to think of a reason why Janet might have taken and concealed her father's poison, but it didn't make sense. Eventually, she decided to go upstairs to the attic rooms to see if Maggie was awake.

Louisa tapped on the door, and Maggie answered, her eyes still swollen and red.

"I hope I haven't woken you," said Louisa, eyeing her pallid face with concern.

"No, Miss," said Maggie. "It is too early to sleep, and I don't think I could anyway, so I've been reading instead." She pointed to a battered book with the fly cover hanging off. "Why can't Margaret see that John Thornton is a good man?" she sighed, "I would marry him in a flash if he asked me."

Louisa smiled. "You like Elizabeth Gaskell?" she asked.

"Oh, very much, Miss.

"Then I will lend you some more of her books."

"Thank you," beamed Maggie. "I would like that very much."

"Are you feeling any better?" asked Louisa. "I realise how distressing Janet's arrest is for you," she continued.

"I feel a little better," said Maggie. "Do you think they will let me see her?"

"I expect so," said Louisa. "Did you know that the suffragists have arranged a march tomorrow to draw public attention to the plight of Mrs Drummond?"

"I had heard," said Maggie.

"Well, they will also march for Mrs McGowan," said Louisa.

"Even though the constable found poison in her cupboard?" asked Maggie.

"Yes," said Louisa. "If that is the only evidence, then it isn't a good enough reason to detain her, and I cannot think of another. Tell me, what you know of Mrs McGowan?"

"She said that she came from a small town in Scotland - Falkirk, I think. She has been a cook or housekeeper all her working life."

"Does she have children?"

"She never mentioned any."

"And did she ever speak of her husband?"

"Not to me," said Maggie. "Funny, I never thought of her having a husband, but I suppose she must have if she is a Mrs."

"Hmm," agreed Louisa. "What did she keep in her cupboard?"

"It was just a housekeeping cupboard, Miss. She kept spare crockery and cleaning items. If we ran out of something, I would ask her, and she would usually have a spare in her cupboard. Mrs McGowan had a weekly allowance from Mrs Russell for the food which she also kept there, and I think there were some vases and silver and that sort of thing."

"That sounds reasonable," said Louisa. "Who else knew where the key was kept?"

"I did," said Maggie. "But anyone could have. It lay in an unlocked drawer in the kitchen. and she wasn't particularly careful of it."

"I didn't know there was such a key," mused Louisa, "although I have lived in this house all my life."

"No, Miss, but then you don't spend much time in the kitchen, do you? Many of the regulars like the baker or chimney sweep or the odd job boy share a cup of tea in the kitchen with us while they are on their rounds, and they could easily have seen it taken from the drawer."

"Oh, dear," sighed Louisa, "that doesn't help us at all."

"Sorry, Miss," said Maggie, "but surely they must release Mrs McGowan when they find out how many other people had access to her cupboard?"

"I think it is likely" smiled Louisa, "And your information has helped me to understand that locating the poison in her cupboard does not convict her, by any means. I have kept you long enough, Maggie. Thank you for your help, and I hope you can sleep properly tonight."

Louisa retired to her room and went to bed but after an hour of tossing and turning, sleep eluded her. She tried again, to no avail, and eventually gave up and lit a candle, deciding instead to look for the two Elizabeth Gaskell novels she kept in her bookcase. She located them with ease and was contemplating re-reading Cranford before giving it to Maggie when she noticed the battered black-covered diary belonging to Anna Tomkins that she had removed from The Old Museum all those weeks earlier.

"I should take this back," Louisa thought removing it from the bookcase. She flicked through and noticed that there was another entry at the back of the diary in Anna's hand but seemingly voicing her own thoughts. The last entry Louisa had read, though written by Anna, was clearly on Mary's behalf. Louisa remembered the last time she'd seen the diary, blushing as she recalled the awkward encounter with Daniel in the carriage. She supposed it was why she hadn't turned the page after Mary's final account.

Dear Daniel. Louisa's feelings towards him had changed so much in the last few weeks. Her heart seemed to beat faster whenever she thought of him, and the butterflies in her stomach were difficult to ignore. Sometimes she sensed his eyes upon her and wondered if he felt the same way, but if he did, surely, he would act on it? Perhaps she was mistaken? Daniel treated her in the same easy manner that he treated Sophia, which was all well and good. They were firm friends now, but when she thought about it, she didn't want him to see her as he saw his cousin. Thinking of Daniel wasn't going to help her sleep, so Louisa turned to Anna's final diary entry, eager to find out more.

She is dead. My friend is no more, and perhaps I could have stopped it, but she made me promise never to tell. She wanted the truth known, but one person in the know was good enough for Mary, so I watched her go to the gallows in the certain knowledge that for all she contributed to James Cage's death, another was equally guilty.

Mary's execution date was the sixteenth of August, which allowed us only a week together from when I first found her in the cell. We made the most of that week, and Mary talked of her life, about good times and bad times, and however horrible her words, I wrote until my fingers were tired to get it all down. Some of what she said was unbearable, and I thought that she was cruel, sad, loose, insane - she conjured manifest emotions in me as I listened to her story, but most of all, I thought she told the truth. I believe that she has given me all the facts, withholding nothing of her life in this final account.

And what a wretched life Mary bore. I never understood the consequences of abject poverty and how it might alter someone and turn them into an unconscionable monster before I heard Mary's story. I would like to think that I might have conducted myself differently if I had lived her life, but who knows? Few of us experience so much bad fortune and so little good. We might like to think that we would behave in a particular way, but only God knows for sure.

I was with Mary for most of the days that passed between trial and execution. Every day the prison chaplain joined us. He prayed with Mary and read bible passages to bring her comfort. Mary needed little attention and bore her situation with a quiet dignity that I had not seen in her before. She seemed fully reconciled to her imminent death and did not fear it. The only time she broke down was on being told that her execution was delayed, as Mr Calcroft, the executioner, was otherwise occupied. Mary did not view this short stay of execution with any kind of relief and thought it was cruel to prolong the ordeal. But she soon rallied and prepared herself for the new date to meet her maker.

Day after day, the prison chaplain implored her to confess to the murder of James Cage, but he did not know what I knew, and could not make her say it. He could not understand why she would risk her mortal soul in this way, especially when she was so ashamed of her other misdemeanours. It did not occur to him for one moment that Mary could not confess, because, in all probability, she hadn't done it.

The chaplain was a kind man. After one of their meetings, he procured bibles and testaments for her benefit, so she might give them to her children to remember her by. He arranged for the children to see her one last time and sat with her as she dictated a final message which he wrote in every volume. Each was inscribed "The dying gift of my dear mother."

I was not in the cell when they spent their last hours together but passed them in the corridor as they left. Richard, pale and wan, held the hands of the two younger girls who watched with detachment. William walked alone; his brother John had not even come to say goodbye. Only Mary Ann and Sibella shed a tear, Mary crying silently and Sibella with great racking sobs that I could still hear down the corridor many minutes later.

By the time I reached the cell, Mary had regained her composure at the sight of her children. She told me that she was happy and ready to die. Mary had not taken any pills for a long time and could see her life with more clarity than she had for many years. She was emotional, almost ecstatic at her ability to feel again. Free from the numbing effects of opiates, alcohol, and abuse, she freely acknowledged her love for her children, a love which gave her the strength to face her impending doom.

Mary said she had given bibles to her children in the hope that religion would comfort them too. Reaffirming Mary's faith had inspired a deep calm within her. The chaplain had taught Mary to read in her final days, and she was proud of this achievement which allowed her to read the inscription aloud to her children in each of the bibles she presented. That she could finally read, after all the years of wishing for an education, filled her with self-respect.

177

Mary faced her final journey with spirit and fortitude on the morning of the nineteenth of August. I stayed at home, hiding behind my curtains, wracked with anguish; unable to find the strength of character to watch the death of my childhood friend. Alfred, as my proxy, remained to the end and accompanied the under-sheriff to Mary's cell, where he ceremoniously demanded the body of the culprit. I shook with horror and rage when Alfred told me. How cruel and inhuman to carry out this ritual when we are supposed to be an enlightened nation.

They made Mary walk in a procession from her cell, through the courtyard and up to the scaffold. She climbed the ladder on her own, faltering a little but standing on her own two feet unsupported by the turnkeys. Then the bolt was thrown, and Mary was gone.

Some things in life should be left in a box and never opened. The violence of Mary's death has forever tarnished her memory. She has burdened me not only with the intimate detail of her crimes but with the knowledge that she was, in all probability, innocent of the murder of her husband. I cannot do much for her now but keep my promise. I will retain this journal for one year, and then I will burn it. I have not revealed Mary's secrets to Alfred, nor will I ever do so.

Like her life, this journal ends today.

As Louisa read and re-read the final paragraph, she realised that if sleep had proven difficult before, it would be near impossible now. There were so many unanswered questions in the little book. Why had the diary been kept when Anna resolved to destroy it? What happened to Anna that she had not done so? Most importantly, who killed James Cage? The parallels between his murder and that of Charles Drummond were astonishing. And there was something else in the back of her mind; something she could not quite grab hold of, and it was bothering her.

Chapter Seventeen

The Penny drops

It bothered her all night, and after a scant three hours sleep, Louisa rose again, dressed, and went downstairs for breakfast. The family were sitting at the table, waiting to eat. Minnie had managed a competent job in Mrs McGowan's absence, cooking toast, scrambled eggs, and sausages sufficient for all.

A smartly dressed Henry Russell was sitting in his usual place at the top of the table.

"Don't you have a business meeting?" asked Louisa.

"No, my dear," he said. "Albert and I are coming with you."

Louisa smiled broadly. "Have we converted you?" she asked.

"Not entirely," he said, "but this is important, and I want to see Janet properly represented, regardless of whether she has done this terrible thing. She shouldn't be confined in gaol, while they make up their minds. I called upon your friend Daniel early this morning," he continued. "Elizabeth Drummond has not been released. Perhaps I would have reconsidered if one or the other had been, but this is beyond the pale. They cannot legitimately hold both women, and I feel I must act."

"Good for you, papa," said Louisa.

"Even I am going," said Charlotte.

Louisa was astonished. Charlotte's apathy to the cause was a source of continual irritation. She must feel very strongly to be willing to participate.

"Are we all going to protest?" Louisa asked.

"Yes, even Maggie," said Marianne Russell. "She's coming along with young Minnie, I believe."

"There will be so many people available to draw attention to the case," said Louisa. "I dread to think what Chief Inspector Briggs will have to say on the subject."

"I heard more than I'd like from Briggs yesterday," said Henry Russell. "He warned me off, in the same manner as he employed to young Mr Bannister. It is one of the many reasons that I decided to attend today."

It was rare for the whole family to leave The Poplars without at least one of the servants being home, so they took the unprecedented step of locking all the doors. Henry, Marianne, and Albert elected to take a carriage to the prison while everyone else opted to walk and take advantage of the glorious weather.

Louisa did not join her family and had arranged to go with Daniel and Sophia. She called at The Rowans, tired but with a heart full of optimism for the coming day.

Daniel and Sophia were waiting in the study, watching for her from the window. Minnie emerged from the side door and walked up the path with Maggie.

"Is that everybody?" asked Louisa.

"Ethel is going alone," said Sophia. "She is attending against her husband's instructions. He disapproves of the protest because of the association with the suffragettes."

"How selfish," said Louisa. "This is not about suffrage. The suffragettes agreed to help us because of the injustice against your mother and only then because you are personally known to them."

"You are right," agreed Sophia. "But there is no convincing him. Poor Ethel has tried."

"I am sorry for her," said Louisa. "I hope she doesn't suffer for her involvement."

"Her husband isn't cruel," said Sophia, grasping an entirely different meaning to the one that Louisa intended.

"Oh, no, I wasn't implying that," said Louisa, wide-eyed.

"Of course, not," reassured Sophia. "And Ethel's disagreements with her husband follow a pattern. They won't speak for a few days, he will cut her housekeeping budget for a while, she will serve him plain food for a week, and eventually, everything will right itself. That is usually the way of it."

Louisa laughed. "Ready?" she asked, turning to Daniel.

"I am. Come now, ladies," he smiled, holding both arms out for them to take.

Goosebumps scattered across Louisa's skin as she held his arm, and they walked quietly together for a few minutes. Desperate to break the silence, Louisa said, "will we have the pleasure of Jane Piggott's or Harold's company today?"

"Good Lord, no," laughed Daniel. "Harold would be appalled at the very idea, and Jane is religious and thinks suffragettes are ungodly. Harold is gardening, and Jane has gone out on an errand."

"Which only leaves Catherine and John Edward, who is at school today," said Sophia. "Catherine can't leave her convent, not even for this. It is a cruel God who gets in the way of a mother's love."

"A mother's love, the gift of a mother," mused Louisa. "Oh, my goodness," she exclaimed. "That's what's been bothering me."

"What has?" asked Daniel.

"I don't want to tell you in case I am wrong. It is too unlikely. Just give me a few minutes and go ahead without me. I need to check something and now is an opportune moment, but I promise that I'll return quickly. Walk ahead, and I will catch you up in ten minutes."

"No, Louisa," said Daniel, but she was gone, hurrying up the road at speed, pulling her olive-green dress a few inches from the ground as she ran.

"Shall we wait?" he asked Sophia, sighing in frustration.

"No, we're still in Henley Road. If we walk slowly, Louisa will catch up in no time."

"What do you think she is doing?"

"I don't know," said Sophia. "But rest assured, Louisa values this protest enormously, and she won't miss it under any circumstances. Whatever she has gone to do must be of the utmost importance."

Louisa was breathless with exertion by the time she arrived at the door of The Rowans. She had already noticed that neither Daniel nor Sophia had locked the door before leaving, and she walked hastily up the driveway, hoping that Harold would not be around. There was no sign of him, so she opened the door and closed it quietly behind her. Louisa tiptoed up the grand staircase to the galleried landing and up the further flight of steps to the servant's quarters. The staircase creaked again, as it had when she first climbed it, but Louisa was not worried as the house was empty.

She walked past Minnie's room and opened the door to Jane Piggott's bedroom. It was tidy and sparse as it had been the last time Louisa had seen it except for an open window with a clothes horse beneath on which a few smalls were drying.

Louisa walked to the desk and examined the pile of books searching for the small burgundy-coloured bible. She found it quickly and opened it, hoping that she had misremembered what she feared was inside. She had not. The inscription, in faded blue ink, read, 'The dying gift of your dear mother'. It was dated August 1851.

Louisa took the bible and sat down heavily on the bed. The inscription inside could be a remarkable coincidence, but the more likely explanation was that it was one of those given by Mary Cage on her death. But what of it? Was it relevant?

Louisa flicked through the pages of the bible, contemplating the chances. Mary Cage had died in 1851. She must have been in her forties, so could Jane Piggott be one of her younger children? It was unlikely. That would make Jane nearly seventy, and although her old-fashioned dress and dour features made it difficult to guess her age, she did not look that old.

"Who are you?" Louisa whispered aloud.

"What are you doing in my room?" A voice hissed from nowhere, and Louisa turned, startled.

She looked towards the door where Jane Piggott was leaning quietly against the door frame, her face as grey as the worsted dress that she wore. "That belongs to me," said Jane, snatching the bible. She crossed herself then advanced towards Louisa with her face contorted in rage.

"I am sorry," stuttered Louisa, "but who are you? What do you know about Mary Cage?"

Jane stopped, holding the bible to her chest. "She was my grandmother," she said hoarsely.

"You're baby Jane," said Louisa, "of course."

"How do you know about Mary?" snapped Jane.

"Did you know her."

"No. I was born a few months before my grandmother died."

"I am sorry. So, your mother was Sibella?"

"That woman gave birth to me," said Jane bitterly. "She was not much of a mother once she had her other children."

"She gave you her bible," said Louisa. "It must have meant a great deal to her."

"I took her bible," said Jane. "She gave me nothing. She still lives, you know, but we do not speak."

"I am sorry for you," said Louisa.

"No, you are not. You are suspicious of me. That is why you are here."

"I have seen this bible before. The inscription made me wonder whether you might have..."

"...and you would be right," said Jane. "Quite right to suspect me and others will too if they find out where I came from and know of my tainted bloodline. I have been with Mrs Drummond for over forty years, and she has never asked difficult questions. She gave me a new life in Wiltshire, far away from the shame of my background."

"Your background?" muttered Louisa.

"Oh, yes," said Jane. "I have tried to be good and god-fearing, unlike the rest of my family. But some people are born bad. It turns out that I am one of them, after all."

"Nothing is inevitable," whispered Louisa.

"How would you know?" snarled Jane. "Wicked things happened to all of us. I am as broken as Uncle John, who was transported for rape - as evil as my brother Arthur convicted of a serious assault. My brothers Frederick and William have been in and out of gaol their whole lives. And, of course, there is Mary. How could I rise above my family history? It's bad blood, I tell you."

"Did you kill Charles Drummond?" asked Louisa, trying to disguise the tremor in her voice.

"I did, and I would do it again," said Jane Piggott, taking another step towards Louisa. "He was an odious being, the worst kind of bully, and he hurt Mrs Drummond once too often. She was the only one who showed me any kindness. I would have died for her, and I will die for her if it becomes necessary."

Louisa shrank towards the wall, terrified of the approaching woman, but Jane stood still again, and Louisa spoke. "Charles Drummond mistreated her for years. What made you act now, after all this time?"

"That man nearly killed her last time he hit her," said Jane Piggott through clenched teeth. "The violence had escalated and was getting worse. Her injuries were awful. The more I thought about it, the more

I realised that there was no choice. He would have killed her eventually. She had already lost two pregnancies because of him, but you won't know that. She only confided in me." Jane sighed before continuing, "I can read, you know. Mrs Drummond's late mother taught me herself, and I read newspapers and books whenever I can. I know all about poison through my reading. I thought about poisoning Drummond a long time ago." She stared dreamily towards the window. "I dismissed the thought, but it kept returning until it took hold of me. When Mrs Drummond told me that we were leaving Wiltshire for Suffolk, I was terrified lest the wickedness of my family returned to taint me. It came as a great relief that we lived next door to a chemist with a household of staff, careless about leaving things around. At least that way, I would have access to a ready solution if things got bad."

"You stole my father's chemicals?" gasped Louisa.

"It was easy," said Jane in her thick, Suffolk drawl. "We are up and about long before you rise from your beds. Did you know how easy it is to get into your scullery? Your servants are lax, and it's easy to get around your house unnoticed. It only took me a few visits before I found the key to your father's study, and once I knew where it was, I helped myself to the poison. It was all very nicely labelled for me. I read about tartar emetic in the George Chapman case. He was hanged for his crimes, but I will not be."

"Then why did Janet get caught with the poison?" asked Louisa.

Jane Piggott raised her eyes to the ceiling, "because I planned it," she said. "I love Mrs Drummond, and I did not expect them to blame her for Charles Drummond's death. She was ill in bed. It shouldn't have happened, and I did not know that she dosed his food with bromide".

For a fleeting moment, Jane Pigott looked sad, "I thought she told me everything," she said. "I could not let her fester in that awful place when my only purpose was to protect her. Then it came to me. I could hide the poison somewhere else and make sure that it was found. I took pains to ensure that your father didn't miss it the first time but was deliberately careless on my next visit. I wanted your father to realise it was gone and I wanted the police to search the house. That way, they would be certain to free Mrs Drummond, and there would be no reason to suspect me. My plan worked."

"But they haven't freed her, have they?" said Louisa. "Elizabeth lingers frail and sick in the gaol house, and it is your fault."

"She won't be convicted now," said Jane, "I am certain of it. There is too much doubt now that Janet has been caught with the poison."

"Elizabeth could die before she is released. She is unwell and delicate, and you must tell them you killed Charles," said Louisa.

Jane Piggott laughed and shook her head. "Never," she said. "I will not die for this. My mistress Elizabeth will soon be free, and I will look after her as I always have. No, my dear, today you will die."

Louisa sprang from the bed and stood with her back towards the window watching the steely glint of a pair of razor-sharp shears as Jane Piggott snatched them from her wide apron pocket. Without moving her gimlet-grey eyes from Louisa, the housekeeper reached behind her back and twisted the key in the door lock. Louisa was trapped.

"No," she screamed, "Get away from me."

"Scream all you like," said Jane. "The house is empty. There is no-one to hear, and they think that I am out running an errand. When they discover your remains, nobody will think of me."

"You are quite mad," whispered Louisa, edging towards the window.

"Don't say that." Jane advanced quickly, pointing the shears towards Louisa who grabbed the bolster from the bed and hurled it at the housekeeper's head, knocking the shears from her hand. Cursing, Jane Piggott bent to retrieve them, as Louisa climbed on the bed, hurled open the sash window and slithered onto the pitched roof below.

Tiles crunched beneath her feet, falling, clattering down the roof like casualties from a tropical storm. She grabbed the windowsill to stop herself falling along with the tiles, watching as the manic face of Jane Piggott loomed through the window.

"Even better," she spat, banging the end of the shears against Louisa's clenched knuckles.

"No," cried Louisa as the pain ripped through her fingers. Jane smashed again, first one knuckle, then the next. Louisa's fragile grip on consciousness almost abandoned her as she felt bone shatter and a stab of pain flashed up her arm.

One more smash on her right knuckle and her tenuous hold upon the windowsill gave way. Her chin crashed against the bay fronted

185

window, and she slipped down the pitched roof, scrabbling against the tiles.

The sharp pitch of the roof did nothing to stall her descent. "I am going to die," she thought before being saved by the dual fortune of her dress snagging against a pipe as her foot found the gutter.

She came to a halt, flat against the roof, hardly daring to breathe while the gutter pitched and swayed beneath her feet. She tugged gently at her dress to test how firmly it held her to the roof, but it did not feel secure. Louisa waited for a few seconds, trembling, terrified and sick to the stomach. Then a rush of water sloshed towards her splashing into the gutter which wobbled precariously. She could not see where the water came from but heard Jane Piggott grunting as a further torrent of water spilt down the roof.

Louisa screamed as loudly as he could. "Harold," she cried. "Help me, please help me."

She stopped screaming and listened desperately for a reply. All was quiet and still, and she realised that the deluge of water had ceased. Her relief was short-lived.

"Die, damn you," shouted Jane Piggott. Something crashed onto the roof above setting tiles jangling into the gutter and spraying sharp shards of clay over Louisa's face and neck. There was another loud clatter of tiles, and Louisa saw a heavy silver tin roll into the gutter, as a section detached from the roof and smashed on the pathway below. Jane had given up trying to dislodge Louisa with water and was launching tins of food taken from the pantry to destroy her fragile grip on the roof. The undamaged gutter had formed a stable hold for Louisa's foot before but barely supported her now as she clung precariously to the wobbling, weakened structure.

Louisa screamed again; her piercing shrieks accompanied by another volley of tins. One hit her directly in the arm, and a fresh wave of nausea assailed her as she heard her bone crack. Louisa clung to consciousness through a hazy mist. In the distance, she thought she could hear a familiar voice penetrate the fog marring her clarity.

"Hold on Louisa, hold on. I am on my way."

It was Daniel - Daniel and Sophia. She could hear them both now, calling her name. "Daniel," she cried weakly.

Another tin clattered past her head, smacking into her shoulder. A crimson welt of blood seeped from under her dress, but she found the strength to cling on, knowing that help was near.

"Daniel, hurry," she whispered.

The sound of raised voices emerged from the window above. Then the window slammed open, and Daniel threw a chain of sheets down the roof and began clambering towards her.

"Louisa, hold on. I am here now." He reached her, breathless with effort and put a strong arm around her waist. Louisa's eyes fluttered as she heard Harold and Sophia calling from above.

"It's all over. You are safe now," said Daniel.

"Thank you," whispered Louisa, and that was the last thing she remembered.

Chapter Eighteen

Whatever happened to baby Jane?

Louisa's senses sprung quickly to life when she woke the next day. She inhaled the smell of freshly laundered sheets, followed by the delicate scent of sweet peas, her favourite flower. The sun shone through the window of her bedroom, casting warm rays over her skin and the bed quilt engulfed her body like a comforting friend.

As sleep fell away, she became aware of a nagging ache from her knuckles. She pulled her hands from the bedclothes, watching them with drowsy eyes, and wondering why they were both swathed in bandages. She looked like a pugilist ready for a fight. Louisa tried to sit up, but the effort of placing her hand on the bed to raise herself was too painful. Her eyes snapped open, and she looked around the room.

"You are awake," said Charlotte. "Thank goodness. We were so worried."

"What happened?" asked Louisa.

"Don't you remember?"

Louisa rubbed her head with her bandaged hands. "Yes, it is coming back. Jane Piggott. She poisoned Charles Drummond."

"We know," said Charlotte, "something must have snapped in her mind. She was raving when they found her and admitted to everything. She was quite proud of her actions and saw herself as Elizabeth Drummond's protector."

"She tried to kill me," said Louisa shivering beneath the bedclothes.

"Daniel stopped her," said Charlotte. "I am afraid he had to restrain her in a very ungentlemanly manner. She was determined to dislodge you from the roof. Harold and Sophia had to hold her while Daniel went to get you."

"Where is Daniel?" asked Louisa. "I must thank him."

"You have been unconscious for two days Louisa. You have hardly been able to thank anyone. Anyway, he has gone back to London," said Charlotte.

"Oh," replied Louisa, taken aback. "How long has he gone for?"

"I don't know," said Charlotte, "but Sophia will. She asked me to tell her as soon as you were awake. She has been distraught."

Charlotte held a glass of water to Louisa's lips. "Drink this," she said. "Now, are you up to visitors?"

Louisa nodded, and soon a succession of people entered her room. First was Marianne, bearing a suffragist sash. She hugged Louisa and regaled her with details of the protest, which had garnered great attention both locally and nationally. The march was so successful that it would have undoubtedly improved Elizabeth's chance of release had events not taken their natural course after Jane Piggott's arrest. Louisa instantly forgot her aches and pains when they told her that Elizabeth Drummond was safely back home.

"Thank goodness," she murmured.

"Ada has sent you a message," smiled Marianne, with a wry smile. "She says that she doesn't consider the state of unconsciousness to be an adequate excuse for missing a crucial march."

When Marianne left, Maggie arrived followed by a grateful Janet who was recovering from her ordeal, after being released the previous evening.

Later that afternoon, Louisa heard a knock at the door, and she looked up to see Sophia peering into the room, wearing a broad smile across her pretty face.

"I'm so pleased to see you," said Louisa as Sophia rushed to her side. She reached for her hand.

"Not as much as I am at seeing you safe and well," said Sophia. "We worried that you wouldn't wake up," she continued. "You were unconscious for ages. Daniel was out of his mind with concern."

"Not enough that it stopped him going to London," said Louisa waspishly.

"It is work, silly," said Sophia. "He has gone back to the electric company."

"How long for?" asked Louisa.

"He wasn't sure, but he won't be coming back soon. He did explain, but it is a boring work matter, and I wasn't listening properly. From what I remember, Daniel said he would be away for at least a few months."

Louisa's heart lurched as a familiar feeling of nausea returned, which she now realised came from the pain of dashed hopes. Just as she was finally able to acknowledge her feelings for Daniel, it was evident that he only saw her as a friend. He hadn't thought her health was important enough to keep him in Suffolk and wait for her safe recovery.

Louisa went through the motions of conversation with Sophia, barely listening, as she described how Daniel had insisted on returning to the house when Louisa did not come back after the promised ten minutes, only to hear her shouting from the rooftops. They had rushed to the rear of the house to see Louisa hanging precariously. They advanced to the housekeeper's room followed by Harold before making the rescue.

"You are quiet, said Sophia. "Are you still feeling unwell?"

"I am a little better, just tired," said Louisa, unable to tell Sophia that the real reason for her quietness was feelings of utter wretchedness.

"You will be better soon," said Sophia. "The doctor said you would be out of danger as soon as you woke up. He never doubted your speedy recovery, which is why Daniel felt able to leave."

"He checked with the doctor?" asked Louisa hopefully.

"We both did," said Sophia. "We are your friends Louisa. We were terribly concerned."

Sophia stayed a few moments longer, but Louisa slipped further into melancholy, which Sophia interpreted as illness and she left, promising to visit the next day. As soon as the door closed, Louisa put her head in her hands and sobbed until the bandages were damp with tears.

It took a few more days for Louisa to feel well enough to leave her bed, and a few more still until her physical injuries began to heal. Her knuckles were smashed and would never be quite right again, but she found, to her relief, that she could pick up a pen and use it, although her writing was shaky.

Louisa received a steady stream of visitors, but nothing improved her mood. She read Mary Cage's diary from cover to cover, trying to understand why Jane Piggott had believed that she was born wicked. It was a mystery to Louisa. Jane was a tiny baby when Mary died. She had lived outside the influence of her family for many years and had no reason to feel that murder was inevitable. Louisa could only assume that Jane was either mad or that that the knowledge of her family history provoked a self-fulfilling prophecy. Jane clearly believed that evil ran through the generations.

Jane's beliefs bothered Louisa and continued to bother her. Eventually, she decided to visit the repository in Ipswich and waded through several decades of the Ipswich Journal quarter sessions, where she soon discovered how much trouble the family had provoked. Every one of Jane's half-brothers had been charged with larceny or assault; one was stabbed to death, and her Uncle John was transported for rape. Almost every man in Jane's family had been in trouble with the law at one time or another. While she didn't believe it herself, Louisa could now understand why Jane felt that a predisposition to criminal acts was almost a given.

Louisa continued to fret about the origins of the diary, wondering how it had fallen into the hands of the Ipswich Museum. Anna had been so clear that nobody would ever read it. The thought became so troublesome that Louisa consulted her father, who suggested a visit to the parish priest. A week later Louisa walked to St Margaret's church on the south side of Christchurch Park to access to the parish register. It could have been a futile visit with no appointment and no knowledge of whether the vicar would be around, but Louisa was in luck. The vicar was in the vestry and listened to her request sympathetically. He asked her what she needed and when she replied, he produced a dusty, red-bound book and laid it on the altar. Louisa thanked him, turned a few pages, and found the entry she had half expected.

"Anna Tompkins of this parish, beloved wife of Alfred was buried 12th April 1852 aged 49." Scribbled in the margin was a single word, "tuberculosis."

The mystery was solved, and the regret that Louisa felt was tempered with relief. She had known from the earnestness of Anna's promise, that only something unforeseen could have kept her from destroying Mary's diary. Death had claimed Anna early, and Louisa felt an unexpected surge of sadness at the prospect of a bereft Alfred struggling to care for his young children.

Another unresolvable matter occupied Louisa's mind in its place - something that Mary's diary did not and could not answer. Who killed James Cage? In time, Louisa rationalised that some mysteries would never be solved and that this was one of them.

Chapter Nineteen

Twilight years

Woolverstone – April 1911.

In the tiny village of Woolverstone, nestled on the banks of the River Orwell south of Ipswich, Abraham Barker trudged wearily down the dirt track of a farm, and into the front yard of the decrepit stone cottage that he shared with his disagreeable landlady and her granddaughter.

He entered the front door of the cottage, stooping to avoid the lintel as he passed from dwindling sunshine into the cold, dank interior of the dwelling. He walked toward the kitchen, rubbing his tired eyes with calloused hands. His once handsome face was weathered and etched with the lines of disappointment gained from a hard life, not relieved by the comforts of old age. At seventy-three years old, he had hoped to have enough means to retire, but fate had been cruel, and he was destined to labour in the fields every day if he wanted to eat. He worked rain or shine, despite his stiff back and painful gout in his left foot.

Abraham opened the latched door to the back room feeling the same surge of resentment that he felt every day. The fire was unlit as usual, there was no food as usual, and the room was filthy; nothing had changed and probably never would. Not until the old girl died anyway. And once she was gone, he would, no doubt, lose his lodgings and would be no better off. Abraham had no prospects and little hope for improvement.

He lowered himself onto the wooden kitchen chair, watching the recumbent form of his landlady sprawled across a mattress on the floor. A dirty, fraying blanket covered her shoulders, and she opened her eyes and examined his face.

"Where is Rose?" she demanded.

"I do not know," he muttered. "There is no food again."

"Rose gave me food earlier," she said triumphantly.

"And left nothing for me?"

"I told her not to bother. You do not pay enough." Her eyes sparkled with pleasure at the unkind words.

He stood wearily to his feet and shuffled towards a wooden kitchen cupboard. The door hung uselessly from a broken hinge. He peered inside. There was a loaf of mouldy bread and a chunk of cheese. Abraham removed a penknife from his pocket and sliced the cheese, then picked the worst of the mould spores from the loaf.

"I will have this," he said gruffly.

"It's mine," she growled, narrowing her eyes. "You cannot have it."

He sighed. Another night; another long night, arguing with this mad, bad old woman as the last vestiges of her mind crumbled.

"You cannot stop me," he said, shaking his head, then he took a mouthful of the dry bread and grimaced.

"I'll stop you," she said, "just like I stopped him. I'll put something in your water until you scream for mercy. You eat my bread, you steal my food, but you don't know what's in it. A little poison, perhaps."

Her face contorted and spittle flew from her mouth with the force of her words.

Abraham carried on eating. He heard this tirade almost every night now. Rat poison, dead father, hanged mother, transported brother - it was sad to see a mind disintegrate this quickly.

She carried on. "I'll get the arsenic from the privy again. Just you wait".

He finished his scant meal. There was no point in waiting up to listen to the ramblings of a decayed mind. He might as well get an early night, ready for the daily grind in the fields tomorrow, providing her incessant, spiteful chatter allowed him the luxury of a good night's sleep.

Abraham shook his head as he climbed the creaky stairs to his mattress in the tiny back bedroom, regretting the poor decisions he had made in his life. When he was looking for lodgings two years ago, he'd had a choice between this room and the ground floor room at the house of the widow Johnson. The rent was the same, but when his old friend Richard Cage said his sister had a room available, Abraham felt obliged. Poor choice, he thought now as he listened to the irrational screams coming from the back room and rued the day that he crossed paths with Sibella Studd.

Chapter Twenty

The final conspiracy

Though Louisa was relieved to discover Anna's fate, she missed having her research to look forward to as a distraction from the pain of Daniel's absence. Every day was endless and filled with wistful hopes that she could not banish. Louisa found no pleasure in the company of others and began to take long, solitary walks to fill her time. After a week of walking around Ipswich alone, she decided to visit Ada and Bessie Ridley. The morning spent with her cousins lifted her spirits immensely, and Louisa returned to The Poplars in an unusually good mood.

She entered the house and made her way towards the morning room, hearing voices through the door of her father's study.

"Who is Father with?" she asked.

Her sister Charlotte was sitting in the morning room with her embroidery on her lap. "Have a cup of tea," she said, gesturing to the teapot.

"Oh, hello. I didn't see you there," said Louisa, as she noticed Elizabeth Drummond sitting on the window seat next to her mother. "Do you know who's in the study?"

Marianne sipped her tea and exchanged glances with Elizabeth Drummond. "I've no idea," she said.

Louisa sighed and poured herself a cup of weak tea, then sat down and stirred the brew with a silver apostle spoon.

"How are you feeling Louisa?" asked Elizabeth Drummond, looking thinner than when Louisa had last seen her, but appearing well for all her recent experiences.

"I am better," sighed Louisa, "just a little tired still, but I'm sure it will pass."

Their conversation was interrupted by a sharp rap at the door, and Maggie entered, accompanied by Sophia.

"Where is....?"

"Hello, my dear," said Elizabeth, standing to greet her daughter, and surreptitiously putting a finger to her lips.

"Oh," said Sophia. "Are you well, Louisa?"

"Quite well. I was just telling your mother I am feeling better. Why does everyone keep asking?"

"We're just concerned," said Sophia absently watching the other women sipping their tea in silence. The conversation faltered, leaving Louisa puzzled.

"Is everything all right?" she asked.

Sophia opened her mouth to speak, then the door to the study creaked open.

From her vantage point opposite the morning room door, Marianne saw Henry Russell emerge, accompanied by Daniel.

"Elizabeth and I are going for a walk around the garden," she said. "Do come and join us."

"No, thank you," said Charlotte.

"Come on," said Sophia. "I'm going too."

"And me," said Louisa.

"No, not you," said Sophia. "You are tired, and you do not look at all well. Stay here in the warmth. Charlotte will join me." She took Charlotte's arm and practically dragged her through the glazed door and onto the lawn.

Louisa sat alone in the corner of the morning room, watching the four women walking in the garden, chatting together. Sophia was talking animatedly to Charlotte, who kept looking back at the house.

Louisa did not hear the door open, nor did she see Daniel enter the room. She was so preoccupied trying to decipher what was passing between Sophia and Charlotte, that she was entirely unaware until Daniel put his hand on her shoulder.

"Louisa," he whispered.

She looked up and the colour drained from her face as her heart thumped wildly in her chest.

"Daniel, where have you been?" Louisa blinked and turned away, but she wasn't quick enough and could not hide the tears that welled up in her eyes. She lowered her head and tried vainly to disguise her hurt.

Daniel knelt beside her, placed a gentle hand on her chin, and tipped her face until she was looking directly into his eyes. Time disappeared in the intensity of his gaze. Then, he kissed her gently on the lips and the clocks ticked again.

"Dear Louisa," he murmured, kissing her over and over, lips like butterfly wings across her skin. "Marry me?"

And she thought her heart would burst.

Daniel and Louisa were so engrossed that they did not see the four women smiling and clapping as they watched them from the garden.

Epilogue

14 December 1918

Louisa peered through the oval mirror in the hallway, adjusting the brim of her dusky-pink hat, as she smoothed imaginary hairs from her matching coat.

"Will I do?" she asked.

"You will do very well," said Daniel putting an arm around her waist as he kissed her neck.

"Come here, Emily," he said to the pretty four-year-old sitting at the foot of the stairs. She ran to her father, and he held her hand and smiled.

"Thank you," said Louisa as the nanny pushed a large wheeled perambulator towards her. She looked inside and smiled at her sleeping son before stroking his cheek with her finger.

"Good luck then," said Mrs Pierce, the nanny.

"Thank you," said Louisa. "I am so sorry that you cannot join us, but it is a start."

"It is," said Mrs Pierce, and it will soon be my turn."

Daniel opened the door, and they walked down Henley Road towards the polling booth to cast their votes.

Note:

When they finally gave the vote to women in 1918, only those over the age of thirty who owned property or were married to men owning property were eligible. It was 1928 before all women were able to vote. Suffragists and suffragettes alike ceased all activity during the first world war. When it was over, they campaigned again, eventually securing their long-held dream of enfranchisement.

THE END

Afterword

My great, great Uncle, Alfred Bird married Rosa Jane Studd, granddaughter of Sibella Cage and great Granddaughter of Mary Emily Cage nee Moise. I first read about the murder of James Cage while researching my Bird family history in Stonham Aspal and was intrigued by the story. Mary Emily was genuinely remorseful for her actions, and although she acknowledged the deficiencies in her conduct, she flatly denied murdering her husband. I wondered what drove her to commit murder and how much the dreadful, gnawing poverty contributed to her crimes.

Ada and Bessie Ridley are also my genetic relatives. They were at the other end of the social scale, leading privileged, middle-class lives. They were both active in the suffragette movement with Ada, a fine seamstress, credited with creating the 1911 WSPU Coronation Banner. The women's 1911 census evasion in Ipswich Museum was a real event. Ada and Bessie Ridley may well have been there, as they were absent from the 1911 census.

I have invented some of the characters in this book, though many are real, and I have taken artistic licence with many of the events described. There are several accounts of the Cage murder available on the internet and in the Ipswich record office as it was widely covered in newspapers during 1851. I consulted several excellent books about suffragism, read numerous accounts on the internet & sought authenticity by reading historical newspaper articles. However, I am no expert and, notwithstanding the census evasion, 1911 was a quiet year for suffragette activity, so I have stretched a few historical points to fit the story into this year. Although I live in Gloucestershire, my heritage is East Anglian. My Suffolk genealogy goes back to the early 1500s, and my family still live there. I know my way around Ipswich, and it was a pleasure to set the book around Christchurch Park.

This book should be considered part fact, part fiction, especially where Jane and Sibella Cage are concerned. I don't know who killed

James Cage, if not Mary and have only speculated on Sibella's guilt and wickedness of character. Equally, I did not find Jane Cage in the census records after 1861, but that does not mean she is not there. A better genealogist than I may find her alive and well in a future census, perhaps living in another country.

Jacqueline Beard, Cheltenham, 2015
https://jacquelinebeardwriter.com

If you have enjoyed this book, please consider leaving a review.

Also, by this author:

The Lawrence Harpham Murder Mysteries:

The Fressingfield Witch

The Ripper Deception

The Scole Confession

Lawrence Harpham Murder Mystery Short Story

The Montpellier Murders

Coming soon –

The Felsham Affair

Printed in Great Britain
by Amazon

16749233R00122